THE HELLION'S
WALTZ

Also by Olivia Waite

The Lady's Guide to Celestial Mechanics

The Care and Feeding of Waspish Widows

THE HELLION'S WALTZ

A Feminine Pursuits Novel

OLIVIA WAITE

AVONIMPULSE
An Imprint of HarperCollinsPublishers

THE HELLION'S WALTZ. Copyright © 2021 by Olivia Waite. All rights reserved. Printed in the United States of America. No part of this book may be used or reproduced in any manner whatsoever without written permission except in the case of brief quotations embodied in critical articles and reviews. For information, address HarperCollins Publishers, 195 Broadway, New York, NY 10007.

Digital Edition JUNE 2021 ISBN: 978-0-06-293181-8
Print Edition ISBN: 978-0-06-293183-2

Cover design by Amy Halperin
Cover illustration by Christine Ruhnke
Cover images © Jenn LeBlanc (women); © rusty426/Shutterstock (background); © popcorner/Shutterstock (face)

Avon Impulse and the Avon Impulse logo are registered trademarks of HarperCollins Publishers in the United States of America.

Avon and HarperCollins are registered trademarks of HarperCollins Publishers in the United States of America and other countries.

FIRST EDITION

21 22 23 24 25   HDC   10 9 8 7 6 5 4 3 2 1

For Grandpa Toby, who has flown west.

Acknowledgments

It's traditional to stack acknowledgments in ascending order of importance, but everything else about the past year has been topsy-turvy so why not get right down to the heart of the matter: neither this book nor its author would be in any kind of shape if it weren't for the incredible love and flat-out heroism of my husband, Charles. This year was our ten-year wedding anniversary, and the fifth year since I came out as bisexual: we'd planned on Paris, and instead we found ourselves spending a year indoors in an apartment like a sealess ship. We've both lost loved ones, we've struggled to feel connected to absent friends, and we've been sick and tired of absolutely everything—except each other.

It is a gift to have you in my life, my love, and I thank you with everything I have.

My editor, Tessa Woodward, always sees where I'm trying to go with a book, and offers me a road map to making the journey more directly. Courtney Miller-Callihan, agent extraordinaire, has a sure and steady hand on the tiller when I am feeling most tempest-tossed.

Katherine Locke read an early version of this story and provided feedback of the most sensitive and invaluable kind; any pain or awkwardness still in these pages is mine and mine alone. Rose Lerner's incredible brilliance (and high standards for heist stories!) made this book so much sleeker and sharper: I am perpetually delighted by her friendship.

Lastly, I want to send my love to everyone who is feeling haunted by this past year and its ghosts. We're all missing someone, whether it's for now or forever. It feels important to remember that we're not alone in feeling alone. I hope the reading of this book may bring you a little of the solace that the writing brought me—this was my escape and my refuge, and its door is now open to you.

The Hellion's
Waltz

CHAPTER ONE

"Carrisford is an honest place," Mr. Roseingrave said happily.

"So you've said, Papa," Sophie dutifully replied.

They were walking out of the center of town, just crossing the north river bridge. On this winter day Carrisford was picture-pretty, all clear blue sky and ancient stone. The River Ethel murmured around the bridge pilings and bore away boats full of merchants, sailors, and oyster fishers.

Downstream the two great mills hulked on the riverbank. Mr. Obeney's stood empty, its owner gone to build a new utopian society across the sea; beside it, Mr. Prickett's mill did work enough for two, quaffing huge gulps of water to power the thrumming steam engines that kept the silk-winding machinery busy day and night. Upstream, the wind swirled through what remained of the ancient Castle Carrisford.

"Look at all of them," said Mr. Roseingrave, beaming at the people on every side. "So busy, so engaged in their labor." He turned to twinkle at his daughter, cheeks flushed with hope, the sharp wind tugging at the ends of his muffler. "No silver-tongued thieves and swindlers here."

Sophie bit her lip. In her estimation, it was far too early to go making judgments about the character of an entire populace. The Roseingraves had lived in Carrisford a scant two weeks, and most of that time had been spent organizing the secondhand instrument shop: checking the stock against the previous owner's inventory lists, setting out sheet music and partbooks, oiling wood and tuning strings, hanging the violins and guitars on the wall, placing the harps where they'd show to best advantage. Even with seven Roseingraves pitching in, the work had felt endless—the more so because it was now a full two months since Sophie or her father had laid hands on a piano.

She flexed her fingers inside her mittens, as though shaking off a weight.

Now, finally, they'd been called out on a piano job. A local widow, one Mrs. Muchelney, had asked them to take a look at some damage to her family instrument. If Mr. Roseingrave thought secondhand sales and repair work were a sad comedown for a man used to designing and building his own pianofortes in his own workshop—including a new type of piano action he was still hoping to patent—he didn't show it. His cheeks glowed rose-red in the wind, and his lanky legs ate up the street beneath him.

Sophie's frozen heart thawed a little to see her father so happy. He'd taken Mr. Verrinder's betrayal so painfully to heart, it had acted upon him like a wasting sickness. When he'd told the family of his plan to move them out of London and to this town near the sea, Sophie'd thought of mineral waters and hot springs and quailed to think her father imagined himself a permanent invalid.

She hoped there was no new Mr. Verrinder to come along and blight his recovery. Thankfully, in all of London, for all her life, Sophie had only ever met one Mr. Verrinder.

Perhaps Carrisford was simply too small to hold anyone with so much wickedness.

They wound their way past bakeries, butcher shops, handcarts with pies of all kinds, and orange sellers. The streets grew more spacious, the houses less squashed against one another. Mr. Roseingrave set down his tools and knocked at the side door of a cozy home of three stories. "Mrs. Muchelney has a Southwell—and five children, I hear," he murmured, hands clasped behind his back, bouncing a little on the balls of his feet.

Sophie nodded. She knew the role she might have to play: keep the children occupied and away from the delicate instrument while her father assessed the work to be done. Hand him tools one by one while warding off small sticky fingers. She'd done it all her life, ever since her younger siblings had started coming along, year by year. There had been four Roseingraves after Sophie, but somehow five Muchelneys seemed like a larger number.

It meant she'd likely be too occupied to set hands to Mrs. Muchelney's piano today. Sophie writhed secretly at the tiny bright note of relief she felt about that.

Mrs. Muchelney was round and warm as a teapot as she greeted them. "Oh, Mr. Roseingrave, I cannot thank you enough for coming today. Harriet and Susan were trying to teach one another fencing and I do not know what harm they may have done to that piano."

"Whatever it is, I'm sure we can mend it," Mr. Roseingrave said, clasping the widow's hands between his and sending her the deferential smile he saved for customers.

She smiled back gratefully, patted his wrist with a soft, pale hand, and guided him to where the instrument stood between a pair of windows overlooking the street.

Mrs. Muchelney's Southwell was an old-fashioned demi-lune variety, the kind that looked like a simple half-circle side table until you lifted the top and found the keys waiting for you underneath. Instead of a pedal for the sustain, which would have looked odd on a table and spoiled the illusion, there was a lever to be pressed at the height of the player's knee.

The underside of the fallboard had been inlaid with paler wood and veneered to look like the spines of a sea-shell, radiating upward and outward when opened—as it evidently had been when the duelists struck, because a gash marred the shining surface, and splinters framed a jagged hole in the wooden lattice that sheltered the instrument's working parts.

Sophie bit her lip, and saw her father's shoulders give a delicate shudder. "You said they were teaching one another to fence?" Mr. Roseingrave asked.

But the widow was attending to a footman, who had bent to murmur in his mistress's ear.

Mrs. Muchelney's sigh had the threadbare quality of

a maternal patience long worn out from use. "Pray excuse me, Mr. Roseingrave," she said. "The boys' violin tutor has just arrived, and I have some similar matters to discuss with him." She vanished through the doorway.

"Apparently this is a very dangerous house for instruments," Mr. Roseingrave said, his low tone shaded by amusement.

"Susan was reading about assassins," a voice piped up. "She said we were woefully underprepared to defend ourselves."

Sophie and her father turned. A girl of thirteen or so was standing there, brown haired and brown eyed, face freckled and currently bright pink with rebellion. Hands clasped before her, shoulders back, chin up. As though she were determined to bear up nobly under some coming blow, like a martyr in a child's book of sermons.

"What weapons had you chosen?" Mr. Roseingrave asked curiously.

"The fire irons." The girl—Harriet Muchelney, presumably—replied. She spread her feet and braced herself for reproof.

Sophie smiled. "I'm sure this piano will think twice about threatening you after this."

Those brown eyes fixed on her, then flickered back to the instrument. "It was a gift from Uncle Albert to Papa," Harriet explained. "We only keep it because Uncle Albert died, and then Papa died, and it makes Mother sad to think of parting with it." She chewed her lip. "Nobody even plays it."

Mr. Roseingrave had taken off his coat and set it aside, and rolled up his sleeves. "Let's see if you've wounded it fatally."

It took his experienced hands only a few moments to

find where the case came apart—the showy lacquered wood fell away and Mr. Roseingrave slid out the action. There were the hammers, the dampers, the springs and shanks and hinges, all the bits of wood and felt and metal that came together for the making of music. The ivory-topped naturals and ebony sharps that were such a striking feature of the piano looked so much smaller when the rest of the mechanism was visible.

And most importantly: the strings. Inside the half-circle case, they crossed over one another in two layers, the thicker, longer bass strings stretched slantwise over the shorter notes for the treble and tenor. Exposed like this, they whispered echoes of every sound that reached them.

Harriet gave a little gasp. The note of wonder was unmistakable.

Mr. Roseingrave looked up at Sophie and smiled wryly.

Sophie smiled and nodded her head gently in return. She knew precisely what he was thinking. He'd shown every one of her younger siblings the inside of a piano, one by one. They'd been vaguely curious—small hands testing the tension of the strings, pressing on the keys to watch how the action raised the hammer and the damper and then brought both back down. But before long their hearts had been claimed by other instruments: Freddie by the viola, Robbie the cello, the twins Jasper and Julia striving to outdo one another on the violin.

Sophie alone had shared her father's love of the piano, with its chorus of voices and hidden machinery.

Now, apparently, Harriet Muchelney had lost her heart to it as well. The girl's eyes were round and her clenched hands had gone slack in amazement. She lifted one hand slightly, as though tempted to reach out and stroke the strings directly, like the harp they resembled. But it was clear she didn't dare actually touch anything.

Sophie knew that heart-struck wonder. There was something irresistibly poignant in an opened piano awaiting repair—like a wounded bird with its feathers splayed. It needed patient attention and a soothing touch to get it to sing again.

"Aha." Her father's voice interrupted her thoughts. "Looks like there's only one hammer broken inside. Not a fatal wound at all." His long fingers worked swiftly to pluck out the damaged part, with its red-and-white felt head, while Sophie rummaged in the tool bag for a shank of the size and length Southwells usually held. The hammer head slid off the old shank and onto the new, and the action went back into its proper place, the bulk of it sliding home like a key fitting into a lock.

Mr. Roseingrave grinned down at the keyboard. "Let's see what she sounds like." He struck the note attached to the repaired hammer: the A in the octave above middle C.

The tone staggered like its knees had been broken.

Sophie and Harriet Muchelney both winced.

Mr. Roseingrave laughed in horror. "I see she needs tuning! Sophie, would you be so kind?"

Her father had a genius for piano design and mechanics—

but Sophie shared her opera singer mother's perfect ear for pitch. So it was Sophie who'd learned the tuning trade, and who'd taken over when her mother's hearing began to suffer. Between them they'd tuned every piano that bore the Rose-ingrave name.

She smoothed her brown skirts down and took a seat on the bench, the ribs of the piano spread wide before her.

Her shaky fingers wrapped around the handle of the tuning hammer and gripped tight, one pinky on the end, thumb extended along the handle for leverage. She put the tuning hammer on the head of the first pin, muted the notes to the side of the starting string, nudged the knee lever to raise all the dampers, and set her left hand on the keys.

The familiar movements ought to have been a comfort. Instead, sweat and fear made her hands soft and slick as melting candles.

Every string was a voice, every pin was an eye—watching her. Waiting.

Her father coughed, softly. She didn't dare glance back at him. The ivory was cool beneath her touch, the winter sun-light spilling in the window not enough to warm it, or to melt the chill of fear in Sophie's bones. She sucked in a lungful of air and struck the key hard before she lost her nerve. The note banged like brass into the semi-silence.

The heaviness of iron, sensible only in memory, clapped tight and hard around her fingers.

It's nothing. She repeated that silently like a prayer. *It's only one note, to test the tuning. It's not really playing. You don't have to think about your fingers. Just listen.*

Sophie tried to ignore the leaden stiffness in her hands, and gave all her attention to her ears.

The note was flat, the string too slack. She moved the tuning hammer—just slightly, a light wriggle back and forth, her fingers sensitive to the tiny movements of the pin where it was anchored in the block behind the soundboard. She struck the key again, and again, the same note thrumming like a heartbeat. Another light twist of the hammer and there it was, the proper pitch, pure and clean as the first breath of spring after a long winter.

Tears pooled in her eyes; she blinked them back.

Sophie's hands and hammer moved up and down the keyboard, skipping higher or lower and then tuning the strings in the gaps. It was slow going. This house had five children, and thin walls—and this piano was slight and small, not meant for pouring out oceans of sound. You had to tune it to blend well with the noises around it, or it would always sound off no matter how accurate the pitch. She tuned the bass to the sound of the carts and horses going by in the street outside, and the treble to the plaintive voice of violins being imperfectly practiced several rooms away. In fact, by adjusting the sharpness just slightly, she could cancel out some of the angrier harmonics from the Muchelney boys' lessons: instead of wolves howling in rage, they became hounds baying on a hunt.

"Oh," she heard young Miss Muchelney breathe, very softly. Echoing her own relief as the jarring harmonics were tamed.

By the time she reached the final string, she had stopped

trying to contain the drops that spilled from her eyes and down her cheeks. Her father quietly handed her a handkerchief when she finished the highest note on the treble; she wiped her face, tucked it in her sleeve, and finished tuning the bass.

When at last she set down her hammer and sighed, rolling her shoulders to get some of the tightness out, her father reached down to the keyboard.

An arpeggio rang out, this one sweet as a bell.

Miss Muchelney gasped again, her voice unwittingly hitting some of the harmonics hidden in the notes.

Sophie wiped her eyes one final time and glanced up at her father.

He gripped her shoulder—lightly, fingers extended, just the way Sophie gripped the tuning hammer. His smile was soft, without any of the sadness he'd carried around like a cloak the past two months. "Well done, my dear," he murmured.

Sophie gulped and nodded. *He doesn't have to know you can't stop feeling that device,* she told herself sternly. *Just let him be proud of you.*

Her father may have begun to recover from Mr. Verrinder's fraud. But Sophie still had a long, long way to go.

This was how great crimes began: with a single secret question and no law around to overhear.

"All those in favor?" Maddie Crewe asked.

And every hand in the room went up.

Really, they ought to have been somewhere seedier for this. Not this small polite room with its whitewashed plaster and homely windows and a decade-old accretion of technical books. This crime should have been born in a proper den of iniquity, with guttering candles and dubious beverages and women of even more dubious morals.

Maddie supposed one out of three would have to do.

The conspirators here tonight were women and girls, ranging in ages from sixteen to sixty, and mostly on the younger side of the scale. Half were factory girls in their pinafores going off to work the night shift after this, the rest were handweavers of silk ribbons, satin, crepe, bombazine, brocade, and velvet. Madeleine Crewe was a ribbon weaver and the current chairwoman of the Carrisford Weavers' Library (formerly Weavers' Library and Reform Society, changed for prudence's sake when the magistrates had started to look askance at any group with the word *reform* in their name).

This crime was half Maddie's idea.

The other half had come from Mrs. Money—"rhymes with stony," as she'd explained in her gravelly voice. She was a newcomer, much better dressed than the others. Maddie had seen the girls' eyes travel along the lines of her rich black coat with real fur at the cuffs and collar, estimating its weight and worth with eyes that knew precisely how much food the weaving of such fabric would have earned them. They'd been quite naturally wary of anyone in such a coat—until Maddie had showed them Mrs. Money's convict love token, the twin to her own, and told them about the scheme, and asked if they wanted to help.

Hence the unanimous yes. Helping was what the Library was for, after all.

It wouldn't be Maddie's first walk on the shady side of the law. She'd slipped away from a shop a time or two with more in her pockets than when she'd come in. She'd let a lonely soldier—or his lonelier wife—buy her a meal and a drink in exchange for an evening's company. Just to help a body get by when bread was dear. And a little light larceny now and again was practically expected of factory girls, as steady apprenticeships vanished and wages sank lower and lower. Everyone had to make shift somehow.

And once, at seventeen, when Maddie had finally had enough mistreatment and walked away from the throwing mill, and away from its horrible overseer . . . They'd sent her to jail for breaking contract and shaved her head so the lesson would sink in.

But hair, like hope, had a way of growing back. Maddie was free, and her auburn waves now flowed past her shoulders when she left them unpinned. She tucked one wayward lock behind her ear now, and smiled at her fellow thieves.

"It's likely to be dangerous," Mrs. Money said. Her voice was soft but her eyes were hard, and she turned them on every weaver in the room, one by one. "They'll transport us, if they catch us."

"Or worse," Alice Bilton said.

"Nothing's worse," Mrs. Money shot back.

Alice put her long fingers to her long mouth and chewed

her nails grimly. At nine-and-twenty, she was older than Maddie, but her thin frame and general air of nervousness made her seem a decade younger.

Mrs. Money continued: "Are you sure you don't want to take that vote again?"

Maddie understood her skepticism. Mrs. Money had met these girls only tonight. If she'd known them better, she'd know the Library had been criminals for years already. Combinations, such as workers formed to agitate for better wages and working conditions, had been outlawed in England for decades. It was legal for workers to form associations to sell wares jointly, or purchase a set of small rooms like this for lectures, or take up subscriptions for their library of technical weaving volumes and pattern books.

But they knew if they tried to protest for higher wages or fewer hours, or any softening at all in their working conditions, the law would come down strongly on each and every one of them. As it had in London and Manchester and Birmingham.

The law hadn't stopped the girls dreaming about it, though. And it hadn't stopped them talking, especially when Maddie's mother had been running things. The late Mrs. Crewe had always said: "There are only two kinds of people, Madeleine. The people you protect—and the people you protect them from."

Maddie believed that more fiercely now that her mother was gone.

So instead of calling for a second vote, Maddie turned to Mrs. Money and asked: "Have you ever heard the story of Jenny Hull?"

The woman's head snapped around.

Maddie couldn't help but grin. She'd known that would get Mrs. Money's attention.

The weavers, long familiar with the legend, snorted and laughed and elbowed one another.

Maddie began: "Here's how they tell it. Jenny Hull was a silk weaver in Carrisford back when silk work was good money. She wove beautiful brocades. The best in all Essex, or so they say. One day a mercer tried to cheat her—saying she'd done less work than she had, so he could give her less money for it. Jenny decided it wasn't right for him to keep a silk he hadn't properly paid for. So she put on her best dress and found a friend and they pretended to be customers, and went by his shop when he was out. The friend distracted the assistant, while Jenny hid the bolt of brocade in her skirts and strode out—but the mercer came back early, and caught them, and brought them before the magistrates. Jenny's friend was found not guilty—they couldn't prove she'd meant to steal anything, when all she'd done was ask to look at the wares—but Jenny was condemned. She was the first woman from Carrisford to be transported to Australia, and the magistrates and the merchants made sure everybody in town heard about it."

"Ever since," Alice chimed in—she'd always reveled in ghost stories, and this was pretty near—"Carrisford weavers have told their daughters: behave, or you'll walk Jenny Hull's path. Be good, or you'll end up where Jenny Hull went. And—well—the children started telling their own versions, after a while."

"Don't stay out late, or Jenny Hull will get you," Judith Wegg added, curving her light brown hands into claws.

"Don't flirt, don't talk back, don't ask questions, don't be ungrateful—" Alice counted off.

"—or she'll snatch you up and swallow you down and leave only your boots behind," Maddie laughed. Mrs. Money was looking rather dumbfounded, and Maddie couldn't blame her. It was one thing to hear about a local legend— quite another thing to actually become one.

"They say she was descended from witches," Alice said, with relish, as Judith quirked an eyebrow at her. "Wicked from birth, and she used to weave spells into her silk."

Mrs. Money made a faint sound of disbelief in the back of her throat.

"So you see," Maddie concluded firmly, "we grew up certain that the law was ready to punish us for something, someday. It's just the way things are."

"Which is not to say we're reckless," Alice hurried to add.

"Not all of us," Judith said wryly, making Alice hide a laugh behind one hand and attempt to look innocent.

Mrs. Money blew out a long breath, carefully smoothing down the fur on her coat collar. "That's good," she said bluntly. "For this to work, the worst thing we can be is afraid."

"How *does* it work?" Judith asked. "What is the plan precisely?"

Everyone looked at Maddie. Twenty-three pairs of eyes, bright and expectant and wary and nervous. Alone they would have been as easy to shake off as scraps of loose thread;

twisted together, they bound Maddie to their cause like the ropes that pulled a sail taut against the wind.

If that made her feel strained and stretched and raggedy as a worn piece of canvas, well, that was just the price you paid for keeping everyone safe.

"We don't have everything worked out yet," Maddie said, "but we have the broad strokes. Here's how we start . . ."

CHAPTER TWO

The Muchelneys' violin teacher was Mr. William Frampton, a pleasant-faced man with close-cropped dark curls and lustrous brown skin. He and Mr. Roseingrave discovered a mutual passion for mechanical design, and by the time they'd reached the Roseingraves' shop Sophie and her father had been invited to next Tuesday afternoon's meeting of the Aeolian Club, a musical and mathematical society that met once a month to perform for one another and discuss topics of artistic and scientific interest.

On the day, however, Mr. Roseingrave received a note about a possible piano for sale—the first such purchase he would be able to make since opening the Carrisford shop. "But you go on, Soph," he said to his daughter, with a wink. "You're a sensible girl. I think Carrisford is safe enough for you to adventure in on your own."

The Aeolian Club met in the oldest section of town, in a room with a plaque that read CARRISFORD WEAVERS' LI-BRARY. It was a small room, clearly well loved and much frequented. Books were stacked haphazardly upon the shelves that ringed the walls, many with samples of textured wool and silk brocade peeking out of the pages. A set of chairs had been drawn into a semicircle around a small dais at the front. The group was some two dozen in number, mostly tradesmen's sons and daughters like Sophie, with a few of the local lesser gentry. Someone brought cakes and biscuits from the corner bakery, a pot of tea was produced, and mismatched cups with chipped handles were lavishly handed round.

Sophie sipped her tea and tried to remember names and was able to relax a little into the music during the performance part of the meeting. Miss Mary Slight played several variations on the harp, after which discussion broke out on the subject of whether or not it was possible to build an automaton that could play any stringed instrument. "The Musician built by Mr. Jacquet-Droz played a working organ," Miss Slight recalled, "but that required only pressure from the mechanical hands. A harp involves a great deal more flexibility in the hand and fingers, and that brings up the question of how to control such complex movements."

"The difficulty is not just in the movements," Mr. Frampton countered, leaning hopefully forward. "The impossible part would be reproducing the real harpist's extraordinary skill and sensitivity. I'm sure you need no enlightening upon *that* subject."

Miss Slight blushed with pleasure.

Sophie hid a smile and slipped out to walk home again, leaving her new friend to his flirtation.

It was a bright morning, if cold, and the streets were

thronged with townsfolk eager to get out and about before the snows returned.

People, Sophie marveled, *are preposterously attractive.*

She'd known this in London: from the highborn ladies to the street singers, Sophie hadn't been able to walk down a single street in town without finding some face or figure that caught her eye and set her heartbeat thundering in her veins. She'd thought it was because she'd been born there, some kind of natural affinity—but she was having the same amount of trouble in Carrisford. People here were *differently* appealing—there was something in the general style that was unlike the inhabitants of London—but the beauty of them all kept Sophie's appetites ready and ravenous.

A woman strode by with her hem swirling around slender booted ankles; the movement of those skirts made Sophie ache with envy and yearning. She hadn't been kissed in over a year now . . .

Not for the first time, Sophie thought what a shame it was she couldn't marry a woman. It's not that men didn't please her—Sophie liked a strong nose and a well-turned calf and a man who knew what to do with his hands—but there were just so many lovely women around. Such a waste to have to discount them as possible spouses.

Unfortunately, she didn't think it was only a matter of it not being legal. Because even adding in the men she'd flirted with and pined for and even kissed once or twice, Sophie had always been the one of the pair to be more tempest-tossed by desire. Nobody had ever seemed to yearn for her the way she yearned for them.

Perhaps she was made wrong, somehow. Perhaps that was what had made her so susceptible to Mr. Verrinder's poison.

The wind coming off the river was particularly sharp today, and by the time she reached the high street Sophie's face was numb and her fingers were chilled stiff even through her gloves. It was only another quarter mile to the instrument shop—but as soon as she arrived there she'd be put back to work. Probably tuning the new Rubini violins.

It wasn't that the job was onerous, really, it was just . . . Today, for the first time in a long while, since well before Mr. Verrinder, Sophie had felt like she existed as something more than her responsibilities to her family. No siblings to oversee, no mother to assist, no father to either make proud or disappoint.

It had been just her. Just Sophie.

She wasn't quite ready to let go of herself quite yet.

Impulsively, she ducked into the nearest storefront. Over the door the silhouette of a bewigged brass courtier proclaimed the owner as Giles & Co., Mercer and Draper, Est. 1794.

It was a palace of a place. Arched upper windows let the light flow through onto a cacophony of fabric on shelves and tables: chintz and bright-printed calico, cotton and linen and lace. Gleaming silks and satins and brocades poured from rods high on the walls, and one corner was a riot of jewel-toned ribbons, edging, and trim. Gilt thread and silver buttons gleamed beneath the glass of the counter at the far end of the room.

After the grays and browns of the town outside so much color and pattern seared the eye. Sophie chafed her hands to warm them, then made her way to the corner with the ribbons. The fabric required for new dresses was costly beyond her means at the moment, but she had enough for a little something to liven up a collar or a cuff.

As a mother and daughter finished paying for their goods and chattered out the door, Sophie reached out to brush her fingers along one bright ribbon: a flight of pink and gold love-birds woven against a cream background. Something in the flow of it reminded her of musical staves—

"There's a story goes with that one," said a voice very near.

Sophie flinched and whirled, startled.

The man who'd spoken laughed, and grasped her elbow to stop her spinning. He had light gold hair and a neat beard running to gray, and his eyes were bright as pennies. Sophie started to tug her arm away—but he held on, though his smile stayed kind, and showed off an appealing set of laugh lines. "Steady, miss, there's nothing to be afraid of. I'm the proprietor here—Mr. Giles himself, at your service—and I only wanted to let you in on the secret."

He shook her elbow a little, then let his hand drop.

"Pleased to meet you," Sophie said, because that's what one said. The elbow he'd grabbed throbbed slightly, and she wondered if she'd find a bruise there later.

"Here." Mr. Giles plucked the ribbon out of the rack and stretched it between his hands like a tightrope for a roped-ancer to walk. "My father created this pattern on the day he first saw my mother. She was the daughter of a comte, back in France under the Bourbons. He was a mere silk weaver, only good for making the ribbons she wore around her throat. Nowhere near good enough to marry."

He spun the ribbon into a circle and tied it off with a flourish, patterned birds fluttering and writhing as the knot pulled tight beneath his fingers.

"My mother wore this ribbon to a garden party, and caught the eye of a duc, who asked for her hand. Her father—my grandfather—was delighted, but my mother refused the match. So my grandfather locked her in her room until she chose to be reasonable." He put one hand through the circle and twisted, so the ribbon banded around his wrist like a manacle.

Sophie shivered.

The mercer's smile flashed a few more teeth. "The Revolution began the next day. My grandfather fought to hold out against the peasants who stormed his estate, but by sunset he had been dragged away to the Bastille. As he was marched to the guillotine, my father ventured into the smoking ruins of his estate and freed my mother, still trapped in her boudoir. They took her jewels and found a ship and crossed the Channel, to England. They wed as soon as they got the license, and were happily in love for the rest of their lives." He freed his wrist and held out the ribbon, balanced like a coronet on the palm of his hand.

Sophie hesitated, chewing on her lip. She was used to shop folk being insistent about their wares: it was part and parcel of the trade. And the ribbon was very lovely. But she had the unshakable thought that by taking the ribbon, she would be accepting far more than just a trinket.

These were the kind of warning thoughts she was trying to pay better attention to.

"Come, come," Mr. Giles said. He grasped her at the wrist and turned her hand over, setting the ribbon in the middle of her palm, where it tickled her fingers into closing around it.

His other hand held longer than she liked, wrapped around her wrist.

Behind him, the door swung open. Mr. Giles dropped her hand and turned toward the door, a little too quick.

A woman walked in, and Sophie forgot about everything else.

This woman was *breathtaking*.

Auburn hair that gleamed gold where the light caught strands slipping free of their pins. Hazel eyes that sparkled with more gold in their rich depths. A perfect pink bud of a mouth, high cheekbones, roses blooming red against the cream of her complexion. A cheap dress of worn gray wool, soft as moonlight—but beneath it a figure that had Sophie's hands curling with the need to shape it, her musician's fingers playing over every curve and contour.

She shook herself. Useless. Sophie'd been with a few pretty girls, but never one so pretty as this. She might as well have tried to pluck the moon from the sky.

This woman was how she'd imagined every cruel heart-breaker in every old ballad she'd ever heard. If you were lucky, you pined away for love of her. If you weren't lucky, you won her, lost her, and were damned.

Here was Sophie, craving damnation.

"Miss Crewe," said the mercer.

Sophie's eyes narrowed. His tone was cheerful enough, but there was a note out of tune.

Miss Crewe nodded her glorious head. "Mr. Giles," she said in return.

Oh dear heavens, beneath the leisurely vowels of her local accent, her voice was low and sweet and just a little bit raspy. Sophie clutched a hand to her heart. She would never make it out of this draper's shop alive.

She pressed herself back into the shadows, the better to be overlooked.

"Have you come with ribbons for me at last, Miss Crewe?"

"Not today, Mr. Giles," the woman replied, matching his tone so precisely that Sophie instantly suspected her of mockery. "I have something else you ought to see instead." The woman heaved up the fabric she had under her arm—Sophie'd missed that detail, too enraptured by the sweet angle of Miss Crewe's cheek—and dropped it onto the sunniest spot of the counter.

Blue silk—but something was odd about it. Sophie held her breath and craned her neck. The blue had other colors running through, just one or two threads at a time. Gold, silver, red, and yellow stood out and made a clash against the hue.

Mr. Giles came around the counter to take a corner in his expert hands. Judging by his face, he approved of it even less than Sophie did. "A satin, Miss Crewe? And with such an . . . unusual color palette? It hardly looks deliberate."

Miss Crewe shrugged, a hypnotic rise and fall of one elegant shoulder. "It's not my finest work, I'll admit, Mr. Giles—but you might take it off my hands, if you like. For half-pay rates."

Mr. Giles narrowed his eyes and folded his hands on the countertop. "Have you started taking in half-pay work, Miss Crewe?"

She snickered. "Not hardly."

"Then the price you've offered me isn't entirely legal, is it?"

Miss Crewe laughed conspiratorially. "I won't tell if you won't."

Mr. Giles snorted. His eyes flickered to Sophie, who hurried to feign a deep fascination with the ribbon rack.

Miss Crewe's voice was a low throb in the quiet of the shop as she leaned forward. "I'll make you a deal," she said to Mr. Giles. Sophie shivered at the musical purr of the sound. "I'll leave this here with you for a bit. I know the fabric looks odd, but believe me: it has a way of growing on you. I'll come by again this evening and if you still don't want the silk, I'll take it back, and happily." She straightened, and smiled, and swanned out the door the same proud way she'd entered.

There was no sign she'd noticed Sophie, heartsick among the ribbons with her fingers tangled up in lovebirds.

Mr. Giles, however, now remembered her—his gaze pinned her in place, though his smile stayed charming. Sophie worked in a shop: she knew the difference between charm and sincerity.

Or she thought she had, before Mr. Verrinder.

"Shall I wrap that ribbon up for you, miss?" Mr. Giles purred.

Sophie blinked down at the coronet in her hands.

"Perhaps . . ." said Mr. Giles. His smile softened as his voice lowered. "You know, I think those colors suit you, miss.

What say you keep the ribbon, as a gift? Just a little secret between friends."

Sophie stared back at him. Uncertainty wound itself round her tongue and held her silent. She couldn't think what to say to him, because she couldn't think what it was he meant by giving her such a gift. She wasn't his friend. He didn't even know her name.

Mr. Giles tapped a thoughtful finger against his chin. "Of course, friends don't repeat one another's private conversations, do they?"

Ah. Confusion clarified. Not a gift, then. A bribe.

Bribes punctured the illusion of politeness, and Sophie sucked in a breath to sweetly reject his offer.

The door opened again, and she swallowed her words as Mr. Giles spun automatically on his heel.

A second woman entered—a lady, older, with plentiful gray threaded throughout the black strands of her hair. Sophie had met a duchess once, in London, while tuning her daughter's new piano, and even though this lady's high-waisted black coat was a little behind the fashion, she had that same aristocratic posture and arrogant tilt of the chin. From the fine leather of her shoes to the silver feathers arching proudly from her hat, everything about her reeked of wealth and luxury.

Mr. Giles offered her a deferential bow as she proceeded forward. "Welcome, madam," he said. "How may I help you this afternoon?"

With his head lowered, he missed the way the lady's lips curled slightly, in unmistakable scorn, though her voice stayed cool and untroubled. "My maid spilled a bottle of perfume and spoiled a silk gown," she said. "I've come to see if you have anything decent to replace it with."

"Our best silks are—" Mr. Giles began, but cut off when the lady gasped and stepped toward the counter.

One fine-gloved hand plucked at the corner of the odd blue silk, turning it back and forth, watching the light play on the threads of color. No mistaking it now: her mouth was a sneer, and her voice had turned positively glacial. "Sir, I must ask you: *Where* did you get this fabric?"

Mr. Giles scrambled forward and began rolling up the bolt of cloth, hurrying to hide the offending article. "My apologies, madam—that was brought to us in error—"

The lady's grip on the cloth tightened into a fist. "It certainly was," the woman said. "I know this weave, sir—and I can tell you one thing: it has *never* been offered for sale."

Mr. Giles gulped and chattered, the trailing ends of explanations hanging from his lips as his eyes darted from the lady to the silk and back again.

"Who brought it to you? They had no right. I shall take this away and report it to the authorities at once." She pulled a little harder on the corner of the silk.

A glint came into the mercer's eye, and he put a hand firmly on the bolt, holding it in place. "Madam," he said, with a little more steel than servility, "if there is some question about the provenance of this fabric, then by all means make your case to the magistrates. But until then, I must regretfully insist my wares remain with me."

Her chin raised. "Is this all you have of the stuff?"

"Yes, madam."

"I will pay you a pound for it," the lady said.

Sophie choked, and even Mr. Giles looked stunned to hear his prices more than doubled. "A pound?" he said.

The lady clicked her tongue. "Have I offended your pride? A guinea, then."

"Two guineas," said Mr. Giles, who even in the midst of mystification was clearly ready to seize an opportunity.

"Done," the lady replied.

Mr. Giles looked as happy as if he'd been offered three wishes by a benevolent fairy.

The lady held up a hand. "Provided—and I cannot insist enough upon this point—provided you let me know *at once* if you come across any more of this silk. Send to Mrs. Horace Money, at the Mulberry Tree." Mr. Giles nodded acquiescence, and the lady reached diffidently into her purse for the guineas as the draper began wrapping her purchase in brown paper.

Sophie set the ribbon on a nearby shelf and slipped out the door. Mr. Giles wouldn't miss such a small sale, not after the windfall he'd just had.

Her footsteps sounded an irritated march in the frost. Two guineas! For one bolt of ugly silk! Poor Miss Crewe. She had obviously been desperate to sell that fabric, and had no idea of its true value. She would come back later and find it gone—and Sophie was not willing to trust Mr. Giles would tell her the truth about what had happened. She would get her half-pay, but not realize she'd been so thoroughly cheated.

A flash of auburn hair—there! Miss Crewe's tall form

was just disappearing round the corner. Sophie hitched up her skirts and hurried to catch her.

It took two turnings before her shorter legs caught up with Miss Crewe's long strides. They were just outside St. Severus's churchyard, winter's first snow draping the headstones in the graveyard like fur stoles on an opera-loving audience. "Miss Crewe!" Sophie gasped. "Excuse me, Miss Crewe!"

The woman paused with one hand on the graveyard gate. Her mitten like her muffler was thick blue wool, with scars where it had been darned and the newer yarn showed brighter against the old.

"Yes?" said Miss Crewe, squinting at Sophie, who had to pause to suck air into her lungs. "I'm sorry, have we met?" The woman's lips pursed, and her head tilted, and a teasing note entered her voice. "Was I drunk?" Her eyes swept down Sophie's shape and then up again, lingeringly.

"No, I—" Sophie gulped again, heat rushing over her wherever Miss Crewe's gaze touched. It seemed Sophie wasn't the only girl in Carrisford with an eye for other women.

Miss Crewe was smiling now, very slightly, as though remembering a wicked secret she was hoping Sophie remembered too.

Sophie's voice was breathy when she went on: "I was in Mr. Giles's shop just now—"

"Were you?" Miss Crewe's hand tightened convulsively on the metal spike of the gate. Her alluring smile stayed in place, but that clutching grip told a different tale: she was on her guard.

"Y-yes," Sophie replied. "After you left . . . Mr. Giles sold your silk—for two guineas!"

Miss Crewe shrugged, as if this was of no consequence. "I left it because I hoped he'd sell it. Obviously."

"But," Sophie protested, "at such a price—you were only asking—"

"Since we do not know one another, Miss Anybody," Miss Crewe interrupted, "I will kindly ask you not to meddle in my business. A girl can wind up in a great deal of trouble that way." She shoved open the graveyard gate with an unholy shriek of rusted metal.

Sophie flinched hard, as the discordant sound scraped raw every nerve she had.

By the time she unscrewed her eyes and straightened her spine again, Miss Crewe had passed the gate and was striding between the headstones. Sophie watched until her tall gray figure vanished behind the corner of the church.

The gate swung slowly shut on a long, anguished moan.

Sophie stared and stared at that empty corner, until a passing carter yelled at her to get out of his way. She scrambled out of the street, putting out one hand on the graveyard fence to steady herself.

Cold and iron bit through the worn leather of her glove. Sophie felt the drumbeat of panic—until she realized it was no memory this time. Her hand was wrapped around one of the gate's iron spikes—the same one Miss Crewe had clutched, when Sophie had asked her . . . No, when Sophie had told her . . .

I will kindly ask you not to meddle in my business, Miss Crewe had said, haughty as any princess.

The wealthy woman's voice plucked at Sophie's memory: *I know this weave . . . it has never been offered for sale.*

Until today. By someone who didn't even care how much it had sold for. Who responded with anger when someone tried to tell them they might have been cheated.

It didn't make any sense—unless you had seen something equally senseless before. Something that turned out to be a lie—and a lie dreadful enough to have ruined her entire family.

Cold spread from her hand, up her arm, and unfolded dark wings in her chest. Suspicion stretched, and fixed itself into a terrible certainty: something was horribly wrong in Carrisford.

Somebody was running a swindle.

And Miss Crewe was in it up to her pretty neck.

Sophie clenched her jaw, clutched her skirts, and marched back to Mr. Giles's shop. She was going to ask him a few questions about Miss Crewe. And she didn't care how many inches—or feet—or miles—of romantic ribbons she had to purchase to get the answers.

She wouldn't ignore her misgivings, or tell herself she was imagining things. Not this time.

Nobody else was going to get ruined, if Sophie could prevent it.

Chapter Three

Maddie Crewe walked home in twilight, past where the new paving stones gave way to the rough medieval cobbles that marked the older parts of town. Once this neighborhood had been a fine estate with gardens, glasshouses, and overwealthy guests. But times had changed, the town had crowded in, and now it was a warren of homes divided up piecemeal and given out as poor relief by the parish overseers.

It was a place you lived when there wasn't anywhere else for them to put you, except the workhouse.

Maddie let herself in the front door and breathed in the smell of Cat's oyster stew. Soft humming came from the kitchen, and the appetizing clink of a pot being stirred. Some knot in Maddie's heart unloosed a little at the prospect of a proper meal, and she hurried to shed her scarf and mittens and hang them up on their peg.

John Hedingham was in the front room, his cotton sleeves rolled up, punching lacing holes in kid leather with an awl. His wife, Emma, was sitting in the last of the light, embroidering a pair of satin slippers with delicate gilt clocks. Dozens of pairs of boots and slippers and shoes danced on the walls around them, the newness of silk and satin aggressively shiny against plain plaster and well-worn wood. Every flat surface in the room held tools or trimming—silk and lace, leather and damask, rolls of cord and thread and ribbon.

Beads and buttons and buckles gleamed like gorgeous insects as Maddie pulled up a stool and sat, taking care not to block the wan winter sunlight. Candles were dear and hard on the eyes.

"We spoke to Mrs. Ravenell today," John began. "And Mr. Colson, Mrs. Doorey, and the Tahourdin brothers. Asked if they'd heard anything about a strange blue silk with . . . unusual properties."

Maddie grinned. "And had they?"

John laughed. "Of course not—though you know Mrs. Ravenell. She *pretended* she'd heard it already." His grin widened, and the awl punctured the leather once more. "So I *pretended* to tell her the next part of the tale."

"Good," Maddie said. "I know the rest of the Weavers' Library has been around to nearly every workshop and draper's in town. We might as well have posted handbills on street corners. It'll be mysterious blue silk for three weeks, at least." She leaned back, rolling her head to stretch the old crick out of her neck.

Emma peered anxiously over at her, though her hands never faltered. "Well?"

"Well yourself," Maddie replied, spreading her gray wool skirts and stretching her feet out to take some pressure off her aching soles. Emma pouted, so with a flash of a grin Maddie took pity and stopped stalling. "Mr. Giles took the bait, no trouble. He paid me the rate I asked, and never let on how much profit he'd made on the sale." Just like Miss Anybody had predicted—and just like Maddie and the Library had planned. "Mrs. Money said he nearly fell over himself trying to wriggle into her good graces."

"Must be that aristocratic French blood of his," John replied.

Maddie snorted. "How many times has he told that lie?" she groused. "His mother was an oyster farmer's daughter—and about as French as I am."

"I hear he asked the magistrates if he could display his comte grandfather's coat of arms," John said.

"If they said no, that'll be the first time the magistrates ever said no to him," Emma replied.

Maddie let it wash over her and pass her by. There had been a time when the mere reminder of Mr. Giles's tricks would have her blood boiling. He'd started as what they called an undertaker: someone who took dyed silk thread from the manufacturers, had it woven up, and then returned it to them for final payment. He'd first hired apprentice weavers at half-pay rates, then bought a number of looms and started charging his weavers for their use, making extra profit on each piece of cloth produced. When demand fell off—as happened often, the trade being seasonal—he would send his weavers back to the parish for relief, having kept all the profit of their labor.

In this way Mr. Giles had spent the last two decades

building up a solid little empire, piece by piece. He'd inher-
ited his father's shop and made luxurious improvements to it
while his weavers strained and starved. He'd shorted them
of payment and materials—but instead of trying to hide his
skimming in the books, where it might have been noticed by
his bankers, he passed off the extra in bribes to the manufacturers, dyers, and traders to get himself more advantageous
rates than his rivals. He'd charmed Mr. Prickett from the
silk-throwing mill into a ten percent discount (and he especially charmed his wife, went the rumor).

Lately, the man had managed to get himself set up as a
factor to buy raw silk in London (the only legal port) and sell
it to local mills and dyers. So now he could increase prices
at any point—and send his profits up at every level further
down the chain—even as the law gave him an excuse to keep
wages down even as profits soared. Now Carrisford's whole
silk industry revolved around him, as though he were the
worm at the heart of the cocoon.

Few weavers in Carrisford could avoid working with him
in some capacity. Maddie had so far been able to manage it,
thanks to her skill with pattern drafting—but she didn't
think that would last forever.

He'd played the game well: the only people who ob-
jected to his business practices were the ones least likely to
be listened to. It had once left Maddie positively shaking
with rage and frustration—but not any longer.

Not now that they were going to take every penny of that
wealth away from him. To take it, and use it to fight back
against the practices that kept so many people struggling.

She could almost taste it already, that tart sweet flavor of revenge. Maddie wondered if this was how prisoners felt, at the end of a long and difficult sentence. Years of cold and salt and hand-ruining labor—and then they looked up, saw the light shining through a window, and breathed the sweet, green air of home.

She would have to ask Mrs. Money about that, when all this was over.

Night fell, and Cat called out the stew was done. They trooped into the kitchen to eat, passing hunks of old bread around as Cat poured out small beer. John and Emma both dropped a kiss on her cheek to thank her, and she blushed happily.

Maddie smiled at the trio, a homey kind of envy flooding her along with the warmth of the oyster stew. It had been a while since she'd had someone—much less two someones—to share nights with. Most of the neighborhood thought Catherine Gray only kept house for the Hedinghams. Maddie knew different: Cat slept so infrequently in her own room that it had become an informal storeroom.

The housekeeper leaned contentedly now against Emma's shoulder, John's lips curving with intent as he watched them both from across the scarred kitchen table.

Maddie sighed into her beer, and thought about a pale face with brown hair and deep, soulful eyes, calling out to her at the churchyard gate. Miss Anybody had been soft and small and a little shy—the kind who always made Maddie go overall protective and commanding. Until Maddie had looked into those brown eyes and caught the flash of a bottomless, ravenous hunger that made it clear that quiet exterior was a lie and a fraud. It had shone for only an instant, that dark star, but Maddie still felt the pull of it, aching in her belly even now.

She wanted to see if she could sate such a hunger. She'd always been fierce that way: the more someone needed, the more she wanted to give.

Too bad Miss Anybody had overheard her with Mr. Giles. It had been a kind impulse, going after Maddie to tell her she was being cheated—but it was the worst possible timing. Where had the girl been when Mr. Giles was stealing Maddie's best patterns and having them copied on the cheap? Why did she have to show up now, when Maddie had no time or attention to spare for flirting and frolics?

It was one thing to involve the Weavers' Library in a criminal scheme—it was quite another to pull in some irreproachable tradesman's daughter. Someone who trusted the authorities, and who could afford to be virtuous.

Dinner ended. John and Emma continued to work in the kitchen, sewing and stitching in cozy warmth as Cat took care of the washing up.

Maddie had some work left yet herself—but she couldn't do hers at the hearth. She took a little more beer and went up to her room in the attic.

In the dimness, the frame of the loom rose high and stern as a guillotine. The moon was clouded over and the gas lamps that lit the silk mill at night didn't quite reach this far, so Maddie lit a candle to work by. Tallow smoked and sputtered as she took off her wool dress to put it carefully away.

There was a little dust on the hem from her long trek around town, but it brushed out quickly enough. In her shift and a comforter, topped by a thick shawl that had seen better days, Maddie sat at her small table and continued working out the pattern for a floral ribbon, one row of colored squares at a time.

The loom hulked in the corner of her vision, waiting to be warped. Maddie wondered how you could love and loathe a thing at one and the same time.

She had grown up measuring her height against its frame. Above it, at first, as the drawboy for her mother, perched on a ladder raising the warp threads in shifting sets as Mrs. Crewe sent the shuttle flying back and forth. Later, Maddie had learned the trick of that herself, throwing with just the right flick of the wrist, humming to keep the pace of the work strong and steady. Steady was reliable, reliable was quicker, and quicker was paid faster. She'd done a few years' labor in the silk-throwing mill, and had taken a few other jobs when weaving work was especially hard to come by—but Maddie had always ended up back again at her mother's side.

Despite the familiarity of the machine, Maddie had learned to hate the loom for the amount of time it stole from her. The soul-numbing hours she had to spend in front of it to produce even an inch of the fabric whose luster was worth infinitely more than the sheen of sweat on her brow.

Fashions had shifted, and these days power looms ate up more and more of the market for cloth. Like Maddie herself, the loom had grown over the years: the Jacquard machine, new warp threads, the multiple shuttles flying back and forth had all been added by Maddie or her mother's hands. The late Mrs. Crewe had scrimped and leveraged every London connection she had to get one of the first Jacquard heads in Carrisford—it was a mass of a machine that sat on top of the loom like a bishop in a cathedral pulpit, pattern cards rattling hollowly as their punched holes stopped or let pass the rods that moved the heddles up and down. Expensive, but it let Mrs. Crewe weave complex patterns in a fraction of the time.

A card punch had come with it, and that's how Maddie had begun designing her first patterns. Simple to start with, but soon she was doing elaborate brocade and figured pieces, swirls of color and shape emerging from the secrets encoded in the cards.

Winter was the low season for weaving work, which followed the currents of fashion and so was busiest at the height of summer. A lot of the girls went into service or found other makeshift work; Maddie filled these months in front of a pin block, arranging the thick pins, setting one card on top, and pressing down the open metal guide to puncture the card in all the necessary places. Some of the more elaborate patterns she sold to the cotton weavers who'd had Jacquard looms in their factories for years now. The money from one of these sales was usually enough to get her through the lean times until she could start weaving ribbon on her own loom again.

She still missed working with her mother, the closeness and company of it. The bright jewel-colored satins they used to produce, before the water- and steam-powered looms came along to make those cheaper from the factories. Maddie still had a bit of one particular weave, a bolt of pure bright gold like liquid sunlight.

Fabrics that, she was sure, could have competed with anything smuggled into the country from the French workshops.

She'd find out soon enough, Maddie supposed. According to the newsmongers, the Spitalfields Acts that forbade French silk imports were under siege in Parliament. British dressmakers and drapers would soon be flooded with exquisite French textiles. Everyone knew the first thing the factory owners would do in reaction was to install more power looms. The black silk mourning crepe that Carrisford had been known for was a weave ideal for power loom production.

Which meant less work for the hand looms.

The handweavers still had the edge in velvets, but that wouldn't last forever. Maddie had lived through the decline of Carrisford's once-robust wool industry a decade ago, when the end of the wars meant wool imports resumed. She'd seen how the wool weavers had struggled to survive on the trickle of jobs that hadn't moved to the more machine-friendly north.

She'd worked factories before, and she never wanted to again.

Fortunately, the newspapers also said that the weavers would soon have opportunities they hadn't had for decades: the Combination Acts were also careening toward repeal. Workers would be legally permitted to band together for better conditions and higher wages. These combinations would once again be able to put pressure on the factories to be less of a nightmare for those who labored there. They'd even be able to strike, if it came to that.

But to survive a strike, the Weavers' Library would need funds. A good amount of money to feed and clothe and house protesting workers until a consensus with the owners could be reached. In times past they'd have had a fund stored up from long-standing member dues and donations—but they couldn't collect that legally now, even if it would be legal in a very little while. They quite simply couldn't afford to wait.

Hence: crime. It was really the only practical solution.

Maddie worked until she was so tired her eyes couldn't tell one pin from another. She swallowed the last of her beer and let loose her hair, braiding it gently down her back instead of keeping it pinned tightly back and out of her eyes.

From around her neck she pulled the one piece of jewelry she owned: a slender silver chain from which hung a two-penny piece, drilled through. One side was Britannia showing off her titties and her trident—the other had been carefully sanded flat and then etched with tiny figures: a woman leaning on a coffin, an anchor linking two hearts, and a ship vanishing into the distance. Thick funereal letters around the edge spelled out a promise: I LOVE TILL DEATH SHALL STOP MY BREATH.

Inside the hearts, in letters so tiny they were almost invisible, were written two names. One: MARGUERITE ARTUS, who would later marry and become Marguerite Crewe.

The second name: JENNY HULL.

After the trial Marguerite had had two of these coins carved, one to keep with her, and one to send across the sea with her condemned beloved. She hadn't told her daughter the same Jenny Hull stories the other parents did: hers were stories of long evenings by the river, or summer rambles through the forest outside of town. She told stories of tricks played on cruel parish officers, of thefts that kept families from starving, of respectable villains and lying heroes and the kind of justice that happened in spite of the law.

Marguerite Crewe had died trying to create a more just world. Her daughter was determined to follow suit—and then Jenny Hull had returned under a new name, with a new fortune, and one old token of a dead woman's love, to match the one Maddie wore like a saint's medal over her heart.

Grief had recognized grief, and two lost souls found a shared purpose in plans for revenge.

The edged letters sparked in the candlelight as Maddie hung the love token from the nail in the wall. She blew out the candle, pulled the blankets tight around her, and was asleep before the thin trail of smoke stopped rising from the wick.

Chapter Four

Sophie's father had indeed found a secondhand piano to purchase from the late Dr. Abernathy's estate. It was a beautiful instrument.

Or, more accurately, it had once been beautiful. Sophie could see it in the curving lines of the case, clean and sleek and true, and the lovingly burnished letters that proclaimed DEWHURST AND FFOLKES as the makers. Short of Roseingrave, Dewhurst and Ffolkes were the names she most liked to see on a piano for sensitivity and richness of tone.

Unlike Mrs. Muchelney's demilune instrument, designed to hide its true nature, this grand piano had been built to flaunt exactly what it was. The cover, when opened, hovered at an angle that seemed to beckon the viewer to move closer and peer inside at the strings that spread out tense and quivering as a wing in flight.

Now all Sophie and her father had to do was put new felt on the hammer pads, replace the rusted bass strings, fit new hinges on the lid, see if the pin block was still solid enough to hold the tuning pins in place, put new tops on the white keys, refinish the mahogany case, and install a newer, smoother action that didn't rattle like a skeleton in a charnel house. And then, of course, to tune it.

Sophie struck one key and thought about hands, as the off-tone wailed and wavered in the air.

You could tell a lot about a person by watching their hands. How they moved, how they held still, what they fidgeted with and what they reached out to grab for themselves.

Mr. Giles's hands had been fluid and graceful, sure and confident—but they'd snatched and tugged; they'd spun Sophie around and twisted expensive ribbon into knots. They'd moved like Mr. Verrinder's hands, gesturing toward what he wanted everyone to see. Hiding what he didn't. When Mr. Giles had seized her wrist, his grip had banded tight as iron.

She ought to have paid more attention to Mr. Verrinder's hands, all those months ago. He'd claimed to be an inventor, but his hands hadn't shown any workmen's marks or calluses. They'd been the deft, deceptive hands of a card sharp, or a pickpocket, or a forger of other men's signatures on letters of credit and counterfeit banknotes. Sophie had been dazzled by their confidence and grace, the teasing way his fingertips brushed the back of her hand when he watched her practicing at the keyboard. The way they seemed to stroke an unspoken apology for the coldness of the iron contraption he insisted would make all of their fortunes in the future.

He'd sold that future several times over, while Sophie was

ensorcelled by his flattery, and Mr. Roseingrave distracted by construction of half a dozen pianos that went unpaid for. His hands had coaxed away everything valuable and left only debts and empty promises behind.

Sophie hadn't gotten a good look at Miss Crewe's hands. She'd been too far away in the draper's shop—and then, outside the church, the woman had been wearing those mittens. Even so, when Sophie had mentioned that blue silk, for whatever reason: her grip had noticeably tightened.

Even through her thick mittens, Miss Crewe's hands had given her away. They were the most honest things about her.

Sophie spread her own hand out over the keyboard and played—well, not precisely a chord. There were a few too many jangly notes, snarling out when they ought to have been blending, soft as velvet. She itched to reach for the tuning hammer.

It was only as the jangle died away that she realized she'd played without feeling her fingers were imprisoned.

Of course, as soon as she realized, the iron came back. She tried shaking it off, but hadn't managed it by the time her mother came out to the front of the shop.

Mrs. Roseingrave was soft and round and a little shorter than Sophie, but had the same brown hair and eyes, the same old-parchment shade of skin. "Sophie, dear," she asked, tilting her head so her good ear was slightly forward, "are you terribly busy with that piano?"

Sophie clenched her cold fingers hopelessly, and sighed. "No," she said, with a shake of her head to make sure the message got through. Tilting her face toward the light, so her lips could be clearly seen, she faced her mother and asked, "How can I help?"

Mrs. Roseingrave smiled, her eyes fixed on the movements of Sophie's mouth, compensating for her troubled hearing. "The twins have grown again," she said, "so I've made a bundle of some of their old things. Our neighbors have told me Mrs. Narayan's shop is the best for secondhand clothes—will you take them there for me? And find a few things to bring back with you?"

"Of course," Sophie said, nodding, and her mother hummed a little in relief.

Mrs. Roseingrave had been a singer as well as a piano tuner, before she lost enough of her hearing range that performing and tuning became impractical. Between the shared talents and her resemblance to her eldest daughter, sometimes Sophie felt as though she were staring into one of those enchanted mirrors from a fairy story, looking forward through the years to her own future.

It was a perfectly acceptable future, she tried to assure herself. A husband, a shop, a family. Comfort enough for the most part, and an abundance of love to go around. These weren't unpleasant things, not at all—in fact they were often considered the very best things in life.

But Sophie was greedy—and deep inside, to her secret shame, Sophie was ambitious. She'd helped raise her siblings while her mother performed, helped her father build pianos and keep the books. She'd lived this life already for over twenty years.

She wanted, desperately, to see what other kinds of life there were. In other places, with other kinds of people. Who weren't so . . . ordinary.

Sophie felt steeped in ordinariness, the dregs of it left too long in the cup, turning her bitter.

Mr. Verrinder had promised the Roseingraves an extraordinary future. But even the shock of that betrayal had not cured Sophie of her ambition. It still pulsed inside her, fluttering its wings and beating at the lock on its cage.

This surely meant she was a selfish person. So she did as her mother asked, and went shopping for her siblings.

Mrs. Narayan's shop was two streets away, part of a row of clothing shops on the edge of Carrisford's Jewish quarter. The buildings here were a bit older, a more somber stateliness than the fresh paint and plaster flourishes of the high street. Sophie found the sign that read NOUREEN NARAYAN, CLOTHING BOUGHT AND SOLD, FINE TAILORING. She stepped in and took a breath—and for a moment it was just like being back in London.

Mr. Giles's shop had smelled new: the bite of fresh dye had puckered the air. His cloth and notions had been dazzling, but they weren't garments yet—he sold the promise of clothing, the potential of something to become a gown or a coat or a cloak.

Here, though, was the soft, human scent of clothing that had been worn and washed and worn again, often by more than one person during its lifetime. It reminded her of the secondhand shops the Roseingraves had known in London. Everything here had to be taken as it was—or nearly, at any rate. A signboard behind the counter listed prices for different types of alterations: hemming, taking in, letting out, mending seams.

A young woman with dark hair and gold-brown skin sat behind the counter, stitching a seam along a chalked line bristling with pins. She glanced at the bundle under Sophie's arm and set her work aside. "Good afternoon—have you brought those to sell?"

Sophie nodded and placed the bundle on the counter. Miss Narayan—the shop owner's niece, as she introduced herself—went through the twins' clothing quickly, tugging to test the strength of seams and checking for marks or damage.

Her hands, Sophie couldn't help noticing, were efficient and remarkably quick, the fingers small but strong and sure.

They agreed on a price for the trade, and then Miss Narayan showed Sophie to the precise shelves where she would most likely find the sizes and garments she needed: dresses for Julia, trousers and shirts for Jasper.

Sophie was going through a stack of linen shirts at the front of the store when movement caught her eye. She looked up and there, across the street, was Miss Crewe. Auburn hair, mischievous smile, enchanting figure, and all.

Sophie was fixed in place by twin spears of righteous anger and irresistible lust.

Miss Crewe was in her gray gown again. She stood chatting with a man holding the reins of a trader's wagon, paint gleaming in the winter sun. He was slender, and the deep blue of his coat made his dark hair shine.

As Sophie watched, Maddie held out her hand—those mittens again—and the man shook it, black leather dark against that bright blue wool. They made a beautifully matched couple: blue and blue, dark hair and red. Sophie's belly clenched with jealousy.

"Do you know her?" asked Miss Narayan.

Sophie swallowed. "We've met. That's Madeleine Crewe, a ribbon weaver." She glanced at Miss Narayan. "I don't suppose you know the man she's speaking to?" Was he also involved in whatever Miss Crewe was planning?

Miss Narayan nodded, though her eyes never left the couple across the way. "That's Mr. Micah Samson. His father is an old-clothesman. He must be on his way here—he usually stops in around this time."

And indeed, Mr. Samson was handing the reins to an earnest young groom to hold. Sophie's hands clenched in the fabric of the shirt she held. "He's very handsome, isn't he?"

"I've often thought so." Miss Narayan began refolding the stack of shirts Sophie had disrupted, smoothing out the fabric, then smoothing it out again.

Not very efficient. Her jealousy set up a sympathetic chime in Sophie's breast. Miss Narayan's lovely lips were pressed thin, her smile a little pinched. She flicked one glance up to the couple across the street, then dropped her eyes again. But that one glance had *seared*. "They look well together, don't they?" the young woman said lightly.

Sophie's stomach twisted again. "Yes," she rasped. "But then, I can't imagine Miss Crewe *not* looking well, no matter whom she was standing next to."

Miss Narayan's hands stopped moving.

Oh dear. Sophie's heart thumped, and she concentrated on breathing normally, even though she wanted to suck in air out of panic. Had there been too much obvious longing in her voice? Had she not hidden herself properly? She'd known, in London, who it was safe to say such things to— but she'd forgotten for a moment she was in a new place, among new people.

Miss Narayan looked at her, her mouth relaxing enough to lift one corner in a rueful smile. "Isn't it *rude* how some people are too beautiful to resist, even when you most want to?"

Relief, pure and sweet, poured over Sophie like spring water. "Especially when you most want to," she replied, with a small laugh. "There must be some magic to it, don't you think?"

Miss Narayan's smile turned sly. "It's only magic if you don't know how it's done. I know quite a few tricks—I was a lady's maid in London until this past summer." She turned to the dresses behind her, a riot of color and pattern. "If you're looking to balance things a little in your favor, I have a few things presently that might help you turn the tables . . ."

She spread out one skirt: muslin dyed forest green, trimmed at the hem and bodice with buds and blossoms made from ribbons of rose-colored silk.

It was lovely in a quiet, inviting sort of way, and Sophie's heart ached to wear it. She'd had to sell most of her best gowns before they left London. "Maybe another day," she said wistfully. "I'm not here today for myself."

The door swung open, letting in a rush of air that cooled

Sophie's heated cheeks. Mr. Samson stood poised on the threshold. "Miss Narayan," he said warmly, and gave a little nod acknowledging Sophie. Oh yes, he was definitely worth looking at closer up: light brown eyes that looked as though they were laughing, an expressive mouth that gave away his every thought.

A lot of those thoughts seemed to center on Miss Narayan, if the intensity of his gaze were any guide.

"I'll be right with you, Mr. Samson," Miss Narayan said. She moved unhurriedly to wrap up Sophie's things, looking as cool and untroubled as spring water.

Sophie's glance darted outside, where Miss Crewe was starting to disappear down the street. Those long legs of hers would carry her far away before too long. "Can you hold that parcel for me for a little while?" she asked. "I have a few more errands to run."

"Of course," Miss Narayan said, very carefully not looking at Mr. Samson, who was equally carefully not looking at Miss Narayan.

Sophie waved farewell, and tried not to sprint out the door.

Sophie kept pace, letting the crowd move between her and Miss Crewe, her eyes focused on the trailing end of the woman's blue muffler. She didn't have far to follow; only two turns away, the Mulberry Tree stood where the London road met the River Ethel. It was a lovely, expansive inn, rich in dark wood, plump with windows and gables.

Miss Crewe strode inside as confidently as if the building belonged to her.

Sophie hesitated on the far side of the street. She had not yet learned which taverns in Carrisford were welcoming and which ones were . . . otherwise. It was one thing to follow Miss Crewe down a public street—quite another to follow her headlong into danger and ruin.

She could see a few shadowy figures through the front window, and as she watched a pair of men in frock coats and polished boots emerged from the inn and strode down the street, walking sticks tapping. They seemed respectable enough to her: not fine enough to be gentry, but too well-dressed to be farmers. Tradesmen, most likely, or merchants. Another such pair entered while she stood debating.

She decided she could risk a look inside, at least. She moved quickly enough that she caught the door before it could fall shut, and slipped inside.

The warmth hit her first: a fire roaring on the hearth, light flickering merrily on old walls, scarred but clean tables, and sturdy chairs. Then the scents: ale and fresh straw and savory pies. Stairs led to the upper floor, and the bar stretched against the long wall at the back. A doorway there was propped open to catch the breeze from a small garden that fronted the river. The soft tick of a tavern clock measured the beats of banter and conversation.

Miss Crewe was leaning with one elbow on the bar, laughing cheerfully at something the barmaid was saying.

Sophie hurried to take a seat in a booth under the stairs, where the shadows were deepest. A pair of soberly dressed women were writing letters at the table in front of her; she mimicked their posture, curving her shoulders forward, hoping her brown clothing would blend unnoticeably into theirs.

Miss Crewe accepted a pint of ale from the barmaid, who winked pertly. She cast a quick glance around the room— Sophie held her breath, but Miss Crewe's gaze passed over the booth without faltering or giving any hint of recognition.

Then, decisively, Miss Crewe rose and slipped through a doorway to a separate room.

In the space between the door's opening and when it clicked shut, Sophie caught a glimpse of an older, unmistakably dignified figure sitting ramrod-straight on a small sofa.

The lady who'd been at Mr. Giles's shop.

Sophie's heart settled into a grim, steady beat. Whatever was happening, they were in it together. Mr. Giles was not destined to keep his windfall profits for long, it seemed.

The minutes ticked by, each one another small cut, shredding her patience. The women writing letters eventually finished their missives, gave the letters to the barmaid, and bundled themselves out the door. Sophie ordered a hot cider, and nursed it resentfully. About half an hour later, her cup empty and cold, the parlor door swung open again. The lady strode out, her turban today silk and velvet, the hem of her gown a foot deep in black silk trimming. She made her elegant way up the stairs.

Miss Crewe, however, did not emerge.

It was baffling and infuriating. Mind racing, Sophie had a sudden wild suspicion that there was a back exit to the other room. The thought had her up and moving across the bar, her hand on the doorknob.

She'd lain in wait too long to lose Miss Crewe now.

It was done in an instant: Sophie slipped through the door, quietly as ever, and pulled it softly shut behind her.

It was a small private parlor, the kind often reserved for the use of guests. Miss Crewe lounged on the sofa, at her ease—but sat straight up, eyes wide, when Sophie entered.

Sophie froze like a mouse before a hawk.

The only sounds were the crackle and pop of the hearth fire, and the hammering of Sophie's own heart in her ears.

Miss Crewe's eyes turned sharp, flickering with firelight. She took a long breath, in then out, in a deliberate way that made something in Sophie go quietly hot.

Then Miss Crewe took a dainty sip of ale, as though they were speaking to one another at a duchess's afternoon tea. "Miss Anybody," she said. "What a surprising pleasure to see you again." She licked her lips, her tongue a flash of deeper pink.

Sophie felt faint and swallowed hard.

Miss Crewe patted the cushion beside her. "Won't you have a seat?"

Sophie sat. Entirely because she didn't trust her shaking knees not to give way beneath her. Certainly not because it brought her nearer to Miss Crewe than she had yet been.

For defense's sake—her own or Miss Crewe's?—she folded her hands tight atop her knees and tucked her feet beneath the sofa, away from the spread of the beauty's skirts, as gray and soft as cobwebs.

Sophie feared she was already caught.

"That's better," Miss Crewe said. She took a last draught of ale, and set the tankard down with a meaningful click. "What is it you want, Miss Anybody?"

"Sophie," Sophie blurted.

Miss Crewe's head cocked. "I'm sorry?"

"My name is Sophie Roseingrave," Sophie said. "Not *anybody*."

"Maddie Crewe," said Miss Crewe, with a flourish of her hand. "But then, I suspect you knew that already." She turned slightly, facing Sophie, those hazel eyes burning with reflected flames. "What is it that you *want*?"

One thing Sophie wanted—badly—was to put a hand on the nape of Miss Crewe's neck and pull her forward for a kiss. It was a disastrous impulse, to be resisted at all costs. Had she learned nothing from the last year? "In order to answer, I need to tell you a story," she said.

"Oh, how nice," said Miss Crewe, her tone desert-dry.

"We used to live in London," Sophie began. "My father, mother, my siblings, and me. Father ran a workshop that built pianofortes—good ones. Not as many as Mr. Broadwood turns out from his factory, but a few of the experts believed ours were better. So when Father was approached by a musician named Mr. Verrinder, who had nothing but praise for his work, it didn't strike him as unusual. Mr. Verrinder was very charming, and had so many ideas about how my father could better employ his talents, and make a great deal more money for everyone."

"Ah," Maddie Crewe said. Her tone was low, almost as

though she hadn't meant to let the sound escape, and the amount of heavy sympathy in it made Sophie's teeth ache. "Which idea was it?" Miss Crewe asked. "The joint-stock company? The patent application?"

Sophie shook her head. "Mr. Verrinder said he could revolutionize the teaching of piano. He believed students could be taught in groups, rather than singly. That way an instructor could charge less per student—meaning more pupils would be able to afford lessons—but still earn more in total than even the masters who charge a guinea a lesson."

"A guinea a lesson!" Miss Crewe whistled, pursing those rosy lips and making Sophie clench her hands until the knuckles went white. "I had no idea piano-teaching wages ran so high."

"They don't, for most of us," Sophie said. "I've never been able to charge a pupil so much. Those who do are the popular concert performers, the composers whose names are known by the public."

"In short, the people you and your father both wanted to impress and to surpass."

Sophie blinked. She had never thought of it that way. But it was true. Miss Crewe was sharp.

Then Sophie remembered: Miss Crewe was sharp because this was the kind of game Miss Crewe was used to playing. She steeled herself against beauty's onslaught. It would do her no good to notice that one wayward auburn curl had slipped free to tremble against the delicate skin of Miss Crewe's long throat.

"Father and Mr. Verrinder set up a piano school," she

said, pulling her gaze away. "Twenty Roseingrave pianos, for twenty pupils, under Mr. Verrinder's instruction. A building rented in a part of town where the wealthy wouldn't hesitate to send their children. Once the enterprise was a success—as it was sure to be, Mr. Verrinder said—we could open more schools, and charge the teachers a percentage of the profits."

"All the money, none of the work," Miss Crewe responded.

Sophie flushed. "He made it sound nobler than that." She rubbed an imagined ache from her wrists, and forbore to mention the chiroplast. A device meant to train and control, and by some measures it had succeeded. But she wasn't about to reveal her deepest shame to a liar and a trickster. "He ruined us," she said instead. "It came out that he'd been selling the project to all my father's colleagues, friends, and rivals, using his connection with us as a sign of his reliability. When he was exposed as a charlatan, he fled—and left my family holding all his debts: the twenty pianos built in expectation, the investments people had made, the teaching fees Mr. Verrinder had already started collecting in some cases. We had to sell everything to recoup what we could—the workshop, the storefront, back stock, our home. We had to let all Father's employees go, and hope the stain of our names and reputation wouldn't follow them. Or us."

"And you came to Carrisford, because it is cheaper to start over here than London," Miss Crewe said, and reached again for her tankard. "It's a very sad story, Miss Roseingrave, but I fail to see how it pertains to me."

"Because you are doing what Mr. Verrinder did," Sophie said bluntly. "You are running a swindle."

Miss Crewe went still, her drink held just shy of those rosebud lips.

Sophie smirked, just a little. "I asked Mr. Giles about you."

"Mr. Giles lies," Miss Crewe said at once.

"Both you and Mr. Giles are liars," Sophie shot back. "I want to know whose lies are worse."

Miss Crewe slowly set the tankard down, as though refusing a poisoned chalice. She regarded Sophie, her head tilted, eyes narrowing. "Why should either of us matter to you? Surely Carrisford is large enough that you could simply avoid us, if you choose."

Fury raced like lightning through Sophie's veins: the sting of the injury was still fresh in her heart. "Because as long as there is one swindler at work in Carrisford, there's a chance it could happen again—to my family, Miss Crewe. To *me*. I am ashamed to admit I spent months quietly ignoring my misgivings about Mr. Verrinder. I let myself believe only the things he said, and not the things he did. And I will be *damned* if I let myself be led astray again by someone with more charm than honesty."

"Charming, am I?" Miss Crewe echoed, and her smile twisted like a key turning in a lock. She bent closer, and some of the heat came back into her hazel eyes. "If it's honesty you're looking for—you really ought to start by being honest with yourself, Miss Roseingrave."

"I'm sure I don't know what you mean," Sophie demurred at once. But her voice shook, giving everything away.

Miss Crewe chuckled, a low throb of a sound that made

Sophie's palms go damp and her mouth go dry. "Aren't you lying just a little bit about your true motives?"

"You're the only liar here."

Miss Crewe went on as if Sophie'd said nothing at all. "You hide in corners, quiet and plain as a sparrow—but I see the way you look at me. My hands, my bosom . . . my mouth."

Sophie's eyes flicked down to each part as it was named. She couldn't help it.

Rosy lips curled into a knowing smile. Miss Crewe leaned further forward, hardly more than a breath away. Her fingers lifted Sophie's chin.

Sophie obeyed that gentle pressure quite before she realized what she was doing. The soft, teasing touch made her head spin. Anger was an anchor; she clung to it. "You are trying to distract me," she said faintly.

Miss Crewe laughed, low and sweet, sliding her hand forward to follow the line of Sophie's jaw. "Is it working?"

"No," Sophie lied. She swallowed, and felt the muscles in her throat move beneath Miss Crewe's palm. "I'll not be put off so easily."

Miss Crewe's eyes burned now, and her voice lowered to a pitch that seemed to pluck at every nerve Sophie had, setting her thrumming. "You can keep following me all around town if you like . . . but be warned, little sparrow. I may take advantage."

Miss Crewe leaned down, closed the gap, and kissed her.

Sophie was too aroused and frustrated and furious for

prudence, so when Miss Crewe's lips touched hers she seized the woman to prevent her from trying to escape.

This was precisely the wrong thing to do. It meant Sophie's hands were now clutching at Miss Crewe's shoulders, pulling her closer. She tasted of apples and ale, tart and earthy and intoxicating. Sophie's gasp for air opened her lips and Miss Crewe did take advantage, as she'd promised— her tongue sank into Sophie's mouth and swallowed up her helpless moan.

Sophie grew angrier, even as pleasure lured her into its drowning depths. How *dare* this swindler kiss so well?

The kiss became a duel, as Sophie battled to take back control. She slid her hands up and wound strong fingers into those auburn curls, her thumb tracing a demanding line across one perfect cheek. Miss Crewe's mouth softened as Sophie held her in place—tempted by that softness, Sophie bit lightly but insistently at her rosebud lip.

Miss Crewe made a noise of surprise and pleasure, deep in the back of her throat, and Sophie pressed forward, desperate to taste it for herself.

Miss Crewe tilted back, a feint of yielding so that Sophie wound up pinning her luscious body with all its curves against the arm of the sofa. Sophie had one moment of wild, predatory triumph—and then Miss Crewe slipped one sure hand up from Sophie's waist, and cupped her clothed breast.

Layers of cloth and stays were no armor against the caress. Sophie nearly went out of her skin with horrified pleasure—and even as her nipple tightened and ached beneath her chemise, she tore herself free and stumbled away, until she stood with her back pressed against the wood of the parlor door.

Miss Crewe stretched languorously, one arm above her head, her hair a ruin, sleek and self-satisfied as a preening tiger. The movement called full attention to the glorious length of her, the dip of her waist, the high, full breasts beneath the worn gray gown.

Sophie's courage failed her, and she fled.

Chapter Five

Sophie managed to stay close to home—and out of Miss Crewe's path—for three days. She knew it was cowardly, and tortured herself further by imagining how many nefarious deeds Miss Crewe could undertake in such a span of time. Perhaps by now she'd swindled half the finest families in Carrisford into giving up their gold.

Or their daughters. But presumably the children of the wealthy and well protected were less vulnerable to a ribbon weaver's appeal than lonely, hungry Sophie Roseingrave, shop owner's daughter; no pampered, comfortable scion of the local gentry would be so unguarded as to let an argument end with a kiss that still had her nerves sizzling days later.

Or perhaps they were just as susceptible. Perhaps Miss Crewe was even now whispering in the ear of some trembling silk-clad maiden, that siren's voice offering seductive promises and lustful threats.

Shame and jealousy were a poisonous combination, and they kept Sophie quite sick until her father sent her out with the new panels for the veneer on Mrs. Muchelney's piano.

The house was as busy as before: Susan was having a singing lesson in the front room, and the boys could be heard in the garden shouting something in delighted rage that Sophie couldn't quite make out. "It's Latin—or something like it, anyway," Mrs. Muchelney sighed, as she led Sophie up the stairs. "Their tutor has been teaching them about Caesar, and now they've apparently decided our creek is as good as a Rubicon."

Sophie peeked out a window where the stairs turned and saw the two boys, leaping back and forth over the small stream, jabbing triumphantly at one another with sticks whenever they ended up on the same side. Oftentimes they'd miss, and end up ankle deep in the wet, which seemed to delight them just as much as when they fought.

She hid a snicker behind her hand.

"At least it will keep them outside for a while," their mother said firmly, as if insisting could make it true. "I'm afraid you'll find Harriet rather underfoot today—she's been banging away on the piano for days now."

"Has she ever had any lessons?" Sophie asked.

"We had someone in to tutor Susan for a while—but she didn't take to it, and I'm sorry to say she rather rebelled against her teacher. And Harriet is always happy to follow where Susan leads." They'd reached the parlor door, and Mrs. Muchelney stopped with her hand on the handle. "I don't suppose—Miss Roseingrave, does your father teach piano?"

"He does not," Sophie said. "But I do. Or at least," she amended, "I used to."

"Oh!" Mrs. Muchelney brightened. "Would you be willing to teach Harriet?"

Sophie hesitated. "I am rather out of practice as a teacher, Mrs. Muchelney."

The widow waved this aside. "I am not asking you for miracles, of course not—it just seems better than letting the poor girl try and figure it all out on her own. She's barely left the parlor for days, and I swear we're lucky if there's anything recognizable as a tune in there." She clasped her hands against her bosom. "Please, Miss Roseingrave, have mercy—teach her something before she drives the rest of us barking mad."

"Let me talk to Miss Harriet," Sophie said after a long moment. "If she's willing to learn, I'm sure we can find someone to instruct her."

Mrs. Muchelney beamed as though Sophie had offered an unqualified yes, and led the way into the parlor.

Harriet was indeed at the piano, slouching with her head almost on the keyboard, pressing individual notes one by one in no good order. When the door opened her head whipped around and she spread her fingers protectively over the keys, as though guarding her treasure from pillage.

Sophie smiled. She knew that jealous feeling. "Hello, Miss Harriet," she said. "I've come to finish the repairs to your piano."

A shout came from Susan down below, and a squawk

from the singing teacher. Mrs. Muchelney slipped back out to deal with this new crisis, and Sophie began the repair work under Harriet's suspicious eye.

She explained every step as she performed it, until the new panels were in place and the shell shape of the fallboard gleamed whole and unblemished again. Sophie glanced at the young would-be pianist. "Is the instrument holding its tune?" she asked.

Harriet blinked in surprise. "How should I know?"

"The sound will tell you, if you know what to listen for." Sophie reached out and played a few light notes, then a few chords, and a few bars of a waltz. She nodded. "It sounds steady to me."

Harriet was staring at her hands, the envy on her face so plain Sophie felt almost embarrassed to witness it. "I never realized it was out of tune before," the girl said. "I like it a great deal more like this."

"Would you like to learn how to play?" Sophie asked.

Harriet lit up as though someone had turned up the wick in her soul.

God, Sophie could remember feeling that way. How long ago was it? She missed it, all at once, utterly and fiercely.

Sophie pulled over an ottoman and topped it with a cushion—it wasn't perfect, but for someone Harriet's size it was a better seat than the stool had offered. She sat the girl on this and stood to one side. "This is called middle C," she began, and struck the note, clear and ringing in the quiet of the room. She showed the girl how to hold her hands—

sitting up straight, elbows low, wrists loose—and taught her a very short, very simple melody with one hand, singing the name of each note as its key was struck.

Harriet soaked it all in like a plant being watered. Sophie was so intent on her teaching that half an hour passed before she thought of Mr. Verrinder at all.

Of course, as soon as she did, her hands were like dead weights at the ends of her arms.

But it was something—more time with the piano than she'd had since London. And thoughts of Mr. Verrinder had reminded her that not all piano teachers were honest—or patient, or kind. Would she trust eager, sensitive Harriet to the mercy of a stranger?

There was only one acceptable answer. Sophie left Harriet happily repeating the simple tune, and went to talk to Mrs. Muchelney about instruction rates.

The widow was so delighted she agreed to the first number Sophie named—a crown per lesson!—and then Mrs. Muchelney insisted that today had counted as the first lesson, and paid Sophie on the spot.

This was the first money of her own Sophie had seen in months. And for once, there was nothing more urgent to spend it on. She held it for a while as she walked home, her hand wrapped around it in her coat pocket, just enjoying the weight of it as the metal warmed from cool to skin temperature.

On a whim, Sophie decided to stop by Mrs. Narayan's and see if the green dress was still available. If she were to be teaching regularly, she could use something more presentable than the gowns she wore for repair work like today's, where she feared oil stains and tool marks.

It had nothing whatsoever to do with looking her best in case she encountered Miss Crewe again.

The green dress was still there, but when she slipped behind a screen to try it on, it was a little longer and grander than Sophie's short frame could fill.

Miss Narayan told her not to worry: "It's easy enough to take in. I could do it in my sleep." The rates were reasonable and Sophie was no great seamstress, so she threw prudence to the wind and soon found herself on a stepstool with arms stretched out, barely breathing, as Miss Narayan set new seams with pins like so many thorns around the rosebud embroidery. Her aunt watched the proceedings with a judge's eagle eye.

The shop bell chimed. "That will be Mr. Samson," Mrs. Narayan said. She flicked a glance at her niece. "Go and see what he has for us today, won't you, Gita?"

"I am sure Mr. Samson won't mind dealing with someone else, just this once," she said stiffly.

Mrs. Narayan only waited, her expectant silence blooming louder and louder until even Sophie was tempted to yield to it.

Miss Narayan gave in and sighed, brushing her hands down her skirts to smooth them. She sent Sophie a considering look and said, "I shouldn't be long." She slipped past the screen and out into the main part of the shop. "Good afternoon, Mr. Samson," she said, clear and strong.

"And to you, Miss Narayan," came the reply. Now that she

was able to listen, Sophie had to admit Mr. Samson's voice was as appealing as his person: a solid tenor with a warm timbre that put her in mind of good lacquer on the back of a violin. It rippled beautifully. "I've saved a few things especially for you to look at today."

"All the way from London?" Miss Narayan asked.

"All the best," came the soft reply, followed by the soft shush of fabric being spread out.

Mrs. Narayan moved closer to Sophie and took up the pinning where her niece had left off. Her hands moved just as swiftly and surely, with a slightly more insistent grip; Sophie kept her breathing slow and smooth as the seamstress slipped a pin into the seam that ran under her arms and along her ribs.

Past the screen, Miss Narayan spoke again: "We've just sold the green linen you brought us, I'm happy to say. Miss Roseingrave is being fitted for it right now, in fact."

"I'm afraid I don't know Miss Roseingrave," Mr. Samson replied, after a pause.

"She's new to Carrisford," Miss Narayan went on, "but you might ask Madeleine Crewe to introduce you."

The silence was exquisite and complete.

"Oh," Miss Narayan went on, "this velvet is gorgeous."

"Isn't it?" Mr. Samson said at once. Almost as though he were eager to talk about anything else. "I thought of you especially when I found that one. Velvet is so difficult to alter, it requires a very skilled hand. And the amber color would suit you beautifully."

Miss Narayan's voice was tense as a wire. "I have to buy for the shop, not for myself, Mr. Samson."

"You don't think Miss Roseingrave would be interested in the velvet?"

"I think she'd be more interested in asking why a seller of secondhand clothes would be talking to a silk weaver."

Sophie gasped in surprise at Miss Narayan's frankness.

Mrs. Narayan's hands stopped. "Did you get stuck, dear?"

"My own fault," Sophie breathed, and attempted a smile. "I will do better at holding still, I promise."

Mr. Samson's voice was tight now too, a violin just before the string snapped. "Miss Roseingrave sounds very . . . inquisitive."

"Oh, one has to ask questions when one is in a new town," Miss Narayan continued. "Everyone is a stranger, and one doesn't know everyone's alliances and enemies. One has to find out who one can trust, and who is best given a wide berth. Like you, Mr. Samson."

Mr. Samson made a wordless noise.

Miss Narayan went on, ruthlessly cheerful. "When I moved here last autumn, I came to depend on you as someone reliable, and observant, and—and kind. Do you have anything more in printed cotton?"

"Nothing worth your looking at," Mr. Samson replied. His voice shook a little. "I'm going to London again next week, though—I will put it at the top of my list." A percussive sound, as if someone were drumming anxious fingertips upon a countertop. Then Mr. Samson rushed forward, headlong: "Listen, Miss Narayan—whatever business I have with Miss Crewe, you must know it's only that. Business." More drumming. "You do believe me, don't you?"

"Of course," Miss Narayan said, her cheer pitch-perfect—but Sophie's ear was good, and she heard the soft harmonics of relief shimmering in the air. "Though you must admit, it is a little odd. Usually you are rather on opposite sides of the industry, aren't you?"

"I'm a trader, Miss Narayan. I follow the opportunities I find. And with that," he sighed, that lovely voice ringing with regret, "I'm afraid I must be going. Unless you've changed your mind about the amber velvet?"

"Do you know," Miss Narayan said, after a moment, "I find I rather have. It feels quite special, doesn't it? As though it has been waiting a long time to be found by just the right person."

"That's worth any amount of waiting," Mr. Samson replied, low and sure.

By Sophie's elbow, Mrs. Narayan muttered something under her breath, and rolled her eyes.

Miss Narayan and Mr. Samson settled up for the clothes she had purchased, as her aunt stuck the last pin into Sophie and helped her out of the green frock, which now bristled like a hedgehog, waiting for the hand that would transform it back into something safely wearable. The plain brown dress felt even plainer than before—Sophie thought of princesses disguised as kitchen maids, and gossamer gowns that turned back to rags at the stroke of twelve.

Miss Narayan poked her head back behind the screen and looked at Sophie with knowing eyes. "I hope that answered at least some of your questions."

"About Mr. Samson, certainly," Sophie replied. But now

she had even more things to ask Miss Crewe the next time she—the next time they—

Sophie's face flamed and she yanked her thoughts away from that precipice.

Miss Narayan cocked an eyebrow. "I don't suppose you are interested in the velvet? It's lovely."

As Sophie shook her head, Mrs. Narayan's patience ran out. "Gitanjali, if you like that boy as much as I think you do, I wish you would let him know it. He brought that dress for you, it was clear as anything."

"It's a rare suitor indeed who brings gifts that must be paid for," Miss Narayan said tartly.

Mrs. Narayan snorted. "They *all* do that, beti, one way or another."

"I didn't leave London and Bapuji just to toss my heart at the first person who comes along," her niece shot back. "I'm here to prove to you I deserve to be part owner of this shop. A husband will only get in the way."

Mrs. Narayan snickered. "Who said anything about a husband?"

Her niece looked scandalized. "Aunty Noureen!"

Sophie, at the counter, gave a little cough.

Miss Narayan's cheeks glowed with embarrassment; her aunt only laughed again. "Youth fades, my dear, and beauty with it—you have both, and you should be getting more use out of them." She winked at Sophie, and took the green dress to the workroom in the back.

Miss Narayan gave a long-suffering sigh and tallied up Sophie's purchase.

"You do like Mr. Samson, though?" Sophie asked hesitantly.

Miss Narayan snorted. "What's not to like?"

Sophie cocked her head. "I suppose a person can be *too* handsome," she said.

Miss Narayan sputtered a laugh at that, and some of the tension in her posture eased. "He is *far* too handsome, and too kind, and—and I find him far too distracting." She sighed, as her eyes met Sophie's curiosity with a wry and wistful confession. "And well-off, to boot. His family supply all the best secondhand shops between Carrisford and London, and if they move into manufacturing like the rumors say, they'll make more money still. All in all, he's a very eligible young man." She handed back Sophie's change and noted the payment in a book. "Either his intentions are less than honorable—in which case, I want no part of him—or his intentions are honorable—and I have no time for him."

"Why are the prettiest ones always the least convenient?"

Miss Narayan's lips tilted at the corners. "Maybe if they were convenient they wouldn't be so pretty?"

Sophie laughed. She left Miss Narayan staring wistfully at the amber velvet, and walked home trying to think of anything but a lying pair of rosebud lips.

CHAPTER SIX

The alterations to the green linen were finished within the week—but the first time Sophie wore the dress was not to Harriet's next lesson, or to any confrontation with Miss Crewe.

She wore it when Mr. Frampton and his father asked the Roseingraves to tea. Mrs. Roseingrave had to decline, as the ringing in her ears was giving her more trouble than usual; when Sophie and her father left, she was lying down upstairs while Robbie took charge of the shop with solemn sixteen-year-old dignity.

Mr. Augustus Frampton had the same rich brown skin and kindly eyes as his son. Last spring he had retired from King George's orchestra, but he still wore the eye-catching silk robes in the Turkish style that had brought him so much attention as a young musician new at court. They were less fashionable now than they had been in days past, but they still gleamed with jewel-bright colors and lush embroidery.

Sophie was pleased to see that Miss Mary Slight was also

present, chatting with the elder Mr. Frampton with the ease of long acquaintance. Mr. Roseingrave came entirely alive when Mr. William Frampton introduced Miss Slight as the most gifted builder of clockwork mechanisms in Carrisford; the mechanical talk soon overflowed the bounds of all but their own enthusiasm, and the three went out to William's workshop to see how his latest design for a calculating engine was meant to work.

Sophie poured herself and the elder Mr. Frampton each another cup of tea.

"I am truly sorry your mother could not join us. I heard her sing Susanna at the peak of her career—her expression was wonderfully moving. I should have enjoyed thanking her for the joy she brought to her listeners."

Sophie's hands fussed anxiously with her teacup. "Mother often finds it hard to catch conversation, even in small gatherings," she explained. "She told me once that the sounds get so muddied and jumbled together, it's as though she were completely, not partially deaf."

Mr. Frampton nodded in sad sympathy. "It is hard to have a talent and lose the full enjoyment of it. I speak from experience." He held out his hands, the knuckles knobbled and stiff. "For five years I attempted to play through the pain, but at last I was compelled to choose between loving the violin and losing the use of my hands completely. Every morning I wake up and wonder if I made the right choice." He sighed, then wrapped both hands around his teacup. His motions were slow, but they still showed some of the fluency of long years of practice and study. The violinist took a sip of tea, and cleared his throat. "My son tells me you teach piano, Miss Roseingrave."

"Oh yes," Sophie said, "though I only have the one pupil, really."

"But is teaching the sum of your ambition?" Mr. Frampton pressed. "Do you compose? Do you perform?"

Sophie flushed. These were topics she rarely spoke of, even among her own family. But he was looking at her so kindly, and had spoken so well of her mother, and her sympathy for his loss of the violin was still chiming in her heart. "I have only given one concert, Mr. Frampton. It . . . was not a success."

It had, in fact, been interrupted almost as soon as it had begun.

She held tight to the teacup, letting the heat seep soothingly into her bones.

"As for composing," she went on, "I have never dared to call myself a composer. But I do write music. Some études, a few waltzes and variations here and there. Half a sonata, once, when Mr. Keats died. But nothing—nothing I'd be bold enough to perform in public, or even send in to a publisher." She shifted on the sofa, squirming beneath the weight of his silent, steady attention. "I haven't written anything this year—what with the move, and—and what came before. Perhaps it was only a whim I have outgrown."

"Could you play one of your études from memory?" Mr. Frampton asked, and gestured at the piano Sophie had been diligently not looking at. "I keep it in very good tune."

Sophie could have demurred, except she felt it would be

rude. So she steeled herself, set down her teacup, and walked to the piano.

It was a Delaval, with an older style of action, but well maintained and tuned, as promised. She spread her green skirts over the bench and wiped her damp palms on them surreptitiously. Before her nerve could fail her, she launched into the first piece she'd ever composed. It was meant to evoke raindrops: the way they'd met and melted into one another on the panes of the parlor window in London. She still could never see rain without humming it, even if only to herself. Over the years she'd refined the melody and added flourishes, ornaments she could put in or leave off as the mood struck her.

She had never played it for another person before, not outside her family. And Mr. Frampton had been a court musician, accustomed to royal standards of performance. He'd spent years with a prince in a place that existed to nourish musical genius and reward accomplishment and endeavor.

Sophie didn't know *what* she was thinking, playing her childish tunes before such an expert critic. Nevertheless, when she reached the end—it was an extremely short piece, after all—she went back and played it a second time through with a different set of ornaments.

It was far from a perfect performance—her hands were stiff and cold still. She was not able to lose herself in the melody as she always sought to. But she got through it without crying, without shivering, and without that sick feeling of regret that had haunted her for so many months.

Mr. Verrinder's harm was healing.

It was such a relief she went a little breathless, and giddily she put a few extra impromptu flourishes on the final crescendo, then brought the melody gently back to earth at the finish. The notes faded away into the silence like water being soaked into thirsty earth.

Mr. Frampton the elder nodded decisively at her as if she'd confirmed a theory. "The next time someone asks if you are a composer, Miss Roseingrave, I gently encourage you to reply: *Yes, I am.*" Sophie blushed in mixed embarrassment and pleasure and he continued: "I know composers when I hear one, my girl—I played with Beethoven, once."

Sophie's self-consciousness fled, and she leaned forward eagerly on the piano bench. "What is he like?"

Mr. Frampton stared off into the distance. "He seemed to bend the world around him; good or bad, everyone was affected. We were friends, until we suddenly weren't—and even that proved a useful lesson for me in the end. Sometimes I think the truest proof of genius is not just what one great mind produces with it, but what it draws out of the others who encounter it." That keen gaze cut back to Sophie and his mouth curved in a wry half smile. "Or perhaps it only looks that way to my lonely eyes—since my retirement, I find what I miss more than anything is the company of other musicians. Performing and practicing. Living and breathing harmonies and counterpoints." He shook his head. "I once hoped my son would follow in my footsteps and surpass my own accomplishments on the violin."

"Every father's wish," Sophie murmured.

"He has the talent and the ear," Mr. Frampton went on,

"but his heart lies elsewhere, and so his genius follows. I encourage him, of course—every father *should* encourage his child in their proper sphere—but I remain a little wistful for my own sake. I spent a lifetime as a professional musician, and I had hoped to be able to use my experience and connections to further William's career. The great temptation is to want to be *useful* to him, and at times it led me to press him toward music more than I believe he wished." He uncrossed and crossed his legs, flicking the bright silk of his robes out of the way before settling back in his seat. "I have spent my months here looking for other talents where my acquaintance might offer some scope." His eyes gleamed meaningfully.

Sophie was surprised into a laugh. "Are you offering to send me to perform at court, sir?"

"Should I?"

Sophie stopped laughing, as ambition welled up and shoved every atom of air from her lungs. It was an enormous idea, so big she'd never dared to dream it on her own. To play before the king and his courtiers—to perform her own pieces, and take students of her choice, at rates that were enough to support herself—to be part of a society of knowledge and talent and passion for music . . .

To hold nothing back. And to have what she wanted most in the world.

She looked up at Mr. Frampton, whose eyes were still watching her so closely. "I do not believe I am ready for that yet, sir. But I—I think I would like to be." She caught her hands fussing with the fabric of her skirts, and clasped her fingers to still and soothe them. Then she looked up, and straightened her shoulders. "I should warn you, I have not proven to be an easy student in the past." So Mr. Verrinder had said, anyway—but it suddenly struck Sophie as odd that she should still believe him in this, when she knew so well how he'd lied.

Mr. Frampton shrugged. "That is of no consequence: I have no intention of being your teacher. My aim is to guide you, to polish you—if it suits you—into a jewel I may present to my old friends and rivals." He leaned forward, his smile sly and a bit fierce. "To prove that whatever may have happened to my hands, my mind and my taste are as sound as ever."

Sophie nodded once, sharply. She had always enjoyed a challenge. "Where do we start?"

Mr. Frampton settled back against the sofa, and nodded at the piano. "Play me something else of yours."

"I think I still recall the first theme of the sonata," Sophie offered. She turned back to the keyboard, and began.

It was worse than the étude—she had to start and stop a few times, until she gave up on resurrecting the actual notes she'd written and just improvised the melody until she got back to the bit she did remember. Mr. Frampton asked a few questions, and offered some suggestions, and Sophie played it once more, incorporating his criticism as best she could.

It certainly *felt* better—more fluid, more like a real composition—and by the end of the theme she actually found herself getting a small sip of that dizzying pleasure she used to find in performing before an audience.

Applause startled her: her father, Miss Slight, and the younger Mr. Frampton had evidently returned while she was playing. The latter two waxed enthusiastic—but it was the proud light in her father's eyes that tied Sophie's tongue and lodged like a ruby in her breast.

It was an early sunset, being so late in the year, and the long orange streamers of light sliding between the buildings felt quietly triumphal as the two of them walked home to the instrument shop.

Mr. Roseingrave was in raptures over William Frampton's calculating engine, which apparently only partially existed. "He's built one section of it, to prove the soundness of the idea—but there is no way for him to complete the project. The precision required of the parts is simply impossible in sufficient quantity. Yet the machine obviously works! It would do precisely what he designed it to—if only the world would allow for its creation." He clasped his hands behind his back, and sighed. "It is the inventor's curse, I think—to have so clear a vision, and to be unable to bring it to fruition."

"Perhaps the world will change, someday," Sophie said.

She imagined being in a concert hall, or a royal pavilion, hands flying over the keys. Sending her own arrangements of notes out into the air, to be heard and appreciated and lauded.

But there were so many things standing between her and that vision—time, money, and the ever-shifting whims of luck and happenstance. She thought of Mr. Frampton's apparatus, all those mechanical dreams. Then she thought of his father, missing his violin—and her mother, retired from public performance. "I have to wonder," she said. "Is it better to have had a dream and lost it, or to have a dream that you know you will never achieve?"

"Neither," her father said at once. "The worst thing is to never dream at all. To go through life with the inward eye shut tight, never dazzled by the light of inspiration, or warmed by the—the sunbeams of, I don't know, imagination? Acclaim?" Sophie snickered, and her father shook with a self-deprecating laugh. "I am better at building pianos than composing panegyrics." His eyes turned thoughtfully to his daughter, as they turned a corner into the street that led them home. "You and the elder Mr. Frampton seemed to have got on splendidly in our absence."

Sophie nodded. "He is very kind—and very critical, in the best way."

"A rare combination."

Sophie chewed her lip thoughtfully, and said: "I might bring Mother for a quiet visit, just the three of us," she said. "He expressed a wish to meet her. He misses having other musicians to talk to."

Mr. Roseingrave sobered a little at this. "Your mother has said much the same since she left performing. She still writes to her friends, but I know she misses the musical evenings she can't enjoy the way she used to. We both love music, of course—but I'm such a technician. She is an artist." His mouth curved again, the particular fond smile he wore only when speaking of his wife. "It is a good union—but often it is good because we are so different. I hope to see you find such a match yourself, someday."

"As the artist or the technician?" Sophie asked. It was a

deflection from what she truly wanted to ask: *What if I find someone I cannot marry?*

What if she's a woman?

"Whoever you please," her father replied affably, and she had the eerie sense he was answering the unspoken question instead of the other one. "As long as you're happy."

Sophie blinked back sudden tears at this—but they had reached the shop door, and her father went inside, beaming as his wife came forward to greet him. "Clara! You were missed, my dear. Let me tell you . . ."

Chapter Seven

The St. Hunger's Day Fair had finally arrived, and Maddie buzzed like a swarm of bees had taken up lodgings in her breast.

The whole household woke early for a hasty breakfast, bites snatched in between the sorting of goods and the loading of the cart. Within the hour the four of them were trundling out into the dark streets. Their breath fogged in the chill air before dawn as they hailed friends and fellow traders, streams of people bundled against the cold, all moving toward the field beneath the ancient oak.

The fair had once been a cattle fair, centuries back when Carrisford was entirely farmers and local fiefdoms. But since the wool and silk trades had moved in, and the traders and shopkeepers with them, St. Hunger's Day had become a celebration of garments and fabric and clothing goods. Handweavers and shoemakers and tailors and merchants of all kinds brought wares with them—some carefully chosen for the occasion, others the unsold remains of the year's work, now marked down to low prices that would hopefully give the maker some return on their labor.

By the time the sun rose, the fair was in full swing. The field became a labyrinth of stalls and tents, each one thronged with people and swathed in all manner of textiles. Secondhand dresses and summery frocks competed with bolts of last year's brocade and boys' shirts, long outgrown by their first wearers. Everywhere hands reached out, testing the weight of a skirt, spreading the lapels of a jacket, handing over coins for a waistcoat shimmering with peacock embroidery. Naturally the food sellers were there, too: the scents of roasting meat and cakes and hot cider and ale breezed through the lanes like eager hounds tumbling over one another in excitement.

Maddie helped set up John and Emma's stall first: shoes and slippers glittering on the table like some hasty to-be-princess's castoffs. Maddie made her way to the Weavers' Library booth, shining with satin and brocade, where Maddie's silk ribbons could flutter like castle pennants from a string stretched from one corner pole to the other.

Business was brisk—it had been a bleak month, and people in Carrisford were eager to celebrate—but just before noon Maddie bid farewell to a customer, put her coins away, and pulled one closely wrapped bolt of cloth from beneath the booth where it had lain hidden since they arrived.

Alice smiled at a prosperous-looking lady who'd stopped to stare yearningly at a length of silver silk. The girl smiled back but moved on, her regret achingly clear. Alice glanced at

Maddie, her eyes flicking to the bolt of fabric under her arm. "Good luck," she whispered.

Maddie squeezed her hand once, and slipped out into the fair.

She walked past the aisles where many of the Jewish old-clothesmen had set up, and stopped as she passed by the Samsons' stall, bursting with colorful garments they'd brought from the great London rag markets and pawnshops. Mr. Samson grinned at Maddie's wave. "Will the yellow silk work out alright?" he asked.

"It's perfect," Maddie assured him. "You are a wonder, Mr. Samson."

He pinkened with pleasure. Maddie hefted the fabric beneath her arm and continued toward her goal.

Beside the food and drink stalls, plenty of traders had come with toys and books and other small goods, eking out the last sales before Christmas. Here was the booth the Roseingraves had set up, small harps and whistles and guitars out for sale, and sheet music pinned up on the tent flaps like feathers on the wings of some enormous bird. Maddie tamped down on a wave of mischievous heat when she spotted the round little figure at one corner of the stall, tilting a violin to show off the shine of the varnish to a skeptical buyer. The man shrugged and moved away.

Sophie's smile faltered and her shoulders sagged. But only briefly. She called out to one of the younger siblings, handed over the violin, and before long four Roseingraves were demonstrating the quality of their instruments with an impromptu concert. An old country tune, simple enough for the younger ones to master, the violin singing over a cello and the strum of a guitar. Eyes bent their way, and fairgoers began stopping to listen.

Sophie Roseingrave clasped her hands in front of her and waited for them to take the bait.

So. She had a little light trickery of her own, Miss Anybody did.

Maddie's walk matched the song's rhythm perfectly, and she hummed along until she turned the corner and lost the tune in the crowd.

And here, at the very center of the fair, in a tent on a raised dais to show his importance, was where Raymond Giles had come to display his wares. It was the largest tent in the fairground, with room enough for a dozen customers as well as the tables full of fabric and finishing. Mr. Giles's name was blazoned over the entrance to the tent, but a closer look showed the paint was cracked and flaking with age. It would have to be redone before next year's fair.

If Mr. Giles was still in business then.

She sent a glance around the other nearby stalls. Relief speared through her when she saw what she was looking for: black silk, heavy-hemmed with trimming, above a pair of soft leather boots.

Mrs. Money bent over a tray of feathers, shafts trimmed for millinery work.

Maddie sucked in a breath and slipped into Mr. Giles's tent.

Her quarry was smiling his charming liar's smile at a

mother and her daughter. Telling them one of his salesman's stories, she guessed—Maddie caught something about *the Bastille* and *the next day the Revolution began* and stopped listening because she knew how that nonsense went.

Instead she focused on the wares on display. To Maddie's expert eyes, the name of each maker might as well have been woven into the threads of the fabric—here was Alice Bilton's emerald velvet, which Mr. Giles had claimed was cheaper single pile and not the three pile he'd commissioned from her. Judith Wegg's pale aerophane, gauzy and crisp, which she was still fighting to get paid for. And, worst of all, the late Mrs. Echard's last brocade—Mr. Giles had sent in the bailiffs to cut the cloth from the loom while the family was out at the funeral, claiming it was his by contract. The merchant had then refused to pay the grieving children for their late mother's work. Because it was unfinished, he'd said.

Maddie pressed a shaking hand down on the richly patterned cloth and breathed a silent vow of revenge to Mrs. Echard's shade.

The mother and daughter went on their way, aflutter with ribbons and flattery. Mr. Giles turned toward Maddie, his eyes glinting. "Miss Crewe," he said, and his gaze darted to the wrapped bolt beneath her arm. "Dare I hope you have brought me something special?"

"You're in luck, Mr. Giles," Maddie sang back. "I'm here to fulfill all your hopes."

He chuckled and waved her eagerly toward the back. Maddie opened the wrapping to show the same blue silk as before—same sheen, same odd threads of different colors. "I think I'll be asking you twice as much this time," she said.

Mr. Giles's eyes arrowed up to meet hers. "Will you?"

"You sold it so quickly before," she said, and folded her arms.

Mr. Giles pretended to consider, but Maddie could all but see the wheels turning inside his conniving head. Twice her last rate would still leave him with an enormous profit—and one he didn't have to record in any account books.

There was no possible way he could resist such temptation.

Nevertheless, he put on an unhappy expression. "I could possibly go as high as one-and-a-half times—"

"*Miss Crewe!*" cried a voice from the front of the tent.

Mr. Giles started. So did Maddie, even though she'd been expecting the interruption. This was the trickiest part of the thing, and her nerves were tight enough that she could feel her bones creaking beneath her skin.

Mrs. Money stood there in black silk, a cashmere shawl tossed over her shoulders like the cloak of some ancient general. She glared daggers at Maddie, who cringed back, playing up her part. "How *dare* you," Mrs. Money hissed, every aristocratic vowel fake as counterfeit coin, her expression accusing. "Mr. Giles, I regret to inform you that this woman has stolen this fabric and has no right to be selling it. At *any* rate."

"*Really,*" breathed Mr. Giles. Maddie could see the hope of retaliation kindle in his gaze when he looked back her way. He'd been searching for a way to destroy her for years, and now it seemed like he had his chance. "What terrible news," he said silkily. "Shall we send for the magistrates to have the miscreant hauled away?"

"Absolutely not," Mrs. Money said at once. She reached up and tugged at the ties of the tent-flap—it fell shut behind her, hiding the three of them from the view of anyone passing by. "Cover that up, you insolent girl," she said. "Before someone sees."

Maddie obligingly folded the blue silk back up into its wrapping, doing her best to look chastened and fearful of the consequences.

Mr. Giles leaned forward. "Mrs. Money—I beg your pardon, but as someone who knows something about silk I must ask: What is so special about this particular fabric?"

Mrs. Money narrowed her eyes and chewed her lip a long while. "Very well, sir—since you have been so open and honest with me, I shall tell you the whole tale."

"Ma'am, I don't think—" Maddie said, on cue.

"Silence, girl!" Mrs. Money's eyes flashed fire. "This secret is my inheritance to keep—or to share—as I see fit." She strode forward, lowering her voice to a conspiratorial throb.

From beneath her lowered brows, Maddie saw Mr. Giles lick his lips.

Mrs. Money began: "My late husband, God rest his soul, was a brilliant chemist. For some years he had been experimenting with dyes—trying to learn how to make them brighter, longer lasting, that sort of thing. But his interests were wide ranging: botany, physiognomy, and in particular the new science of electricity. At one point he wrote a letter to a scientific journal—I forget precisely which—about a hypothetical process that combined weaving techniques with electrical charges produced by—oh, I forget the term. Some kind of pile." She sniffed. "It didn't sound like the kind of thing a lady should inquire into."

"Power looms are hardly a secret," Mr. Giles interjected. "Though electrical power would be—"

Mrs. Money cut him off. "This was not some mere mechanical device," she said. "The electricity produced a chemical reaction in certain dyestuffs he had discovered. It is a discovery of no small genius, and many are the men who would be jealous of the knowledge. You see . . ." She lowered her voice. "When properly prepared, running an electric current through a silk fabric dyed in this manner can apparently produce some fascinating chromatic effects."

"She means it changes color," Maddie said bluntly.

"*What?*" Mr. Giles's shock was evident and delicious. He flipped back the wrapping to stare at the blue silk—his eyes fixing on those odd-colored threads with a new and avaricious light.

God, but you could practically *see* the gears turning in his head. Winding the net even more tightly around himself. Maddie hid her smile in a scowl.

"Crudely put, but correct," Mrs. Money sniffed. "Mr. Obeney saw the letter and wrote to Mr. Money asking him about producing such effects commercially. I believe they had some kind of contract. Certainly money changed hands, as my beloved Horace suddenly had all the funding he wanted for large-scale replications of his early results. But Horace knew others were always hunting for the secrets that he'd found, so he guarded the process most closely—Mr. Obeney became impatient, and went off to America to found his believing the experiment a failure. And then poor Horace . . . passed away."

Her voice wavered, and her gloved hand trembled as she wiped a nonexistent tear from her eye. It was all Maddie could do not to applaud.

"A handful of Carrisford weavers—Miss Crewe being one of them—had been put to work creating a stock of the new fabric." She tapped the blue silk meaningfully. "The weaving takes no particular skill, once the dye itself is understood. But with Mr. Money dead and Mr. Obeney gone, there is no one to sell that silk. It molders in the storehouse, unsold, unclaimed, and quite useless to anybody." She whirled on Maddie again. "Which is why I assume this little thief thought a bolt here or there would not be missed."

"I did the work," Maddie said stubbornly. "I deserve some payment for that, don't I?"

Mr. Giles's confident fingers stroked one long red line amid the blue. "I confess, Mrs. Money, your story has astonished me. I am speechless with wonder." His fingers tapped, tapped. "It seems a waste for your late husband's achievements to go unrecognized. Surely you wish his genius to be made known to all the world. I know I would, in your place."

"It does pain me, I confess," Mrs. Money murmured. "Horace worked so hard on his creation. But what can I do? Mr. Obeney is not here to sell the fabric."

Tap, tap went Mr. Giles. "There might be a way around that," he said slowly. "If this cloth were to make its way into the market by some roundabout means . . . Mr. Obeney is so far away, and so busy with his utopian society. Surely far too busy to take note of every little ebb and flow of the silk supply here in Carrisford."

"Doesn't sound proper to me," Maddie pouted.

"This from a proven thief," Mrs. Money retorted.

"An unsuccessful thief," Mr. Giles added, and straightened. "What you need, madam, is someone more subtle. Someone who has connections with the traders and merchants of the town—and with the fashionable ladies who are their best customers for something like this." He stroked the corner of the silk again possessively. "Can you control the color change? Is it permanent?"

"There is a range of hues the process produces," Mrs. Money said. "They are reasonably permanent—so long as the fabric is properly maintained." She indicated a red thread, then a gold and a green. "This silk was charged to turn it blue, but the hue is deteriorating in storage."

"Could it be corrected?"

"An electric current would refresh it, yes." She sighed. "That is one of the problems that has yet to be solved—any gown made of such fabric would need to be refreshed periodically, to keep its color true."

"So the customers would have to come back at intervals?" Mr. Giles asked. His hands flexed like a musician's, limbering up.

Maddie thought of Sophie Roseingrave, and said: "Like a piano that needs to be kept in tune. Who has the time or the money for that sort of thing?"

"Who indeed?" Mr. Giles murmured blissfully. Maddie

could practically see the visions of profit dancing in front of his bright and eager eyes. "Would it be possible to witness this color change in person?"

Mrs. Money pursed her lips, pretending to consider. "I suppose it might be possible. I still have the equipment Mr. Money had made up for just such an event." She narrowed her eyes at Maddie. "You might atone for your sins by granting us the use of the Weavers' Library for a demonstration."

Maddie grumbled. "Long as you promise the electrics won't harm me."

"It is that or the bailiffs," Mrs. Money said.

"Oh," said Mr. Giles too quickly, "I don't think we need involve the bailiffs, madam. It would make everything so much more public—we ought to let discretion be our watchword. At least until we are ready to trumpet Mr. Money's brilliance to all the world." He spread his hands with a deferential little bow.

Mrs. Money simpered beautifully.

Maddie had to bite the inside of her cheek to keep from chortling.

"Would one week from now be acceptable?" The date fixed, Mrs. Money took back the blue silk, permitted Mr. Giles to kiss her gloved hand, and swanned out of the tent like a queen stepping forth to her coronation. Mr. Giles tied up the tent flaps again, his glee apparent in the tilt of his smile and the avaricious gleam in his eyes.

Maddie slipped out soon after and hurried back to the stall to tell Alice and Judith the good news.

Perhaps it was the elation from their success: they did

so well the rest of the day that Maddie had sold all her ribbons by evening. The fair didn't close until midnight, however. Normally Maddie would have stayed for the dancing and drinking that happened between midnight and dawn. But her secrets were hot and sweet on her tongue, and she didn't dare risk letting them slip free in a moment of tipsy carelessness.

So Maddie said goodbye to her friends and walked home to enjoy the rarity of solitude.

She took her time, stopping for a late meal and wondering at the emptiness of the town, the thrum of the silk mill loud and hungry without bodies to absorb it. The night wind seemed to flick at her heels and skip her down the road the whole way home. *We've done it*, she chanted, a secret song of triumph. Mr. Giles had responded to their lures precisely as they'd hoped: he'd leaped on the opportunity they offered and had been eager to keep the law out of it.

At least for now. Maddie laughed silently. He'd probably change his mind about that later—but by then it would be too late.

As she turned her key in the lock, a sound behind her had her whirling around.

Chapter Eight

For a moment all Maddie saw was the dark street, its shadows deep and deeply familiar. Then movement—and a figure stepped out onto the sidewalk. Short, round, and judging by the way her eyes flashed, extremely angry.

Sophie Roseingrave. Cloaked in gray, her muffler wrapped to hide the lower half of a face that shone like the moon in the dimness.

Maddie's heart was still racing from surprise, and it sped up still further as Miss Roseingrave moved close. "Won't your family miss you, little sparrow?" Maddie breathed.

Miss Roseingrave tugged the muffler loose. "You were at Mr. Giles's tent. You and your—associate."

She made the word sound like a curse. As if that was the worst thing she could think to call someone. Maddie sputtered a laugh.

Miss Roseingrave bristled like an angry hedgehog. "If I had a shred of any proof of what you're about, I'd be standing before the magistrates right now to denounce the pair of you."

"But you don't." It was a guess, but Miss Roseingrave's scowl deepened, so Maddie knew she'd guessed right. Nevertheless, the girl could cause trouble, if she made enough fuss that the people in authority took notice of Maddie's activities.

She had to be distracted somehow.

Seduction leaped to mind. It had halfway worked before, and Maddie had certainly enjoyed it. But it had proved temporary—for here the girl was again, still angry, still in pursuit.

Because she was trying to do what was right. She'd come here to a strange neighborhood, all alone and friendless, to confront someone she believed to be a liar and a cheat—because she wanted to stop people being hurt the way she'd been hurt by Mr. Whoever in London.

The best way to stop her would be to show her Maddie was doing the same thing: defending people she cared about from someone who would do them harm. It was a risk—but everything was a risk, these days.

The trick was knowing which risks were worth taking.

Maddie flung the front door wide. "You might as well come in," she said. "This is no conversation to have in the street where anyone could hear."

She stepped into the hall, trusting Miss Roseingrave to follow. A lit candle spilled gold across the walls and floor just as the girl stepped into the doorway. She paused there, one hand on the door frame.

Maddie took pity. "It's only us—everyone else will be at

the fair until dawn." *So the only threat to your virtue is me.* She bit her lip not to say it, in case it sounded more like a threat than a tease.

Miss Roseingrave pulled the door shut and hung her cloak and muffler beside Maddie's on the hook. Maddie tried to ignore how fine the wool was, especially compared to the chunky blue handspun beside it.

Then Maddie saw what was beneath the cloak. Surprise washed through her. "You're wearing my ribbon."

"What?"

Miss Roseingrave looked down as Maddie stepped closer, the candle flickering with movement. Soft light flashed over cream-and-pink lovebirds that edged the neckline of her brown linen frock.

The same pink spilled into Miss Roseingrave's cheeks. "You kept calling me a sparrow," she muttered defensively. Her eyes widened. "Wait—you made this?"

Maddie put out one finger and traced the line of the ribbon. Down from the shoulder, across the collarbone. She let her fingers stop right above where Miss Roseingrave's heart beat like wings in her chest. "All the best ribbons in Carrisford are my designs," Maddie said, smug and sure. "I send them to the Weavers' Library when the fashions change. Sometimes they come around again, though. This is one of mine from a few years back. Very popular—so much so that it's been copied quite a few times." She stroked with her fingertip, just an inch of a caress.

Miss Roseingrave made a faint, high sound like a violin

string under strain. "Is there—is there any special story behind the design?" she asked.

"Story?" Maddie laughed. "Once upon a time there was a girl who needed the money."

Miss Roseingrave sucked in a breath, then exploded. "That *bastard*," she hissed. "That lying, poisonous piece of *shit*!"

Maddie's eyebrows shot up almost into her hair. Well. Miss Roseingrave knew worse words after all.

The girl's bosom heaved with her fury—a sight Maddie secretly appreciated, modest though the beribboned neckline was. "He told me his father designed it for his mother, back in France. Before the Revolution—"

"—daughter of a comte, escape to England, et cetera," Maddie went on. "It's Mr. Giles's favorite tale. And not a word of truth in it."

Miss Roseingrave's hands fisted and her eyes looked downright murderous. "I once asked you whether your lies or Mr. Giles's were worse. I think I have my answer."

"I have never lied to you."

Miss Roseingrave's mouth snapped shut.

Maddie folded her arms, smirking.

"Well." Miss Roseingrave's tone when she spoke again was more grudging than gracious. "You're lying to other people, though."

"That's true," Maddie admitted cheerfully.

"To what purpose?"

Maddie grinned. "Come up to the attic and I'll explain."

Because the house had stood empty the whole day, she

warmed some cider in the kitchen. The drinks steamed in the cold air of the attic while Maddie and Miss Roseingrave slipped off their shoes and sat on opposite ends of the small bed. To further fight the chill Maddie brought out her two best coverlets, one for her and one for her sparrow: velvet piecework in a riot of colors, stitched by hand during the seasons when weaving work was scarce.

The girl stroked a wondering hand down the velvet pile. "These are lovely."

"I'm very good with my hands, Miss Roseingrave."

The girl blushed and scowled together. "It's your tongue I am concerned about," she said tartly, and blushed harder when Maddie chortled. "And you may as well call me Sophie."

"Sophie, then." The blush deepened, blooming from Sophie's cheeks down into her throat. Maddie wanted to see just how far down she could get it to go . . .

No. Truth before seduction.

A swallow of cider for warmth and courage, then Maddie told Sophie all about Mr. Giles: the mistreatment of his workers, the bribes and the lies, every horrible secret of how he'd built his fortune. It was a bit of a test, if Maddie were being honest with herself: How would respectable Miss Roseingrave, tradesman's daughter, react to this revelation about a man of her class?

She needn't have worried. Sophie steamed nearly as much as the cup she held. It was almost fun, watching such a small person simmer in righteous fury. The tipping point for Sophie seemed to be that so many of Mr. Giles's stories were so transparently, *obviously* false. "He isn't even a *careful* liar!" she hissed.

Maddie dissolved into laughter.

Sophie fumed. "I've been deceived by a very talented swindler, Miss Crewe. It was deeply painful and I've no wish to repeat the experience. But at least I could appreciate the effort and the artistry he put into his deception! Mr. Giles just cobbles ideas together however he pleases, no matter who he's speaking to. It's shallow. It's insulting! It's—it's like he's tied twine to a picture frame and I'm meant to pretend it's a harp!"

"He doesn't have ideas," Maddie said. "He has scraps of cunning that he stitches together." She snickered. "You prefer your lies well tailored, little sparrow?"

Sophie produced the most adorable imitation of a teakettle boiling over. "If you call me that one more time, I swear I'll scream—"

Maddie's voice was flat and final. "You've never screamed in your life." She tilted her head, eyes gleaming. "We could change that, if you like."

Sophie sputtered. Sophie grit her teeth. And just when Maddie thought she would surely stand up and flounce charmingly out of the room, her eyes flew to Maddie's mouth and fixed there as she said bluntly: "Later. First I want to know: What is it you're doing to stop him?"

Here it was: the secret. "We are selling Mr. Giles something that doesn't exist," Maddie said. "A new fabric nobody else has: a silk that can change hues if you put it in a special machine. He's going to give us all his money in exchange for the whole supply—we keep the money, and he'll be left with a pile of ugly silk and metal scraps, instead of the miracle he thought he was buying." She shrugged. "It's a swindle, like you said."

Sophie's brows rose. "And all this was your idea?"

"Not entirely." Maddie's fingers tightened around her cup. This next part she hadn't even told the Weavers' Library. "You are new here—has anyone told you the story of Jenny Hull?"

Sophie shook her head.

"She's a local legend—except that she was real, too. Jenny Hull was a silk weaver here at the end of the last century. Transported for thievery—but she was only trying to steal back her own work." Maddie swallowed. "From Mr. Giles, who'd refused to pay her properly for it." She reached up and pulled her necklace over her head, then held it out for Sophie to see. "My mother tried to help her. She would have done anything for her, she told me. But the law came between them. Jenny Hull was sent away, and my mother died after Peterloo. She took a saber slash to the side, and it suppurated. They never saw each other again."

Sophie took the convict token and examined it for a long while. Clever fingers traced every line of every letter around the edge, but forbore to disturb the small figure mourning in the center of the coin.

The threat of tears made Maddie's throat ache; she washed them away with another gulp of cider. "My mother is gone—but Jenny Hull came back. Under a new name, with nobody the wiser. She came to find my mother. She found me instead. And she found Mr. Giles more prosperous than ever, his stature and his fortune growing with every cheat and trick he played on those less fortunate than him." Her cup was empty now; she set it aside. "If you can't have love, I suppose revenge is the next best thing."

"How much longer until your plan is finished?"

"A week, at most." Maddie met Sophie's gaze staunchly. "You probably couldn't stop it now short of going direct to the magistrates."

Sophie took a deep breath. "How can I help?"

Maddie blinked. Surely she hadn't heard that right. "Help?"

Sophie nodded. "Is there anything still left to do? Any loose ends or—or last details?" She tugged the piecework comforter more tightly around her shoulders. "I am quite good at being overlooked, in case that comes in handy."

Maddie stared—at Sophie's brown hair pulled back so demurely, those dark eyes so soft and earnest, everything about her solid and steady and true. She'd been a thorn in the side when she'd thought Maddie needed thwarting; now that she knew Maddie's cause was just, here she was offering to pitch in.

The words were out of Maddie before she'd realized she was thinking them: "Anyone who overlooks you is a fool."

Sophie's eyes went hot, and an answering longing stole Maddie's breath.

Sophie tilted forward, still holding the convict coin, and clasped the chain back around Maddie's neck. Her hands tucked the pendant carefully beneath the bodice of Maddie's gown. The warmth of the metal seared into Maddie's skin like a brand, even as Sophie's fingers came to rest against the tender hollow at the base of Maddie's throat. "You said you'd never lied to me," Sophie murmured.

"I never will," Maddie promised recklessly.

"You said you could make me scream."

Maddie's throat went dry, and her voice roughened. "Little sparrow—"

Sophie growled.

Maddie felt goose bumps prickle all down her arms. God, but she wanted to hear that sound again. And every other sound Sophie made. "I would love to try," Maddie said, licking her lips.

Sophie's eyes flared. Her hands slipped around to the back of Maddie's neck and pulled Maddie forward into a kiss like drowning.

Maddie had been kissed by so many people she'd lost count, but Sophie's kiss eclipsed all the others. It felt like more than a single kiss—as though they picked up precisely where they'd left off in the tavern more than a week ago. As if the fire they'd started then had only banked itself, waiting for this moment to burn higher and hotter.

So why go slow? Sophie's hands were clutching at her, insistent and irresistible—Maddie gave in to their pull and tipped forward, sliding her own hands beneath the coverlet and filling them with Sophie's plump and perfect breasts.

The noise Sophie made in the back of her throat was half surprise, half plea.

Maddie let herself taste those noises for a moment, licking hungrily into the heat of Sophie's mouth. Her hands rested above layers—too many layers!—of gown and underthings. Maddie wanted skin beneath her touch, and more sounds to fill her ears. She told Sophie so without words, by curling one finger and scraping the fingernail over the peak of one breast, so that all those fabric layers buzzed with friction down to the nipple hidden beneath.

Sophie tore her mouth away to pant for air. "*Oh.*"

Maddie kissed her throat, tracing her lips over that most delicious spot where Sophie's pulse fluttered. "Not screaming yet," she purred. "How many of your clothes am I allowed to remove?" She added a scrape of teeth to make Sophie squirm. "I could do it without removing any, if you'd like."

"No," Sophie said at once, though it was more than half gasp.

Maddie stopped. Slowly she pulled away, her grip loosening even as her breath still came panting in her lungs.

Sophie blinked up at her, dazed and dazzled. "You stopped."

Maddie nodded. "You said no."

"Oh." Sophie cocked her head. "I did. But what I meant was: *No, please get me as naked as possible.* I see I shall have to be more explicit in future." She bit her lip, a sight that made Maddie go hot from head to heels. "Please Miss Crewe, help me out of this gown. Tear it off, if you have to."

Maddie gasped as if scandalized. "Tear it? Why on earth

would I do such a thing?" Clothing was costly—and it revealed a person's secrets. If you were someone who knew how to read it.

Maddie was an expert in that code. She let her hands coast over the brown linen again, from the ribboned neckline and over the swell of Sophie's breast. "This is good whole cloth, without a mar or mend anywhere. What has it done to deserve harm at my hands?"

Sophie shook her head, even as she arched into the caress. "It's plain linen. Dyed plain brown."

Then why the ribbon? Maddie fought a smile. Sophie Roseingrave was practical but wistful; sensible and sensual both.

Maddie slipped her hands around Sophie's waist, then up to the laces at the back of the dress. Her hands busied themselves untying. She leaned forward to breathe her next question into Sophie's ear. "How could you ever go home if I destroyed your dress?"

"I wouldn't," Sophie said at once. "I'd have to stay here helpless, to be used however you pleased. Utterly at your mercy." She sounded anything but fearful, wriggling close to give Maddie's hands more room to work behind her back.

Maddie chuckled and bit Sophie's earlobe as the dress loosened; the other woman gasped and giggled. Together they pulled up Sophie's skirts and got the dress over her head and arms. Sophie's petticoat and light stays went next—unboned, as Maddie's were. "Your turn," Sophie said, and reached for Maddie's gray gown.

Maddie caught her hands by the wrists and spread them wide, one to either side. "Not so fast," she said. "Let me look at you."

Sophie squirmed. "If your plan is to make me scream in frustration . . ."

Maddie simply looked—at the breasts curving so temptingly beneath the linen, true, but also at the garment itself. Sophie's chemise was good cloth, but old. It had been much mended by a hand clearly hurrying through the job. Maddie dropped one of Sophie's hands so her fingers could trace seams like old scars. *She embellishes her sensible gown, but wears these wounds close to the skin,* Maddie thought. *She doesn't expect anyone ever to see them—or to take notice of them when she's being laced up at home.*

"Is this your stitching?" she asked. Meaning: *Did you hurry through a task you disliked, or were these marks made by someone else's hands?*

"I'm not much of a mender," Sophie muttered.

Impatient, Maddie thought to herself. She ran her fingers over the soft fabric, almost transparent with age and wear. That thinness hinted at what waited beneath: softness and skin and sweet, slippery places. And somehow, despite all her teasing promises, Maddie hesitated to strip that last scrap of cloth away from Sophie's body. It veiled her form—but it said so much about her choices.

Of course Maddie yearned to see what Sophie Roseingrave looked like when she was bare and wet and willing. But apparently Maddie was greedier than she'd realized—because suddenly she wanted more than that. She wanted to see as deep as she could into Sophie's mind and heart, too. To learn every secret that lived in the darkness there.

The shock of all that wanting made her hands shake like leaves in spring wind.

The impatience Maddie had deduced apparently got the better of Sophie. Her voice turned tart and teasing: "If my poor sewing bothers you so much, you need not look at it so closely." She covered Maddie's eyes with one hand and climbed into her lap, knees straddling Maddie's hips.

Her next kiss brooked no denial. Sophie slanted her lips hard over Maddie's, her tongue stroking almost angrily.

Maddie's soul soared in the darkness and she yielded gladly. Who would have thought justice-minded Miss Roseingrave had such wonderful lechery in her? Sophie was a plump and perfect lapful, all hungry mouth and quivering thighs as she guided Maddie's hand beneath the hem of that thin chemise. Tender skin, sweet curves, and—ah, yes, slickness and heat beneath soft curls. Maddie teased those soft folds until Sophie growled again—oh, that sound! Maddie drank it like wine, her eyes squeezed shut beneath Sophie's palm.

Sophie broke the kiss to offer a threat: "If you don't fuck me now I'm going to do it myself and make you watch."

Maddie shuddered in delight. "Next time," she gasped, then took two fingers and slid them deep and fast into Sophie's cunny.

Perhaps too fast: Sophie squeaked.

Maddie went still.

Sophie breathed out, long and low, and her hand trembled where it covered Maddie's eyes. "Oh, yes," she sighed, and spread her hips a little wider. "More of that, please, Miss Crewe."

Maddie didn't need to be told twice. She pushed her fingers up again, heat engulfing her up to the last knuckle, feeling her way for the deepest, silkiest slide.

Sophie's hips bucked insistently. Maddie pressed up with the heel of her hand, grinding against the throbbing pearl just above where her fingers played. "*Yes,*" Sophie gasped. She kept talking, breathing pleas and encouragements and demands, her fingers pressing against Maddie's eyelids, her palms going damp as her pleasure built. She rode Maddie harder, straining up on her knees to give her hand room to work. This had the delightful effect of bringing her breasts high enough that Maddie could lean down, eyes still covered, and suck at one linen-veiled nipple until it went tight beneath her tongue.

Sophie cried out and came, her cunny rippling as Maddie's fingers worked within her. She cupped Maddie's face in her hands and kissed her desperately, small sounds almost of pain pouring from her throat.

Maddie kept her eyes shut tight through it all, drinking in every gasp and whimper, every sound of pleasure made by the woman above her. It was only when Sophie slumped with release, panting and spent, that Maddie realized she'd never removed so much as a stitch of her own clothing.

The church bells of St. Severus tolled midnight.

Maddie opened her eyes.

"Oh!" Sophie sat up. Her face was mottled white and red, her dark hair all but falling out of its pins in tousled locks.

Her chemise had rucked up around her hips, the neckline wantonly askew, and the linen clung wetly at her breast where Maddie's mouth had been.

Miss Roseingrave looked utterly ruined, lust dampened and pleasured within an inch of her life.

"I'm meant to be asleep at home," she said, "ready to open the shop in the morning while everyone else sleeps late."

Maddie allowed herself the luxury of one more kiss—a slow savoring of lips and heated breath. "Then let's get you set to rights."

Back into the soft stays Sophie went, all her small scars hidden again from ravenous eyes. Maddie stood behind her to pull the laces tight and do up the brown gown, and consoled herself by dropping a kiss where the lovebird ribbon ended at the shoulder seam.

Sophie finished putting her hair back in order and glanced at Maddie over her shoulder. "You will come see me if there is anything I can do?"

"I will," Maddie said. "Though we shouldn't have to trouble you. We have plenty of hands available."

"Of course." Sophie ducked her head.

She looked so forlorn that Maddie stepped forward and embraced her, pressing comforting lips to the nape of that bowed neck. "You never did scream," she murmured. "I have to keep that promise, don't I?"

Sophie nestled against Maddie's chest, fingers twining together. "If you insist," she said, in a tone so pristine and proper that it tempted Maddie to undo all that lacing and ravish her a second time.

Maddie stole another few kisses on the way down the stairs, and again as Sophie wrapped her cloak and her muffler back around herself. She melted back into the night as quietly as she'd arrived, leaving Maddie to mount the stairs again one lonely step at a time. She undressed, wishing it were Sophie's hands instead of hers on tapes and laces and linen, then she burrowed into the sheets in search of the ghosts of warmth and company.

The bed smelled of Sophie's pleasure, tart and luscious.

Maddie's hands dove between her legs. She made herself come, over and over, until her eyes drifted shut in wanton exhaustion.

From the doorway of the Weavers' Library, Maddie declared: "Miss Slight is a genius."

In the few short weeks since they'd begun planning their crime, the young lady had designed and built something truly terrifying: a tower of metal discs, half-corroded in a deeply alarming way and ringed by bubbling jars, linked to one another by twisting coils of wire. A branch of candles nearby sent light through the liquid to ripple on the floor in eldritch waves. The occasional spark spit out from this mess to extinguish itself on the thick fire-dampening cloth beneath.

A thick coil of wire snaked out of the tower and connected to a wooden cabinet—a tall, varnished, hulking thing with six palm-sized holes drilled front and back like the pips on a playing card. It loomed in the center of the room, looking like nothing so much as a coffin stood on its end. On the side of the cabinet where the wire went in was a large lever, painted crimson.

The whole apparatus looked like a device that could destroy the world.

"Of course it's perfectly harmless," Miss Slight explained, as she and Alice Bilton dropped more dye and soda ash into the jars. "Anyone who knows anything about voltaic piles can see it's all smoke and nonsense."

"I think we can trust Mr. Giles not to be one of those people," Mrs. Money said, looking alarmed in contrast to the brave military cut of her gown. "But since I am *also* one of those people, I will ask again: Are you certain this is safe?"

Maddie had been to the Slights' shop—a place Miss Slight's hands had filled with pocket watches and children's toys and miniature mechanical birds that piped realistic calls. It was work that took imagination, care, and a zealous attention to even the smallest details. "I'm sure," Maddie said firmly, and smoothed down her silk skirts.

Tonight Maddie would be garbed in blue—the same blue silk they'd used as bait, but without the red and gold and green threads. It was the first time in years she would wear fabric so fine: she used to make herself things out of leftovers and the odd ends of bolts, back when she and her mother were weaving broadcloth, but since she'd moved to ribbon weaving she didn't have scraps to play with the same way. She'd missed the weight of silk, as she held the bundled gown over her arms. She couldn't seem to stop her hands from stroking the nap of the cloth.

She wanted Sophie's hands on this dress, and on the body beneath. Maddie had walked by the instrument shop once or twice, but otherwise she'd been keeping her distance from the quiet and too-tempting Miss Roseingrave, who knew too many of Maddie's secrets. *When this is over,* she told herself. *When it's safer.* But her resolve to hold that distance was weakening day by day. The feel of silk against her skin might shred it utterly.

She wanted Sophie to peel this dress from her layer by layer, hungrily, until only Maddie remained.

But that would have to wait. First, she had to put on a little show for Mr. Giles.

He arrived precisely five minutes late—punctual enough that he couldn't be faulted for it, but tardy enough that he didn't have to waste any of his own time waiting for anybody else. Mrs. Money greeted him and permitted herself to be kissed and complimented.

Her smile never wavered, not even as Mr. Giles's lying lips touched the back of her glove. Maddie wondered what it cost the onetime Jenny Hull, to bear that touch and stay so cool and aloof.

"I must ask you, sir, to never divulge the secrets I am about to reveal to you."

"Madam," he said, and for once Maddie could believe him sincere, "I wouldn't dream of it."

Mrs. Money waved Maddie forward; she put on her best sulk and obeyed.

"Miss Crewe will be donning our dress for this transformation," Mrs. Money said. "We have refreshed the color specifically for tonight's demonstration, so that you may see how completely it transforms. Horace was very careful to make it so a lady didn't have to remove any clothing for the process to work—in fact, he found it more reliable when it was on a person than when he used a mannequin. Something about animal magnetism, I think?" She waved a hand. "It's in his notes somewhere, I'm sure."

"May I?" asked Mr. Giles, his eyes on the cloth. Maddie held out the gown, and let him poke and pull at the silk until he was satisfied to its quality and construction.

"If you would, Miss Crewe," Mrs. Money said, and Maddie stepped behind a screen with Alice and Miss Slight.

"Would you like a closer look at the cabinet?" Mrs. Money asked.

Maddie shed her plain gray wool and stepped into the pooled skirts Alice held as footsteps tapped a circle on the wooden floor, Mr. Giles murmuring soft questions and comments. "Are we sure it will fit over the hips?" Maddie asked, though the dress was already at her waist and she was sliding her arms into the sleeves.

"It is a trifle snug," Alice lied, her hands flying from button to button up Maddie's spine. Only about a third of the buttons actually held the dress together; the rest were for show. "One good tug should do it—there."

"I can't reach to do it up," Maddie complained, slipping her wrists through the prebuttoned cuffs.

"Of course not," Miss Slight said, with an impatient

huff. "It buttons at the back. I'll get them. Start on the sleeves."

"I can't—Alice is doing up the one sleeve, and I can't button the other one-handed."

"Stop wriggling, or this will take twice as long."

Maddie grinned, already dressed, ready to play her part to the hilt. She made her voice turn petulant. "What kind of woman wears something so hard to get into?"

"It's very fashionable," Alice retorted sharply, though her eyes were laughing.

"Is getting dressed what great ladies do instead of work, like the rest of us? Three hours to get everything buttoned and laced, an hour for tea, and then three more hours just to get it all off again?"

Alice hid a silent snicker behind her hand.

At last, Maddie stepped out from the screen, blue silk draped around her, her fingers supposedly struggling to do up the last of the small and fiddly buttons at her wrist.

"Finally," Mrs. Money muttered, then frowned. "Your hair, girl."

"What about my hair?"

Mrs. Money held out her hand. "You can't wear hairpins in the cabinet—unless you fancy ending up with a singed scalp, or worse?"

As Mr. Giles watched avidly, Maddie pulled every last pin from her hair one by one. She dropped them in Mrs. Money's hand and combed her fingers through her long auburn locks to ensure she hadn't missed any.

"Now then," Mrs. Money said, pulling open the cabinet door. "Inside with you."

Maddie twisted her hands nervously. "Are you sure it's safe, ma'am?"

Mrs. Money's voice was all impatience. "Come, Miss Crewe, we've tested it a dozen times, with but a handful of accidents. Have a little courage."

Mr. Giles looked at Maddie and twin hopes warred in his eyes. Either the experiment would succeed, or a woman he loathed would be grievously and painfully injured.

There was no chance he'd look away.

Maddie took a deep breath, made sure he could see her hands trembling, and stepped into the cabinet. Mrs. Money shut the door behind her, circled the cabinet once as if checking it over, and moved to the lever. Maddie could just see a slice of her through the cabinet holes on the left.

At her back, Maddie could feel the hook Mrs. Money had set, tight and sure in a loop of blue silk that went unseen against the trimming and detail of the dress.

"Is everything ready?" Mrs. Money called.

"Yes, ma'am," Miss Slight said, as she and Alice pretended to scrutinize the bubbling jars.

Mrs. Money pulled the crimson lever.

Sparks flew up, blinding the eye, and an agitated hum came from the cabinet. The blue gown gleamed through the holes in the cabinet front—then gleamed a little brighter, as the secret seam tore, the blue pulled away and the gold beneath was revealed. Fabric twisted up behind Maddie, the two layers of silk whispering softly against one another as the hook turned and turned.

After another moment Mrs. Money threw the lever up and the awful humming stopped, sparks dying down and leaving everyone's eyes dazzled.

After a beat, Maddie hammered on the door. "Mrs. Money? Mrs. Money, let me out!"

"Oh!" The widow rushed forward, struggling with the wooden latch.

Maddie wailed and pounded on the wood, as Alice and Miss Slight ran forward to help.

The bolt opened and Maddie flew out, not stopping until she had put Mr. Giles between her and the cabinet. Her hair was wild around her, her eyes wide. "Oh, that was *strange!*"

Miss Slight gasped dramatically.

Maddie looked down.

The silk dress she wore was now a bright, blinding yellow that seemed to gather all the light in the room.

Mr. Giles strode over to grasp Maddie's arms and pat his hands up and down the seams of this gown—totally ignoring quiet Alice, who snatched the torn blue silk from the cabinet and stashed it out of sight beneath the thick fireproof drapes.

Alice, after all, had been a magician's assistant for some years with a traveling fair, and had adapted this trick from something the Wizard Falcetti used to do to change the color of a tablecloth spread beneath full goblets of wine. The mechanism to accomplish it had barely challenged Miss Slight's abilities at all.

Alice straightened up from the concealing drapery and

folded her hands demurely in front of her, professional enough not to grin with triumph.

Maddie turned her own grin into a preen and a simper for the cloth merchant's benefit.

"Incredible," Mr. Giles murmured, his hands still gripping Maddie's forearm, turning it back and forth to watch the firelight flicker on yellow silk. His eyes were wide and his face paler than before, with two eager red spots high in his cheeks. He fixed Mrs. Money with an expert eye, like an angler reeling in a catch. "Are these the only colors the process can produce?"

"Horace's dye produces a complete spectrum. He was able to replicate any hue found in nature—and one or two more besides."

His fingers pinched at Maddie's sleeve, testing the cloth. "Incredible," he repeated. "It feels like fine silk."

"It *is* fine silk," Mrs. Money replied.

"And the transformation is quick," Mr. Giles went on. The gleam in his eyes was almost feverish now, his fingers tightening convulsively on Maddie's cuff.

"Very quick," Mrs. Money said. "Imagine being able to change the color of your dress during an afternoon's walk."

Mr. Giles's mouth was fox-like. "Imagine being able to charge a customer more than once for the same dress."

"You can see why it was so disappointing when Mr. Obeney left for America," Mrs. Money sniffed. "Such an opportunity going to waste."

Mr. Giles dropped the silk—Maddie had to fight the urge to step back out of his reach—and turned. "Madam," he said, with his most portentous delivery, "I have a proposition to make."

Here we are, Maddie thought. *Here's where we sell him the stored fabric, the useless device, the whole set of props. He'll have it on his store shelves by the end of the week—and I'll bet he won't even bother to test it himself first. He's a cloth merchant and an opportunist: he won't be able to resist this fabric.*

"I don't want to buy this fabric," said Mr. Giles.

Maddie's heart stuttered to a stop.

Mrs. Money, wiser and more controlled, only cocked a head curiously.

Mr. Giles's lips parted in a cunning smile. "I want to make more of it," he said. "I want to buy the whole process from you, start to finish." His charming smile grew wider and wider; it was all Maddie could see, just that line of sharp white teeth. "This new discovery is going to change everything—and I want to take full advantage."

Maddie had turned to stone. The horror of this failure froze every bit of her body, from the back of her neck to the soles of her slippered feet.

Mrs. Money only shook her head apologetically. "I believe Mr. Obeney owns all the legal rights to the fabrication process, sir."

"But not the ideas behind them. And Mr. Obeney is in his American utopia and unlikely to object for some time." He lowered his voice as though imparting some great secret. "Think how much money we could make in the time it takes for the news to reach him. Enough to handle any small legal matters that crop up, I am sure."

"But I had planned to travel, sir, once my business in Carrisford was completed, and my year of mourning over. I had not thought to stay for any lengthy commercial venture."

"You wouldn't have to stay." Mr. Giles spread his hands. "You would only have to explain the process to me, take your money, and go."

Mrs. Money narrowed her eyes. "How much money, precisely?"

"I was going to offer you fifty pounds for the existing stock," Mr. Giles said. He shifted from one foot to the other, and tucked a hand into the lapel of his coat. "Of course, I would expect your price to be much higher for the technical knowledge than for a simple stock of fabric. Trade secrets and all that. I am prepared to be extremely generous. By a factor of two, possibly three."

"I want a thousand pounds."

Maddie's mouth went dry, and even Miss Slight couldn't repress a quick gasp of shock.

Mr. Giles's mouth went agape, before he got hold of himself. "Done. But in return . . ." He took a breath. "I would expect to know every step of the method, from start to finish. You show me how it works—and you relinquish all rights to the process thereafter."

Mrs. Money pretended to consider—but of course she couldn't agree. There *was* no process, nothing beyond the tricks in this room. Maddie ground her teeth together in anguish. This wasn't supposed to happen. This wasn't what they'd planned.

This was supposed to be their moment of victory!

Mrs. Money held out a hand. "Very well, Mr. Giles. We have a deal."

They shook on it.

Mrs. Money went on: "It may take me at least a week to reassemble the production line Horace established. Particularly since one wants to be discreet."

"Of course—discretion is an absolute watchword," Mr. Giles answered.

I'll bet, Maddie thought grimly.

He bowed, and his eyes when they met Maddie's flickered with reflected flames. "I will look forward to our next meeting," he said.

Maddie curtsied, cursing inwardly.

This was a *disaster*.

Chapter Nine

The shop bell chimed a welcome. Mr. Roseingrave peeked up from the keyboard of the now-repaired Dewhurst and Ffolkes as Sophie entered. "Hello, my dear—you're looking cheery. I take it Miss Muchelney's second lesson went well?"

Sophie nodded, still warm in the glow of success. "The girl is a natural. And enthusiastic—she barely leaves off practicing to eat, her mother tells me. Harriet's even asked if we have any simple pieces for both piano and violin so she and her brothers can play something together."

"God help Mrs. Muchelney," Mr. Roseingrave laughed.

Sophie sat beside her father on the piano bench, her green skirts looking even greener against the new varnish. "I think Harriet has a real gift," she said softly. "She's quick and she already seems to understand how the piano wants to be played." She stroked the repaired keys, enjoying the sleekness of them. "She's been composing, too—she calls it 'fiddling,' but it's more than just childish noise."

"It is a joy and a wonder to see such talent in one so young.

Reminds me of another brilliant young woman I know." Mr. Roseingrave set his hands to the keys and began the first bars of his favorite piece, an adagio by Haydn. His voice was much softer when he spoke next: "I never apologized properly for putting you in Mr. Verrinder's path, did I, child?"

Sophie glanced up, startled.

Her father always smiled; he was not smiling now. Without that happy curve his face fell into deeper lines and shadows, the worn stone portrait of a king in exile. His hair used to be gray streaked with white: somehow while Sophie wasn't paying attention it had become white streaked with gray. His fingers trilled over an ornament, a brief bit of birdsong in the melody. "I ought to have protected you better," he said. "Instead I let my own hunger for renown lead me astray—and lead you into danger. I regret that more than I can say."

"You did nothing wrong," Sophie insisted staunchly, despite the guilt that hung around her throat and threatened to choke her. "It was all Mr. Verrinder's crime."

Mr. Roseingrave shook his head, white hair bouncing insistently. "He could not have led me so far down that bad road without some fault in me to latch on to. My love of well-built systems and machinery, my desire for praise, for wealth . . . These were my weaknesses, but they were used against all of us. You, your mother, your siblings—you did not deserve to suffer for my failings." His hands faltered, dropping the rhythm, stumbling over wrong notes that interrupted the smooth flow of the song.

Sophie reached out at once and picked up the thread of the adagio. Soft bass notes and the light clear tune on top.

Her voice still felt thick when she replied: "We lost money and a little pride, that's all. We can recover from that. We still have each other."

Mr. Roseingrave sighed. "I've missed hearing you play, you know. I've missed hearing the songs you create."

Sophie's hands slowed.

Her father took over the left hand of the piece while Sophie played the melody to match. They'd played solo works as duets like this when Sophie was learning—it had helped to break down difficult compositions into manageable halves. Together they could play much more ambitious things than either could play separately.

They brought the movement to a close, notes fading away. Sophie pulled her hands from the keyboard and into her lap.

If anything, she should be the one apologizing. Mr. Verrinder might have deceived her father—but he had not deceived Sophie. At least, not entirely.

"Six months between London and here," Mr. Roseingrave said into the silence. "I think it's the longest I've ever seen you go without touching a piano. And I was so wrapped up in my own guilt and shame that I didn't even notice—until I walked in and heard you playing for Mr. Frampton the other day."

Sophie flushed. She felt as though she had betrayed him somehow. Piano had always been the thing they shared with each other. "I didn't mean—"

"I know." He did smile now, comforting her. "That was another of my weaknesses, you see. I wanted the entire world to know how brilliant my daughter was. I wanted everyone to think as highly of you as I do. I still want that."

Sophie's hands clenched into fists against her thighs, an echo of the way her heart twisted and tightened in her throat. "Love is not a fault," she said, low and fierce.

"Love may not be—but negligence is, and I let my love for you blind me to Mr. Verrinder's true nature." His eyes gleamed in the light of the dying day. "I swear to you, child, I will protect you better in future."

Sophie swallowed. "I hope you do not mistrust Mr. Frampton for offering me his advice?"

Mr. Roseingrave chuckled. "Quite the opposite. Look at him and his son—they are very different, but they take such good care of one another. You can tell so much about a person by what they do, not just the flattering things they say. I should have paid more attention to what Mr. Verrinder did and less to what Mr. Verrinder promised. Because for all his lofty words, Sophie—he treated you very badly. Very badly indeed."

Sophie's eyes prickled with tears. The confessions clustered so close in her throat that she didn't know which one to start with. To explain she'd been more deluded by ambition than he had? To confess she had apparently not learned her lesson, and had fallen in again with someone whose motives were far from aboveboard?

What would he say if he'd learned she'd offered to help Madeleine Crewe?

The shop bell chimed again. Her father's customer smile came out. "Hello, sir," he said, lowering the fallboard and rising from the piano bench. "Welcome to Roseingrave's . . ."

Sophie dashed the droplets from her eyes before standing and turning to help.

The rest of the afternoon passed dreamlike: Sophie sold a violin and a harp and several copies of the *Harmonicon*. She talked about Beethoven and Broadwood and the newest set of ballads from Griffin and Brinkworth's. She smiled and answered questions and pulled instruments from the wall by rote—but inside she carried around a miniature maelstrom of emotion. Pride because her father thought well of her. Anger that her father had to worry about her welfare on top of everything else. Shame because she should have hidden her pain better. Guilt because she hadn't protected him, either. And the low, flickering flame of determination, like a torch in the darkness, lighting her way forward.

It was too many things for a single heart to contain. She had to get them out—and there was only one sure way to do it.

So she lingered by the piano while her father closed up the shop. He glanced at her hands, twisting and flexing, and a knowing gleam came into his eyes. "Make sure to lock up when you're finished," he said, and vanished upstairs to the floors where the family lived, and where her mother and siblings would be gathering for dinner.

But for now, she had the shop entirely to herself.

She turned the lamps down at once and pulled the open-work shutters down over the window and the door. The gas-lights in the street outside provided just enough low light to see by through the wooden scrolls and cutouts.

Then she took a seat at the Dewhurst and Ffolkes.

For a moment she only sat, calming her racing heart and flexing her fingers to limber them up. But before long she was opening the fallboard like a pirate lifting the lid of a long-buried treasure chest. Sharps and naturals gleamed in welcome.

This was no time for subtlety. Sophie raised her hands and set to playing the fastest étude she remembered, the one crammed with more notes than the listener's ears could hear at once. Some of the notes she hit weren't the right ones but she barreled onward anyway, trying to outplay the stiffness of her wrists and that iron chill that still froze her sinews. That cold pushed against her, she pushed back, but the piece ended before the battle did.

She plucked up one of the newer concertos that had just arrived from Vienna. And tried again. But she found herself wrestling with the same problem: it was as though there was a wall between her and the music, some barrier that kept her emotions from flowing down her arms and into the song like she wanted them to. With no outlet, those wild feelings could only swirl faster and faster around her, until they trapped her as completely as if they were walls of stone, and Sophie left with only a spoon to chisel her way free.

She might never get out.

Sophie wanted to weep at the thought—so she shifted to the most lugubrious funeral march she knew. Minor chords, stately rhythm, a melody heavy as teardrops down the face of the bereaved. On more than one occasion playing it had made her sob aloud with mournful ecstasy.

But even that once-familiar agony felt muted and distant. She let the notes die away.

With the piano quiet, other sounds flowed in. Footsteps on the stones outside. Human voices from sidewalks and the street. The rush of the river. And a low, repeated thrum that Sophie had learned was the sound of the silk-throwing mill, that ran all hours. Not just a sound but a heartbeat, like the pulse of some great devouring beast. The rhythm of Carrisford. For the first two weeks here it had kept Sophie from sleeping; now she couldn't imagine going to bed without sensing it just below the threshold of hearing. Like a lullaby.

No, not a lullaby—a waltz. The distinctive *one two three, one two three* fit so neatly into the spaces between the thrums that Sophie's fingers were on the keys before she realized she was moving. She found the bass note that harmonized with the silk mill for the *one*. *Two* and *three* were soft, higher chords, the footsteps of a woman walking lightly down the street. A woman in gray wool (the simple melody began)— escaping into a churchyard (a brief flutter of a minor key for the gravestones)—then a powerful torrent of notes as her pursuer caught up with her and was trapped in turn by a single fiery kiss.

A second theme: languid and sensual. Caresses over linen and hands stroking skin. Building to a climax . . .

But now there were too many possibilities for the tune. Sophie frowned and went back two bars to refine the shape and structure. Not perfect yet, not entirely right—but she kept working at it, so focused on following the magnetic pull of that internal compass that she lost track of everything outside her hands and the keys and the shapes unfurling in the air . . .

A noise—one she didn't make—broke through her trance. Someone knocking.

She whirled around to see Maddie Crewe peering

through the scrollwork. Almost as if she'd been conjured by Sophie's song.

Sophie hurried to the door and let her in, closing the shutters again behind her and hoping the haste would explain the flush that burned on her cheeks. "Miss Crewe," she breathed, then all breath stopped as the other woman whirled off her cloak with a flourish: Miss Crewe wasn't in her usual gray wool.

No, tonight Maddie Crewe was wearing a silk gown of bright sunshine yellow.

It was bold, utterly vibrant, and Sophie couldn't have called up a more alluring vision of sin if she'd been a hermetic saint with nature's full range of pharmacopoeia. The skirts were voluminous with tucks and flounces. The bodice was tight and trim against Miss Crewe's waist; the neckline a long, wide line. Her throat—her hips—the high, generous breasts beneath the silk—Sophie had never seen anyone so beautiful in all her life.

She almost snorted. Of course the day Sophie wore her fine new gown was the day Maddie Crewe turned up in silk.

"Good evening, Miss Roseingrave," murmured Miss Crewe—but there was a siren's song in her voice and a fire in her eyes that scorched Sophie down to her toes.

She clearly relished the effect her frock had on Sophie.

Miss Crewe strode into the instrument shop and turned, making yellow silk twirl and show off her slender ankles. "I hope you don't mind me showing up so late."

"I was only practicing," Sophie rasped. She coughed to clear her dry throat. "You look splendid. What's the occasion?"

Maddie's smile dimmed, and she ignored the question to peer curiously at the dark shelves and shadowed music racks. Instruments gleamed as the gaslight played over wood and lacquer. "Was your London shop as grand as this?"

Sophie laughed. "Not grander, but much larger. We only have room for one or two pianos here. In London, we never had fewer than six on display at any moment—plus another six in the workshop—every one of which my father had built."

Maddie walked to the Dewhurst and Ffolkes and ran her hands over the smooth curves of the piano case. "That must have kept him busy."

"He had journeymen and apprentices, of course—but yes. He was always looking for improvements he could make: differences in the frame, in the shape of the case, in the actions to make the keys more responsive to the touch." Sophie couldn't stop staring at Maddie's hands. The way her gloved fingers stroked over sleek wood was doing awful things to Sophie's pulse.

Maddie tilted her head. "Is your father here at the moment?"

"Yes." Sophie swallowed. "Upstairs, with the rest of my family."

"So we won't be overheard?"

Sophie's mouth opened on a gasp. Was Maddie Crewe going to ravish her right here on the floor with all those windows around them? The idea was perverse and dangerous—and it sent a bolt of searing heat through Sophie's core. She imagined sitting Miss Crewe down on the piano bench, flinging up those lush skirts and diving beneath them, every string instrument in the place sighing in echo at every wanton cry. Sun-bright silk warming beneath her mouth, being torn away by her hands . . .

She stepped closer—but paused when Maddie sighed. Her mouth was tight, her brow slightly furrowed. She looked . . . worried.

She hadn't come here for seduction.

Sophie shoved lust aside for the moment. She guided Maddie to the piano bench and sat them both down: Maddie on the right, Sophie on the left. Green skirts folded against gold, contrast brightening both hues even in the low light. "If we are quiet, we'll hear anyone coming long before they'll hear us," Sophie said. "Now: What's the matter?"

"We gave our demonstration to Mr. Giles tonight," Maddie replied. "Mrs. Money and I, along with Alice Bilton and Miss Mary Slight."

She wriggled; Sophie felt the shift of figure and fabric and had to suck in air to steady herself.

Maddie brandished one silk-sleeved arm. "This gown, you may be astonished to hear, can change from yellow to blue and back again with a simple electrical charge. It would be a smash hit among the fashionable sort. A guaranteed moneymaker for any silk merchant."

"Sounds too good to be true," Sophie said wryly. She put out a fingertip—just one, for restraint—and stroked a line along Maddie's knee. "It feels quite fine. Did the trick not work?"

"Oh, it worked." Maddie's laugh was low, almost a sob. She

began pulling at her gloves, removing them in frustrated little jerks and tugs. "It worked too well. Our Mr. Giles doesn't just want to sell this fabric—he wants to make more of it."

"Make *more*—oh." Sophie huffed out an appalled sound of horrified amusement. "Oh, I see." She shook her head. "You underestimated your own gift for persuasion, Miss Crewe."

"We underestimated Mr. Giles's greed, is what. We thought we were bringing him an easy, lazy way to profit— but he had to exploit it further, didn't he? You could offer to sell him the whole world for sixpence and he'd demand you throw in the moon as well." Maddie folded her gloves into an angry little package and set them on the piano case. "So now we have to find something even more outrageous to sell to him . . . and it means one more *big* step before the part where we get the money."

"And where you get revenge."

Maddie nodded confirmation. "I admit I don't know which of those I'm more impatient for. And now there's a whole other element to plan. It'll have to involve weaving—or fake weaving, which is faster—and it will have to be even more complicated and persuasive than tonight's trick. We'll need people, lots of people, and that just means more chances for things to go wrong. And for us all to get caught." She let out a sigh, which seemed to take all her momentum with her. Without it she looked vulnerable, anxious, and lost. She turned her head, one auburn curl quivering along the line of her throat. Her hand covered Sophie's and Sophie could feel how she trembled. "Did you really mean it when you offered to help?"

She sounded wistful, almost forlorn; Sophie charged

recklessly to the rescue. "Of course I meant it." She spread her hand until Maddie's fingers slipped between hers and she could catch them close. "What do you need me to do?"

Maddie shook her head, but her hand gripped Sophie's tight. The tense lines around her mouth softened and her shoulders were freed of enough weight to let her shrug in reply. "I'm not even sure yet. I'll have to work everything out with Mrs. Money—and we might need Miss Slight to help us with some machinery again . . ."

"Ask Mr. William Frampton, too. He's brilliant. Better yet: get Miss Slight to ask him for help. They're . . . friendly."

"So I've gathered." Maddie's lips curved, a hint of her usual sharp humor coming back into her face. "It's good to have friends in times like these," she said. Her thumb curved underneath their twined fingers and stroked Sophie's palm. "Friends with strong hearts—and beautiful hands." She raised their joined hands and brushed a kiss over Sophie's knuckles. Like a devoted knight in some long-lost ballad, paying tribute to his lady.

Sophie broke out in a sweat. "It's the piano playing, is all," she demurred. "It keeps the fingers nimble."

"So teach me something," Maddie replied, low and teasing. "There are so many ways I could use nimble fingers. You'd be astonished."

"I'd be *delighted*," Sophie retorted. Maddie's answering snicker was ample reward. "Start with your hands like so," she said, demonstrating on the lower keys.

Maddie tentatively reached out for the piano. Sophie showed her a simple melody, just a brief phrase. Then the same phrase, a third higher. Then the resolution that walked the melody down the scale again to its close. "Good," Sophie said. "Just keep doing that—I'll take care of the rest." They started from the beginning, laughing and having to start over several times on account of missed notes and errors. Maddie was a quick study, though: before long she was banging away at the tune while Sophie filled in the more complicated lower parts. The bounce of the melody brought some of her usual good humor back, and chased away some of the shadows hanging over her.

It was a duet Sophie had known for ages; she took this chance to observe Maddie's hands closely and at leisure.

Maddie Crewe's hands were the furthest thing from delicate—they were sturdy, strongly muscular, callused in numerous places. If once they wrapped around your heart, those hands would never let go. Sophie could still feel the pleasing pressure of them. Her chest was tight with longing—and with fear.

The last time she'd wanted something this much—the last time she'd trusted someone this much—it had almost destroyed her.

Maddie Crewe was beautiful—but even apart from her beauty, Maddie Crewe could ruin a person. She was certainly set on ruining Mr. Giles. But she could ruin Sophie, too, even without intending to—especially now that Sophie knew how those hands felt on her skin.

Perhaps that was all just part of the game for Maddie. The thrill of breaking the rules could extend to far more than just the law. Perhaps Sophie was only a different kind of thrill. Someone to be enjoyed and then discarded when some new challenge beckoned.

It wouldn't be the first time. And Sophie was so tired of being left behind.

Her father's words ghosted through her mind: *You can tell so much about a person by what they do, not by the flattering things they say.*

So: What had Maddie actually *done?*

She had warned Sophie away at first—but she hadn't threatened her. She had teased her and kissed her senseless and more—but she hadn't done anything Sophie hadn't wanted her to do. Maddie Crewe had seen a man profit from hurting others, and she had put together a band of people determined to do something about it. And yes, their solution was technically illegal—but the more Sophie learned about Mr. Giles, the more she came to realize that doing what was legal was not always the same thing as doing what was right.

Sophie realized she had already chosen. Law be damned: she was on Maddie Crewe's side.

She slowed her hands and brought the duet to a close. Maddie was laughing, playfulness back in her eyes, making them sparkle. Sophie's heart ached with joy to see it. "Come to dinner with me," she blurted.

"Of course," Maddie replied at once. "Where?"

"Here. I mean: home. I mean—come join us. All of us." Sophie shook her head, cheeks heating. Why could she not be graceful, just this once? She tried again. "Have dinner with my family. Meet my parents, endure my siblings. Then ask me to walk you home."

Maddie cocked her head. "But then you would have to walk home alone. In the dark. And so late at night . . ."

"Yes, it does sound a little alarming, doesn't it? Perhaps I shall just stay the night with you to be safe. Come home in the morning."

Maddie hummed with pleasure at that, but the crease between her brows said she wasn't fully convinced yet. "Is this some sort of test?"

"Naturally."

Maddie's eyes narrowed.

Sophie chuckled. "Haven't you ever met a lover's family before?"

Maddie's hand dove into her pocket and came up full of hairpins. "Just let me make myself respectable again," she muttered, and began putting up her red hair into proper twists and coils.

"Not too respectable, I hope."

Maddie let out a strangled noise.

Sophie laughed. Imagine: she had managed to flummox someone as self-possessed as Madeleine Crewe.

She immediately wanted to do it again.

Maddie's reply was tart. "I suppose your family has met everyone you've been *friends* with?"

Sophie leaned closer. This was going to be fun. "Actually, my father dropped a hint the other day that they're both aware some of my friendships have been more . . . *friendly* that others." She heaved a heavy sigh. "And I thought I was hiding it all so cleverly."

Maddie reached out and played her part of the duet again,

slow and sad. "My mother never said a word about any of the girls I flirted with—though she must have heard rumors. It's a small enough town that everyone knows pretty much everything. It was only when she was dying that she told me about her past with Jenny. I wish . . ." She sighed and pulled her hands to her lap again. "I wish I'd been able to talk about it with her sometimes, is all." She glanced ruefully at Sophie. "I'd thought I was so daring and depraved a seductress, an innovator of perversity. And my mother'd been doing it all years before I was born!"

"It's hard to keep secrets from people you care about."

"Yes," Maddie said, with a significant gaze. "It is."

That was so close to a confession that Sophie's courage failed her. She knew in her heart that she wasn't the kind of person people like Maddie Crewe made impassioned declarations to. Flirtation, seduction, yes—people enjoyed having someone to touch and toy with—but anything that sounded like love proved too temporary, in Sophie's experience. Her stomach twisted in a way she chose to pretend was hunger. "I'm famished," she said. "Let's go in."

Chapter Ten

They heard the first echoes as soon as they entered the stairwell—but it was only when Sophie pulled open the door at the top that the full cacophony hit them.

Maddie stopped dead right there in the hall. Sophie could hardly blame her. Between the sounds of Annie setting the table in the dining room to the right, and the ceaseless noise from her siblings in the parlor to the left overlooking the street, there was barely space to hear oneself think. Jasper and Julia were racing each other through a violin piece, repeating it faster and faster to see whose fingers faltered first. Mr. Roseingrave was reading aloud to Robbie from a history of the French Revolution, and Freddie was embellishing with the goriest details a twelve-year-old's mind could dream up, while sixteen-year-old Robbie pedantically attempted to correct him on matters of anatomy. "Heads on pikes can't grin, you ghoul."

"Why not?" Freddie complained. "If the man with the frog legs can make 'em kick without the rest of the frog—"

Jasper missed a note, and groaned as Julia jeered in triumph. "They go rotten, is why."

"What about the princess who nailed the horse head up—"

"That was a fairy tale!"

"What about the Frank monster?"

"*Frankenstein*. And when did you read that, anyway?"

"Borrowed it from you."

"You *stole* it—and you'll give it back or I swear—"

Julia's bow shrieked on the violin strings. Jasper stopped playing to argue that was a fault; Julia argued vehemently that it didn't count because it was a deliberate expressive choice, *on purpose*—

Maddie clutched at Sophie's elbow, looking rather green around the gills. "No wonder you're so quiet," she muttered. "How does anyone else get a word in edgewise?"

Sophie chuckled and leaned close. "You have to find other ways of getting attention," she said, and nipped at Maddie's earlobe.

The soft gasp that resulted was the most musical sound in the world. Maddie's smile was shy and charmed, as if Sophie had surprised her in the best way.

Sophie's heart buoyed her up, and courage propelled her into motion: she grabbed Maddie by the elbow and led her inexorably into the parlor. "Good evening, everyone, I'd like you to meet—"

Mr. Roseingrave closed his book and stood up; everyone else carried on.

Sophie tried again. "This is my friend Miss—"

Mrs. Roseingrave looked up from her mending, and took a breath to fill her singer's lungs. *"Quiet!"* she called—it was less of a shout and more a sword of sound, tempered to slice through the tangle of voices.

The noise cut off abruptly.

Sophie tucked her arm through Maddie's and spoke into the silence left by the trailing ends of sentences. "Everyone, allow me to introduce Miss Madeleine Crewe. She'll be joining us for dinner tonight."

The Roseingrave siblings scrambled to attention, instruments and arguments cast aside. One by one they bowed and curtsied and offered their names, as polite as any parent could hope.

Sophie's mother came forward last, offering her hand and a gentle smile. "So pleased to meet you, Miss Crewe."

Maddie's eyes flicked to the ear trumpet Mrs. Roseingrave held in her other hand, its narrow end resting in the shell of her ear. "And you, ma'am," she said. She spoke clearly but not overly loud. "How are you finding life in Carrisford?"

Mrs. Roseingrave's smile grew. "We like it more with each new friend we find." She turned and waved at her son. "Freddie, go tell Annie we'll need another place set for dinner." The boy scampered out.

Mr. Roseingrave bowed over Maddie's hand. "So tell me, Miss Crewe—how did you and my daughter meet?"

Sophie felt the weight of the whole world slam down on her.

Heavens, in all her lust and longing she'd forgotten that she would have to *explain*.

Mr. Roseingrave's brow furrowed ever so slightly.

Maddie sent Sophie a slantways smile, mischief lighting her up like a lamp. "She accosted me in the street, sir."

Robbie snickered.

Mr. Roseingrave's eyes widened. "Our Sophie?"

"Oh yes."

Sophie's face was stiff with horror. Was Maddie going to tell them everything? It was one thing to know herself that Maddie was planning a swindle for justified reasons. It was quite another to present the scheme to her father over small talk in the parlor.

Maddie nodded, seeming quite at her ease now that she had found some trouble to stir up. "I am a silk weaver, you see, and I'd left some fabric behind in a draper's shop, while negotiating over the price. Your daughter noticed and came running to make sure everything was alright." Her hand patted Sophie's where it rested in the crook of her elbow. "It was a kind impulse, and made a very strong impression on me."

Sophie was torn between wanting to bask in the compliment and wanting to tear her hair out by the roots.

Mr. Roseingrave made an approving noise. "You're a weaver, then . . ." he said, and so the conversation continued until Annie announced dinner.

Dinner in the Roseingrave house was never a quiet affair. Voices murmured and laughed; conversations flowed over and around and through one another like currents in a mighty river. It made it easy for Sophie to let herself be buffeted by the stream while she tried to calm the racing of her heart.

Maddie sat next to Sophie and made herself agreeable to everyone—asking Robbie what he was reading, helping the twins tease one another, answering a volley of questions from Freddie with a patience that Sophie could never have sustained. "Do you weave in a factory?"

"No, I have a loom at home."

"Have you ever worked in a factory?"

"For a little while."

"Did people get injured?"

Sophie was aghast. "Freddie!"

"What's the worst injury you ever saw?"

Mr. Roseingrave set down his silverware. "Frederick, you will save that topic for after dinner. Or never."

Maddie's eyes narrowed, and her voice turned slightly sinister. "Instead of a factory story, I know of a particularly gory murder. I'll save it for dessert," she both threatened and promised.

Freddie grinned. Robbie rolled his eyes with all the native aloofness of his sixteen years, but Sophie knew he'd find a way to listen if he could.

"Miss Crewe designs her own Jacquard patterns," she said firmly, scrabbling for a safe change of subject.

"Really?" Mr. Roseingrave's ears perked up at the start of any mechanical talk. "I should be interested to see how that works . . . Do you think it would be possible to weave music notation into silk?"

"If I could read it, it would," Maddie said with a laugh.

"Sophie could teach you that," Mr. Roseingrave said with a sidelong smile at his daughter. "She's already teaching one young lady how to play. Her first pupil in Carrisford—the first of many more to come, we hope."

Mr. Roseingrave went on: "You seem clever, Miss Crewe— I'm sure instructing you how to read music would be a trifle. You wouldn't have to worry about the fingering, for instance."

Sophie choked on a bite of potatoes.

Maddie's expression stayed innocent. "Your daughter has a great talent for making people pay attention, sir. I think it's safe to say I'd learn anything Sophie wishes to teach me."

It was just shy of innuendo—or it would have been, if Sophie hadn't caught the eye of her mother, sitting serenely at the foot of the table and watching her daughter and Maddie quite closely.

Mrs. Roseingrave *winked*.

Maddie caught that wink. She flashed Sophie a gaze pert with accusation before smoothing out her features again.

"Your parents are *far* too knowing," Maddie grumbled.

"My parents," Sophie countered, "have five children. I think we're long past pretending they don't know what goes on in a bed."

It was late. The wind was a knife that sliced through clothing. But nothing in the dark and the cold made Sophie feel half as exposed as the memory of Maddie saying: *Your daughter has a great talent for making people pay attention.*

It couldn't be true. Yes, Maddie had promised never to lie to her—but what was the distinction between flattery and a lie? Sophie didn't command attention: she was quiet, small, and round. A natural blender into backgrounds. If she'd been a line in an orchestra score she'd have been the basso continuo floating beneath the melody: pleasant enough, but not what entranced the ear.

Maddie, though—Maddie was better worth attending to. She strode at Sophie's side, gaslight turning her hemline to gold and her hair to flame. Her thick cloak obscured all but glimpses of her figure as she walked: the long line of a thigh pushing forward, the soft swell of her hip as the wind pressed the fabric briefly taut.

The first time they'd spent a night together none of Maddie's clothing had come off. Sophie had been too distracted by what Maddie had been doing to her. And then she'd had to hurry away before she'd gotten to indulge her own curiosity.

She wouldn't make that mistake tonight. Hopeful heat burned through her veins. It tempered her, turned her hunger sharp as a blade.

As if to quench her determination, it began to rain. Droplets pattered the stones around them. Sophie could swear they hissed where they struck her skin.

One drop landed on her forehead, cold as a pearl. She grasped Maddie's hand. "Come on!"

They ran the last few blocks, gasping and laughing, but even so their hair and hems were wet through by the time they arrived at Maddie's door. They brushed raindrops off one another in the hallway, breathless and shivering.

Maddie craned her neck to glance down the hallway. "The kitchen's dark. The others must have gone to bed already." She and Sophie crept to the attic as carefully as they could, and only breathed easier when the door was closely shut behind them.

Sophie shook more raindrops from her hair as she unpinned it and tried to rub feeling back into her chilled hands.

"Let me," Maddie murmured. Her own hands had stayed warm, protected by those thick blue mittens. She chafed Sophie's palms and wrists.

Sophie sighed with relief as sensation flooded back into her fingers. "I hate it when my hands get cold. It reminds me of—" She stopped.

"That's alright," Maddie replied after a moment. "You don't have to tell me."

Sophie felt embarrassment scorch her cheeks. "It's just that it's hard to talk about."

Maddie's voice was a deep, cool pond, a mirror-like serenity. "You're allowed to keep secrets, you know."

"It's not a *secret*. It's just . . . distressing."

"You're allowed to keep embarrassing things to yourself."

Sophie snapped, "You're being kind on purpose!"

Maddie dissolved into giggles.

Sophie grumbled, but the corners of her mouth tweaked upward despite herself.

"We'd better get you out of that wet dress," Maddie murmured.

They undressed, wet cold locks of hair sending shivers down Sophie's spine. She all but whipped her clothing off and over the back of a handy chair. She burrowed into the bedclothes, wriggling until her naked limbs were safely sealed away from all that cold air.

She looked up just as Maddie sat on the edge of bed. Her laces were loose and the yellow gown gaped at the neck, but she seemed in no hurry to take it the rest of the way off. Sophie wished she would. It wouldn't take more than the slightest motion to pull the neck down, bare the breasts beneath the linen.

"Sophie." Maddie's voice cut through Sophie's lustful thoughts. Her gaze was steady and soft. "What is it you think of when your hands get cold?"

Sophie only shook her head. Not so much in denial of Maddie's question—but in confusion about where to begin to answer.

Maddie waited. One remaining raindrop sparkled on her collarbone and slid down to her breasts, vanishing into the shadowed space between them.

Sophie wanted to follow its path with her tongue.

"Tell me," Maddie pleaded.

Sophie blew out a long and tortured breath. She knew she could say no. Maddie would understand. Sophie could almost hear how she'd say it. She'd be very calm and very kind—but some part of her would know it was a poor trade that Sophie kept her own secrets after she'd demanded Maddie offer up so many of hers.

And Sophie would feel like the worst kind of swindler.

"Fine," she said, deciding. She sat up and huddled amid the blankets like a troll beneath a bridge.

Maddie leaned back, radiating attention like a stove putting out heat.

Sophie looked away. This was the thing she liked least about herself, and she was going to tell it to the person she most wanted to think well of her. "I don't suppose you ever heard of a chiroplast?"

"Never," Maddie said. "Sounds horribly medicinal."

"It's a sort of a framework," Sophie said. "Designed to train students in proper hand position for playing the piano." She demonstrated, hands out, wrists flat and flexible, fingers softly curved. "It's a long piece of wood that goes the length of the keyboard, with metal frames you put your fingers into. They hold your hands in correct position, and they slide left and right along two guide rails. The theory is that it forces the student's muscles to only move the proper ways, and the teacher does not have to struggle with constant correction or explanation."

Maddie shivered and rubbed at her hands. "It sounds awful."

"It was." Sophie swallowed. "I wore one every day for a month. It was all to lead up to a concert. The day when we would demonstrate the true success of Mr. Verrinder's method of teaching. There were twenty of us—some as young as seven or eight. We would be playing the same piece at the same time. One teacher producing almost two dozen students in one class."

Maddie's eyes were sharp and her rosy mouth pursed in disapproval. "Sounds like a factory."

"It felt like one sometimes." Sophie shivered. "Every one of us strapped to the keyboard, playing in unison. The sound was . . . not beautiful, but somehow mesmerizing. Mr. Verrinder walked from each to each, checking the fit of the chiroplast. Several of them I'd been instructing already, individually, but many of the youngest were brand-new to the piano—I could only show them enough to perform by rote the part they were assigned. According to Mr. Verrinder, we didn't have time for *real* instruction before the concert."

"Ah," Maddie said knowingly. "He was leaning on your teaching as much as on the device."

"He promised I'd be well compensated—and famous, too. Applauded. Appreciated." And he'd seen the stars in her eyes when she'd looked at him, and he'd smiled, and he'd managed to promise a thousand other things without ever once saying the words.

Somehow that was still the part that hurt worst of all. Probably because of the small voice in her head that whispered that on this point, Sophie had deceived herself.

"Go on." Maddie put her hands demurely in her lap.

Something about the prudishness of the pose, even as Maddie's dress threatened to fall down to her waist, gave Sophie something solid to fix on, and pull herself back to the present. She took a breath and pressed on. "The crowd for the concert was enormous—twenty students' families and neighbors—every music teacher and piano maker in London must have been there. I thought I was going to be sick I was so nervous. Mine was the most complex part, the showy center of the whole piece. Before I knew it we were walking out into the room, twenty Roseingrave pianos gleaming and ready for us. Mine raised a little higher than the rest. My father fit to burst with pride. And then . . ."

"Yes?"

Here it was: the worst part. Sophie steeled herself. "We didn't even get through the first movement before someone stood up from the crowd and denounced Mr. Verrinder as a fraud. He'd stolen the chiroplast from someone else—an inventor and teacher. And the inventor was *furious*. Not least because—as it turned out—the invention didn't really work as he promised. It was a supplement to teaching, not a replacement for it."

Maddie let out a long breath.

"Mr. Verrinder protested his innocence, but the man claimed he could prove the device's failure. He turned to the youngest pupil—Sarah Prewett, her name was—and demanded to see her play a scale." She still felt her stomach twist at the memory of the look on Sarah's face. "And she couldn't. One of the first things every student learns, the foundation for everything that comes after—and she couldn't play it. Because a scale requires you cross the thumb underneath the fingers—and the chiroplast doesn't allow for that motion. So Sarah had never practiced it." She hunched her shoulders as the echo of the crowd's mockery rang in her ears. "I'd been playing for years before Mr. Verrinder came along. I should have noticed that lack. But we'd been so focused on the concert piece that I hadn't thought about what we *weren't* teaching the girls." She swallowed against the sour bile of regret and pushed onward. "Sarah started crying and ran off. When we looked for Mr. Verrinder—well, turned out he'd run off, too. And he'd taken hundreds of pounds of investments with him. The whole time we'd been practicing he'd been collecting money for lessons, for unbuilt pianos, for a license to use his method. My teaching career was over before it had even really begun."

Maddie breathed out. "That's awful."

"It hurt even to look at a piano after that," Sophie said. "We sold everything from the warehouse for less than its value, then sold the warehouse too. To move here and start afresh. And do you know what I keep selfishly thinking?"

"What?"

"That if I'd been a better performer—if I'd held the audience enraptured as I was meant to—everything would have gone off without a hitch." She hunched beneath the weight of her own failure.

"That's absolute nonsense," Maddie said, "and I can tell you why."

Sophie clutched the coverlet at her throat, hardly daring to breathe.

"Mr. Verrinder was *counting* on people watching you and not him. I'd bet good money that at the end of that concert he was planning to disappear anyway. He knew you'd hold their attention. You would have, if the original inventor hadn't interrupted."

"But I'm not . . ." Sophie curled half in on herself.

"You're not what?"

"I'm not anything," Sophie all but whispered.

Maddie raised one hand and curved it against Sophie's cheek. "That's not true," she murmured.

"You can't tell me I'm beautiful," Sophie warned. "You promised never to lie to me."

Maddie leaned forward. Her voice was low and firm with no room for misunderstanding. "You gladden the eye. It's something better than beauty. There is something in the way you move, in your expression, that draws people in." She pressed one steady hand to her chest. "I feel it here, every time, like a hook. You pull at me."

Sophie hadn't let herself dream of declarations of love from Maddie Crewe. But she found herself utterly conquered by this simplest of phrases: *You pull at me.*

Her wondering eyes took in everything. The candlelight faint on Maddie's skin and a gold halo on her hair, the way the rain had spattered the yellow silk with drops of darker amber. The true and steady light in Maddie's eyes.

Maddie slipped one shoulder free of the silk. Sophie's eyes snagged there, ravenous for the sight. The linen of her chemise was as fine as any Sophie had ever seen: light and airy and all but translucent where the rain had dampened it. Maddie peeled the bodice down to her waist—and then rose and stepped back. She was all cream and silver from the waist up and billowing gold below.

Sophie smothered a groan. "Where on earth did you come by so fine a gown?"

Maddie grinned, her arms buried in the fallen bodice fabric. "Mr. Samson found it in London—he's been supplying us with items for Mrs. Money's mourning wardrobe, as well." She slid one hand along her hip, smoothing down the fabric and making Sophie sigh at the curve it outlined. "I like to imagine this one belonged to a scandalous young widow who wanted bright colors as soon as she was out of mourning—she's got control of her late husband's fortune and has gone in search of debauchery."

Sophie's skin felt tight and hot; she squirmed in the heat of the blankets. "Does she have a partner in mind for these debauches?"

"Oh yes." Maddie pushed the dress off her hips so it pooled on the floor with a hiss of sliding silk.

Sophie felt that sound in every fiber of her being.

Maddie gathered the gown up and put it away. She strode back across the room and presented her back to Sophie. Ribbons climbed up her back. "These stays are new and a bit stiff—would you help me?"

Sophie's fingers fumbled with the laces. This garment was far more fashionable than the soft stays Maddie usually wore. The cotton had the telltale gloss of sateen, and tiny silver stitches dotted it like stars. "Who is the widow looking for?" she whispered with a voice gone bone-dry.

Maddie cast a temptress's smile over one creamy shoulder. "There is a brilliant young woman—a pianist—that the widow met at a dinner party. She was soft-spoken so everyone thought her shy. But then she began to play. And all the widow could think about was her hands. How they'd feel, where they'd stroke and caress and pinch."

Sophie's fingers shook as they untied the last ribbon.

Stays loosened, Maddie let the garment fall to the floor like a shed cocoon. She turned, the chemise an insufficient veil against the keenness of Sophie's sight. Slowly Maddie pulled the garment up by the hem and tossed it aside. And there she stood, better and more beautiful than all of Sophie's frequent and fevered imaginings. A creature of flesh and flame and desire, long legs and rounded hips and lovely breasts—but other places, too, that Sophie yearned to know more intimately. The dimple in her knee. The tender skin of her wrist, and the long muscles of her forearm. The dip where her throat met her collarbone, and where one last raindrop still lingered, waiting for Sophie to lick it away.

When Sophie's eyes reached her face again, Maddie actually trembled. As though she'd felt that gaze like a touch.

Sophie lifted a hand and beckoned Maddie closer. "Let me tell you a secret about that pianist. One your scandalous widow doesn't suspect."

Maddie's lips parted on a breath of surprise and sharp delight. She walked over, step by teasing step, until she stood by the side of the bed. She bent and tilted Sophie's chin up with a brush of her fingertips, her lips hovering a bare inch away from kissing.

Sophie went up on her knees on the bed. One hand curled possessively around Maddie's hip. "She's very gifted with her hands—but she's even better with her mouth."

She stretched up for a kiss and swallowed Maddie's gasp. It turned into a moan halfway through, as Sophie pulled her close. Chill skin met Sophie's blanket-warmed body, sending the most delightful shudder through both of them. Sophie skated her mouth down to suck at one pearled nipple, then kissed a trail down the tender expanse of Maddie's stomach. Maddie spread her thighs wide as Sophie bent to slide two insistent fingers into the soft curls between her legs.

She stretched out low and kissed Maddie there, where she was hottest and sweetest.

God, but she was delicious, rain and salt and honey. Sophie licked and sucked and hummed with pleasure, until Maddie was shaking and panting and on the verge of release.

Then Sophie raised her head and pulled Maddie down into the bed with her.

For a moment they were a tangle of limbs and movement, two bodies tumbling and inseparable. Sophie spun Maddie beneath her, breathing hard. She couldn't keep the smugness from her voice when she asked, "Is this debauched enough for you, madam?"

Maddie's laugh was thready, almost a plea. "Nearly," she said. "So very nearly."

Sophie grinned hungrily and redoubled her efforts. She was going to use every musician's trick she had to ruin Madeleine Crewe for anybody else, ever again.

Composers often wrote tempo suggestions between the staves of sheet music, prompts to the performer about how fast or how slow their fingers should fly at every stage. The language of Maddie's moans and sighs likewise gave Sophie sensuous cues to follow. *Andante* was a deep kiss, long savored, Maddie's mouth opening wide as summer roses beneath hers. *Accelerando* as Sophie's pulse and her hands sped up, two sets of legs twining together, Sophie's tongue curling around one delectable nipple. *Allegretto*, then faster to a driving *allegro*, as her fingers stoked the heat between Maddie's wanton thighs. Maddie groaned encouragement and Sophie shifted down to lick—*presto*—just above where her fingers plunged.

No music had ever sounded sweeter than the notes of Maddie's cries as she came beneath Sophie's mouth.

Sophie let them both breathe for a patient five minutes before attempting an encore performance.

Chapter Eleven

Sophie woke before dawn—because *someone* was shaking her. She threw off Maddie's hand and burrowed deeper into the bedclothes.

She growled a protest when the coverlet was whisked off and cold air hurried in on every side. "Cat will be in the kitchen by now," Maddie said. "Come down and meet everyone."

"In this state?"

"There's tea."

The promise of hot beverages was enough to tip the scales. She scrambled out of bed and into her clothes.

Maddie checked the sunshine-yellow silk one final time as Sophie pinned her hair at her neck. "I hope Mr. Samson won't mind if I have to keep this a while longer."

"Why should he mind?"

Maddie grimaced. "Because if I'm wearing it, he can't sell it. Anything he brings us from London takes up space that could have belonged to a garment he could sell."

"That sounds like quite the sacrifice," Sophie said, sliding the last pin home against her scalp. "Why is he helping you?"

"Mr. Giles has been preventing Mr. Samson from purchasing Mr. Obeney's factory," Maddie said. "I don't quite know why—normally the man's reasons are painfully obvious—but in this instance he appears to be motivated by pure spite."

Freshly dressed, they padded down two flights to the kitchen. The stove was putting out great gouts of heat and the smell of bread lured Sophie like manna in the desert.

Cat—"Don't call me Catherine and we'll be friends for life"—was small in stature but her soul seemed to fill the room to the corners. She kept an expert eye on the porridge on the stove while flirting with John and a sleepy Emma. Sophie watched the casually comfortable way they all touched one another—hands brushing elbows, a touch on a waist or shoulder in passing—and found herself shaken by the sweetest sort of envy. What must it be like, to be so confident in being loved?

Emma perked up with tea and porridge, and before her bowl was empty her waking eyes were looking closely at Sophie's green dress. "That's Judith's work, isn't it?"

Sophie stilled, while Maddie's expert gaze passed over the ribbon rosettes. "I expect so. Most satin ribbons in Carrisford are."

"I found this in Miss Narayan's shop," Sophie said. "I thought perhaps it came from London."

"Plenty of their things do—but there's also plenty from the folk right here in Carrisford," Emma said. "Trying to keep step with London fashions. There's a lot more money around than there used to be."

"Not that any of us see much of it," Cat added.

John merely grunted.

Cat quirked her lips at him and topped up his tea. "Pay no attention to him," she said with a sidelong glance at Sophie. "He rarely gets words out before breakfast is over. Oh, and this came for you yesterday, Maddie." She handed over a letter, a single sheet folded craftily to prevent it from being casually opened.

Sophie saw Maddie's rosy lips go flat. "One of my father's." With a few knowing movements of her hands, she managed to get the sharp folds to relax and give up their secrets.

Sophie sympathized with the paper: Was there anything in the world that could resist Maddie Crewe's hands?

Maddie raised an eyebrow. "Actually, it's my stepmother who's written."

"Is that better?" Sophie asked.

"Don't know. I never met the woman." She skimmed the letter and let out a long-suffering sigh.

"What's he done this time?" Emma said with sympathy.

"It seems he had a brilliant idea about stealing clothes from his neighbors' washing lines and trying to pawn them practically on the same block. They stopped him with an armful of Mrs. Plumpton's petticoats and his pockets full of pawnbroker's duplicates—but he managed to escape arrest. Lord knows when he'll turn up next." Her eyes glinted at Sophie's questioning gaze. "I'm sorry to say not everyone in the family has my talent for criminality."

Porridge, Sophie found, was an awful thing to snort up one's nose in surprise and dismay.

While she recovered, Maddie finished the letter and set it down, frowning. "His wife is being sent back to Carrisford to apply for relief from the parish here. She asks if we can take her and my sisters in for a time. They don't know anyone else to ask."

Emma glanced at Cat—who glanced at John—who shrugged.

Emma looked back at Maddie. "Would your stepmother look askance if Cat gave up her room for them and moved in with John and me?"

"Emma, I don't mind—" Cat began.

"But I do," Emma finished firmly.

"She's used to living with my father," Maddie said, "so I know she's seen worse things than three people caring for one another. He's always described her as an absolute nightmare: a scold and a termagant, impossible to please. Then again, I shudder to think what he says about me when I'm not there, so." She looked up at her friends. "If she makes you uncomfortable, even for a moment, we will find her someplace else to live." She flattened the letter against the table, though the precise geometry of the creases sprang up again as soon as the pressure of her hand slid away.

Sophie had always been there for her family—just as they'd always been there for her. She'd always connected that with loving them, as if love and help were synonyms. But now, looking at Maddie, she realized it was possible to help someone you didn't love—that you might not even like—

simply because helping them was the right thing to do. There was a whole new kind of strength there worth admiring.

Maddie, still frowning lightly, toyed with the letter's edge. "She says the girls have been offered work at Mr. Prickett's."

"How old are they?" Cat asked.

"Eleven and thirteen. The older girl has done a stint in a mill before, I think. Their mother will teach them what to expect. She makes bobbin lace."

"She can step into our parlor then," said Emma, trying to lighten the mood. "Between the four of us we can completely outfit any titled lady who happens to come calling in search of clothing."

"A countess," Cat laughed.

"A duchess!" Emma added.

"A princess," Maddie put in wryly. "Which is about as likely."

"A princess might come in disguise," Sophie countered. "All the best ones do, in the fairy stories."

Cat looked at her consideringly. "And what do you do, Miss Roseingrave?"

"Me?" Sophie blinked, as three people's attention perched on her shoulders. "My father has a secondhand instrument shop. I work there—tuning instruments, selling music sheets, that sort of thing."

"And you teach," Maddie said, nudging Sophie with a gentle elbow.

"Oh yes, my one pupil," Sophie said with a self-deprecating laugh.

"Two, if I count," Maddie purred.

Sophie blushed. "That was a bit of fun."

Maddie's smile widened into pure sensuality. "It certainly was."

Emma kicked at her beneath the table. "Don't embarrass the poor girl, Maddie. I'm sure she takes her work quite seriously."

"I do," Sophie said. "I've rather missed it. There's something about the moment when a student makes a breakthrough—conquers a difficult piece, or remembers last week's lesson—it's quite satisfying."

"And the pay's good," Maddie said.

"The pay is sometimes good," Sophie corrected.

"Enough to support you?" Emma asked.

"Not yet," Sophie replied frankly. "I'd need more than one pupil for that—or more demand for my services."

"Quite a few piano masters in Carrisford these days," Maddie said. At Sophie's narrowed eyes, she shrugged. "I've been asking around. There's Mr. Nelthorpe, Mr. Perrin and his son, Mrs. Halban . . . They're all doing quite well, from what I understand. Carrisford is hungry for piano teachers at present."

Nelthorpe, Perrin, Halban. Sophie repeated those names like a descant as she walked home in the rising light of day. Sunrise suited Carrisford: it added rosy tones to the gray stone and brought out the bright silver traces of last night's rain. The air was fresh and Sophie's lungs expanded with it; she breathed out on a long silent sigh. *Nelthorpe, Perrin, Halban.* Perhaps someone in the Aeolian Club knew them and could introduce her. Other teachers were the best way of finding other students—they would know which families paid on time and which tended to let the bills languish.

Her mother and father exchanged a knowing glance when Sophie arrived just as they were opening up. Her cheeks heated but she kept her head high and her dignity intact. She hurried off to change clothes and took her usual place in the shop.

Mrs. Roseingrave made one last note in the account book and kissed her daughter good morning. "So nice to meet your young friend last night," she said. "She certainly is a pretty one, isn't she?"

"She is." Sophie's blush became a bonfire. Scrabbling for a change of topic, she looked down at the columns of numbers. "How have we been doing on the profits?"

"Not bad at all, considering we're so new. And look." Mrs. Roseingrave placed one slender finger next to a new column at the end of the row. "I've started to track your teaching wages." The first couple numbers were already penciled in.

Sophie chewed her lip. "Not very impressive, are they?"

"Not yet." When Celia Roseingrave's eyes glinted, Sophie caught a flash of the ambition and fire that had made her such a celebrated performer.

Her father moved closer so his wife could see his face as he spoke. "You just need more pupils, Soph—that needs time, same as the shop does."

"It needs more than time," Mrs. Roseingrave countered. "She needs a bit of displaying, too. People will be more ready to hire a teacher if they think she is impressively talented."

Mr. Roseingrave chuckled. "You already have an idea, don't you?"

"It's quite simple," his wife said. "We should put on a concert."

"Me?" Sophie was appalled. "Perform?"

"Why not? You've done it before."

"And it was a disaster for all of us!"

Mrs. Roseingrave waved this aside with a flick of one graceful wrist. "That goes on Mr. Verrinder's account—it had nothing whatsoever to do with your talent or skill."

Mr. Roseingrave stroked his side-whiskers thoughtfully. "I like it. We could raise funds for some charitable concern or other."

"And improve the shop's reputation in Carrisford," Mrs. Roseingrave pointed out.

Her husband grinned. "Naturally." He cocked his head at his daughter. "You know a few other musicians in town from that club, don't you? I remember you mentioning a harpist— and of course Mr. William Frampton might grace us with a piece on his violin. His father might be able to secure some attention from his connections in the court . . ."

One Roseingrave alone could be stubborn enough for three ordinary people—but when they banded together in favor of something, that stubbornness became truly vast and overpowering. You might as well try to soothe the storm by shouting into the gale.

If Sophie didn't put a stop to this, they'd have her on a stage by the end of the week—only to be humiliated when she broke down in tears of embarrassment at her own inca- pability. It was one thing to play for the elder Mr. Framp- ton, or to imagine performing before a throng of admiring aristocrats in all their grace and glitter. That was a dream, insubstantial and perfect.

It was quite another to stand up in front of people who already knew her and attempt to demand their approval. She could already feel the burden of expectation pressing down on her—all those eyes, all those tongues so willing to wag. Even if she played well, the praise would sting: *Who would have thought she had it in her, the little sparrow . . .*

Desperate, she threw out a lifeline. "How about this: I will put a placard in the window advertising my services as a teacher. Once I get five pupils, I will *think* about giving a concert."

Her parents mirrored one another's dubious expressions. "That certainly seems like a slower approach," her father said.

"It seems like a waste of time," her mother said bluntly.

"It will be a very *good* placard," Sophie said.

Judging by their faces, the inadequacy of this argument was as plain to Mr. and Mrs. Roseingrave as it was to Sophie herself.

She spent the rest of the morning making the placard: clear black letters, a border of musical notes, some splashes of watercolor to catch the eye. PIANO LESSONS, it read. INQUIRE WITHIN. She put it in the front window, trying to ignore how small it looked within the window frame. Rectangles within rectangles: the sign contained within the pane, the pane within the window, the window within the shop, the shop within the street, the street within the town. The letters that had seemed to take so long for her hand to trace were but a minuscule speck in the scope of the wide, wide world.

As small and insignificant as Sophie herself.

The shop bell chimed; she sighed and put on her most helpful smile.

Maddie's stepmother and sisters arrived two days later. Their belongings were meager and their clothes dusty and worn from the strain of the journey. The girls were solemn and shy as introductions were made, then Maddie showed them to Cat's room.

Her stepmother nodded her silver head just once, leaning on the wooden cane she used, she said, on account of a tubercular hip. "It will do." She reached into her pocket and extracted a few coins. "Bridget, take Susanna and find you both pinafores from the pawnshop down the way. Plain ones, mind—you can always embroider them later if Mr. Prickett doesn't look askance at that sort of thing."

The older girl gravely took the coins and her sister's hand. "Yes, Mama."

"And what do we do?"

"Count the change twice!" the girls chorused.

"That's my little nightmares. Now go." Mrs. Crewe watched them hurry down the stairs and into the street before turning to rake Maddie with a glance that seemed to take in every wrinkle and flyaway strand of hair. Her own thick hair was pulled back as though letting even one strand escape would mean the whole world would unravel at the seams. Her hand tightened on the handle of her cane, the knuckles white. "Thank you for your generosity in opening your home to us. I hope we shall not be trespassing too long upon your kindness."

Her stepmother's reputation was at least a little justified: Lydia Crewe could make even gratitude sound like a judgment. Maddie smiled without baring her teeth. "You're very welcome, ma'am."

The second Mrs. Crewe regarded her stepdaughter narrowly. She was shorter than Maddie by a good six inches, but the keenness of her gaze made it easy to forget that fact. She looked like a person who went about constantly sizing up the world, as if weighing it for purchase. "There is something you aren't telling me," she said suspiciously.

"There are many things I'm not telling you, ma'am," Maddie retorted.

Mrs. Crewe's lips twitched briefly before she pressed her lips together in reproof. "I'd say you're as shifty as your father—but from what he says, I suspect you're a good deal cleverer. I'd like to trust that means you won't get caught. But I am not, in my soul, the trusting sort." Her voice was sharp and icy as the northern wind outside. "I intend to watch you, my girl. I've had my household uprooted by dishonest behavior: it shan't happen again, if I can prevent it."

"Then let's find ways of helping you be independent, ma'am," Maddie said. "So the only honesty you have to worry about is your own."

A very startling dimple flashed in Mrs. Crewe's cheek. "Smart," she said. Maddie wasn't sure if it was a reprimand or a compliment.

They went down to the kitchen to introduce Cat, then retreated to the front room, where John and Emma were already at work: Emma piecing together a gentleman's embroidered waistcoat, and John adorning satin slippers with tiny silver beads. "I understand you're a lace maker, Mrs. Crewe," John said. "I can refer you to a good workshop, if you like."

"That's kind of you," Mrs. Crewe replied. She lowered herself to a seat on the stool and settled her cane within reach. "As soon as I am drawing a wage, I hope you'll let me contribute something to the running of the household."

John and Emma glanced at one another. "We thank you, of course," John said, "but wouldn't you rather save those wages for a place of your own?"

"I hope you're not suggesting this house is not a safe place for me or my daughters?"

Neither John nor Emma nor Maddie had an easy answer to that. They cast anxious glances around in the silence.

Mrs. Crewe's lips thinned again and she narrowed her eyes at Maddie. "Let me be blunt: your father often said you kept the worst sort of company—that you had loose morals and depraved habits—that the loss of your mother had warped you in some way and sent you down a ruinous path of debauchery and rebellion. And then I learn that you have a room to lend me only because three of you are sharing a room—and I see with my own eyes that room has only a single bed in it."

John's shoulders were stone-still; Emma's eyes were on her work, but not her attention; she gave a sharp gasp when she jabbed herself with her needle.

Mrs. Crewe waved a hand at them and pinned Maddie with her gaze. "Is this one of the things you weren't telling me?"

"One of them," Maddie said frankly.

Mrs. Crewe's mouth tightened. "I'm sure I don't judge."

John bristled and Maddie snorted audibly.

Mrs. Crewe sighed. She turned to Emma, one corner of her stern mouth tilting upward. "Let me speak more plainly still. I am sorry to have worried you, and I thank you and Mrs. Grey for your kindness," she said. "This world holds many virtues—but no virtue is higher than love. However it may differ from convention."

Emma beamed with relief, the expression making her painfully beautiful.

John let out a long breath.

Mrs. Crewe quirked an eyebrow at her stepdaughter. "That's one secret out, anyway. Care to confess any others while I'm here?"

"Not just at the moment," Maddie said, leaning one shoulder against the wall.

"Then I might as well unpack." Mrs. Crewe levered herself up and nodded to the room. Her cane struck the stairs one by one like the solemn, sinister beat of an executioner's drum.

"Maddie!" Emma hissed. "You're not going to tell her about the swindle."

"Of course not," Maddie replied. "What good would it

do? Hopefully we'll be done with the whole thing before she has time to notice what we're up to."

John said, "The lacemaking will be picking up speed in a month or so." It always did in spring, when those who could afford lace wanted more of it to flaunt as the weather warmed.

"Yes—and then she'll be in the center of that web of rumor," Emma said. "Nobody gossips like a lace maker."

"If she's listening to any gossip, she'll hear plenty about Mr. Giles," Maddie said firmly. "I can't imagine any world in which my stepmother would approve of anything he's done."

"Having only just met her, I agree," Emma replied.

CHAPTER TWELVE

Winter was showing no signs of yielding to the tender on-slaught of spring. Icicles still hung from eaves and branches, and buds still hid beneath the dark earth. The whole world felt like it was in a long, enchanted sleep.

And yet Sophie felt spring-like. Sometimes she felt so restlessly joyful she was surprised it didn't come climbing out of her skin like leaves or feathers. Part of it was Maddie Crewe, who had become a frequent visitor at the Roseingrave house.

Part of it was feeling like she was finally getting music back. She had no idea how she'd done without it for those six months. She hadn't realized how deep that shadowy place had been until she found herself slowly emerging from it.

She and her mother had made several subsequent visits to the Framptons. The violinist wore powder in his hair, and Cecilia Roseingrave put on the one best gown she'd kept, in which she'd performed before crowned heads and admiring courtiers. The two musicians had a great many acquaintances in common, all of whom were distant or deceased—both conditions which made them well worth talking about. Sophie lost track of the names in the wealth of anecdotes. In Mr. Frampton's company, Mrs. Roseingrave bloomed like a cut rose given water.

It gave Sophie a queer feeling in the core of her, as though she were trying to remember tomorrow night's dream. She spent most of the conversations silently listening, trying to puzzle herself out.

Sophie had learned the art of silence from her mother, who used her voice more strategically than the other, noisier Roseingraves. Her confused hearing was an impediment in a crowd, but it was much less trouble in quiet conversation with only two people who knew to speak clearly. She had stopped even bringing her ear trumpet after the second visit, as Mr. Frampton learned how to pitch his voice to suit the strongest range of her hearing. And when Mrs. Roseingrave talked with Mr. Frampton—reminiscing over past concerts, discussing shared friendships, turning over old pieces of gossip like heirloom gems—Sophie heard the echoes of an extraordinary career. She'd known this, of course, ever since she was little. But it was one thing to have heard of it; to *feel* it now as it unfolded in story after story was something of a revelation. It illuminated the shape of the world, the way a sound from two streets over could make one newly aware of the geography of houses and buildings.

She couldn't remember the last time she'd heard her

mother sing. Properly sing, for an audience, not just hum a tune under her breath. She was still trying to remember when Mr. Frampton waved her over to the piano.

These weekly private performances were also now a habit—and, since Sophie was still thinking of her mother, she played one of the few pieces she'd written with a sung accompaniment. Sophie's voice would never fill an opera house to the rafters, but she could decorate a sitting room prettily enough. The lyrics had been printed by Griffin and Brinkworth's in Melliton, but Sophie had changed the traditional tune out for one of her own devising.

Mr. Frampton thumped approval with his cane when she was finished, in lieu of hurting his hands with applause. "I particularly enjoyed the flourish at the end," he said. "But I have to ask: How is the waltz coming along?"

Sophie had played him parts of the waltz she was writing for Maddie. "I'm still working on that second section," she said. "It's improving, but I'm not sure it's ready for you to hear more just yet."

"You are aiming for perfection," Mr. Frampton said sympathetically. "It's understandable. What musician worthy of the gift doesn't wish to be perfect? But it's unattainable. Either you're on the upward slope and still learning how to achieve your designs, or you're past the peak and tumbling down into overanalysis—forms without feeling."

"So then how do you stay at the top of the hill?" Sophie asked.

"You can't," her mother replied, setting her biscuit on the

side of her saucer. "You have to pick yourself up and keep going, try again. A musician gets only so many chances to stand in that place and give everything she has."

"Only so many perfect moments," Mr. Frampton agreed. "The trick is to recognize them when they're upon you."

"They're worth it," Mrs. Roseingrave sighed. A wistful smile curled the corners of her mouth.

Sophie suddenly wanted to give her mother more than wistfulness. "Will you sing for us, Mama?"

Mr. Frampton sucked in a breath.

Mrs. Roseingrave looked into her teacup for a long moment, then set it aside with a click. "Perhaps just a little something," she said.

"My music library is entirely at your service," Mr. Frampton said at once.

Sophie rifled through the sheet music under her mother's eye. "This one," her mother said, snagging the corner of a piece for voice and piano.

Die Alte, the title read. *The Old Woman*. Sophie cast an eye over the lyrics and their translation: the first verse was all about older, better days and maidens not provoking their mothers. She raised an eyebrow. "A little pointed, don't you think?"

"Who is singing it—me or you?" Mrs. Roseingrave's lips pursed teasingly.

Sophie snorted, and spread the music out on the piano. Her mother rested one hand on the case, the better to feel the rhythm.

Mr. Frampton laughed in surprised delight as soon as she

struck the first notes. Cecilia Roseingrave's voice was a little rusty at the start, as she sank into her character's delicious grumpiness to complain about controlling husbands, indiscreet youth, and a comet that threatened the whole social order. But once warmed up and fluid, there was such a wealth of stodgy offendedness in her tone that Sophie was giggling outright by the time she brought her hands down on the closing chords.

Mr. Frampton pounded approval on the floor as Mrs. Roseingrave curtsied. "Brava!" he cried, using his cuffs to wipe away tears of mirth. "I should like to see any new young soprano do half so much justice to that piece."

"The young sopranos are too busy filling the opera stages and concert halls, I'm sure," Mrs. Roseingrave said. "Getting up at dawn for rehearsals, staying up past midnight for performances, charming the composers so they'll write an aria specially for you." She resumed her seat on the sofa and put her hands round her teacup again. "What is youth for, if not to be used up?"

Mr. Frampton nodded assent. "I only wish I could return the favor and play you something—but my hands will not permit it, I am sorry to say. They are only good for broad strokes these days." He gave another thump of his cane for emphasis.

Mrs. Roseingrave tilted her head. "Your hands have earned their rest," she replied. "I heard you play for the prince in Brighton."

"Ah," Mr. Frampton said, leaning back regally against the sofa. "One of my perfect moments."

"You were a marvel," Mrs. Roseingrave agreed.

Later, after they passed through the loud, busy town and returned to the shop, Mrs. Roseingrave kissed her husband hello and elaborated for Sophie's benefit. "I wish you could have heard Mr. Frampton in his prime, my dear—such a light touch, so expressive. You'd have thought the violin was a human voice, he brought such meaning out of it."

"I believe it," Sophie said. She went to the counter, where the week's new sheet music was stacked and ready for shelving.

Her mother's eyes turned sharp. "And he believes in your potential, Sophia. He thinks you could be the equal of any musician at court."

Sophie turned away to begin putting out the new ballads and concertos. The paper was crisp and cool in her hot and shaking hands. Her mother and Mr. Frampton had talked of hills, but all Sophie saw in front of her was a cliff, and they were forcing her to either climb straight up or leap from it. "We can't afford to send me to court."

"Not yet," Mrs. Roseingrave said, peering down at the account book. "But a year or two like this one, and that could change."

"Maybe next year—"

"Many's the musician I've heard say that, and next year never comes," Mrs. Roseingrave pressed. "Take the chance! You only have so many years to be a performer. You shouldn't squander the best ones." She flipped the ledger closed, jammed it under the counter, and strode to the door.

Turning back, she sent one more volley her daughter's way, projecting as only an opera diva could. "I was a singer before I was your mother, girl. What you're dreading is something I lived through, so you should believe me when I tell you that you're more than capable of it. If you want to be afraid of something, fear running out of time."

She spun on her heel—denying Sophie a chance to reply—and exited, head high.

Sophie stubbornly finished her task, ballad after ballad, song after song. When she turned, her father's glance darted too quickly away, proving he'd been watching her closely. "Well?" she ground out.

"Oh no," her father said, and looped a new string through the peg of the violin he was repairing. "I don't argue with either of you when you're set on something. Although . . ."

Sophie clenched her jaw so as not to scream. "Although *what?*"

Her father raised his hands. "You don't think you're ready to perform yet, I know. All I'm wondering is: What would you need to become ready?"

"I—" Sophie started, then stopped, then chewed her lip, then sighed. "I don't know," she admitted. "I only know that when I think about going on stage, I get a sick feeling in the pit of my soul."

Her father nodded. "I get that every time," he said. "I love the piano, but I'm not a performer. So it could be you're like me, and you don't want the limelight at all."

Sophie thought about the prince's pavilion, and applause

she could almost feel washing over her, and blushed dully with shame.

"Or," her father went on blithely, "you could let yourself feel that feeling, but do the concert anyway."

Sophie shook her head, his words incomprehensible. "What do you mean?"

Her father shrugged. "You let the fear exist inside you, where it belongs. And you go up on stage and you play for people anyway." His fingers tightened the violin string, plucking at it to test the tone.

"Sharp," Sophie corrected automatically.

Her father nodded, and adjusted.

"Better."

Mr. Roseingrave set the violin aside. "You're used to listening to your feelings," he said. "It's what you do whenever you tune an instrument. Your instincts there are precise and helpful. But perhaps—perhaps what Mr. Verrinder did changed your tuning a little bit. So your intervals don't harmonize the way you expect them to."

Sophie shuddered. "What an appalling thought. Am I going to be broken forever?"

"I don't believe so." Mr. Roseingrave came over and clasped his hands around hers. His smile turned mischievous. "You're already almost back to an equal temperament."

Sophie groaned.

Mr. Roseingrave allowed himself a chuckle, and continued. "It's hard, especially because you are young and sensitive, and you feel things keenly. Like your mother." His mouth curled up in the wondering smile he wore only for

Cecilia Roseingrave. "But being young, you can only see the damage. It distracts you. Once you're older, you'll be better about ignoring the scrapes and letting the wounds heal up."

"Oh good," Sophie said wryly. "Something to look forward to."

Her father laughed. "See? Three months ago you wouldn't have made that joke. You're getting better every moment." He squeezed her hands. "And let's say the worst happens. Let's say the concert goes terribly. You forget your music, the crowd throws vegetables, a storm blows in and tears the roof off the concert hall—"

"Someone interrupts my performance and denounces me as a fraud," Sophie muttered.

"—at least you'll know you tried," Mr. Roseingrave said gently. He squeezed her hands to emphasize his point. "It might be worth a little failure to learn how strong you truly are."

For the next part of the swindle, they needed to make an impossible fabric. So Maddie invited Sophie, Miss Slight, and Mr. Frampton up to her attic, to show them precisely how a Jacquard loom worked so that they might devise a convincing impossible process with which to cheat Mr. Giles.

And then, because it was the end of a long, bleak winter, she decided to make it a party.

Maddie made the room festive with unsold ribbons and silk scraps, and Sophie brought lamps to brighten the attic to its corners. The odd blue silk made a dazzling cover for a small table heaped with pies, and beer was served in whatever mismatched glasses people chose to bring along with them.

By sunset, the attic was full and chattering, the noise a chorus above the beat of the silk mill thrumming through the house. John had stayed below to finish a difficult pair of slippers, but Emma had persuaded Cat to take a glass with her; the two sat on the bed with their knees tucked up, laughing at something Judith Wegg was saying. Alice Bilton joined Miss Slight, Mr. Frampton, and a bright-eyed Sophie as Maddie demonstrated the working of the loom and the action of the Jacquard head.

Mr. Frampton, it transpired, was familiar with the theory of M. Jacquard's invention, but not the practice. "Show us again," Mr. Frampton asked, watching keenly.

Maddie flicked her wrist and sent the shuttle—threadless—flying through the shed. The pedal shifted the warp threads—the up went down, and the down went up—and the beater pressed the weaving tight and ready for the next thread row. Another flick and pass of the shuttle, another thump of the beater.

The mathematician nodded. "I assume you'll want something more showy than substantive?"

"I agree," Miss Slight put in. "You need the Jacquard head because its presence tells Mr. Giles that the process is a fast one. He'll know that much about the machinery, I'm sure. But you need the illusion to be *here*," she said, pointing to the shed—the space between warp threads where the shuttle flew back and forth. "This is where his focus will be, so this is where you want the trick to happen."

"You have to decide what you want it to look like first," Alice put in expertly. "Always start with the sparkle, that's what Wizard Falcetti used to say."

Maddie's hand tightened on the handle of the loom cord. "I want it to dazzle him," she said, low and fierce. "I want it to be so beautiful that he can't resist it, and so impossible that only sheer greed persuades him of its truth."

"If it's beauty you want," said Mr. Frampton, "then Miss Slight is your expert. I've never seen mechanisms as lovely and elegant as the ones she builds."

Miss Slight's blush was a lush and lovely thing. She turned wide, pleased eyes on Mr. Frampton, who went ruddy under her gaze but offered her a shy smile in return.

Alice elbowed Judith, who snorted, and the spell was broken.

Miss Slight traced her clock maker's hands over the warp threads. Maddie hadn't changed them out for the new season yet: they were still the soft cream she'd used as a background hue for gold brocade ribbons. "What if you had the full spectrum of hues showing—but only here? The resulting fabric stark white. Like a prism in reverse."

"That would save us having to purchase dyed silk thread, at least," Maddie murmured.

Alice leaned forward to peer up into the mechanism. "Could we put a magic lantern in the Jacquard head? The Wizard Falcetti used one for some of his effects. Easy enough to paint panes of colored glass and turn undyed silk a whole rainbow of colors."

"Yes!" Mr. Frampton leaned forward. His voice warmed with excitement. "You've got the holes and the punch cards already—why not make them work for you?"

"How do you mean?" Maddie asked.

"The cards already pass in front of the lantern. The holes block or allow light from certain panes. Certain colors." He let his hand hover over the warp. "Not just a rainbow: a rainbow in motion."

"We could go even further with that," Miss Slight put in. "There are certain ways of arranging colors next to one another so that they appear to move and shimmer, even when they are quite still. They can quite confuse the eye." Her smile was broad now, her gray eyes sparking with excitement. "The harder he looks, the less he'll see what you're actually doing."

"But how do we explain it to Mr. Giles?" Maddie said. "We need the story to go with the show."

"Resonance." This from Sophie, who'd been standing silent at Maddie's elbow until now. She stepped forward, her musician's hand stroking the warp threads as though they were a harp. "You've got these strings in every color. You tell him that's the special dye Mr. Money discovered. But it's not stable on its own: it only fixes into one hue when a magnet is passed over it." She tapped the shuttle. "You fix a magnet here—maybe with a wire or two, for show."

Maddie felt like the idea was so close to complete that she could reach out and take it in her hand. "So how do we explain the color change of the finished fabric?" Maddie asked.

"Chemical affinity?" Mr. Frampton suggested. "Or perhaps—something about tuning the dye to a particular frequency."

"What beautiful nonsense," Miss Slight said. "I rather wish it were true."

Maddie nodded sharply. "That's perfect. That's the feeling we want him to have. He's an opportunist—we want him so focused on reaching out to seize this chance that he overlooks any risks or dangers."

Miss Slight, Mr. Frampton, and Alice continued to consult with one another about the best way to create the magic lantern and install it in the Jacquard head. Maddie let them; once they'd worked out the structure, she could make the punch cards to fit. Or even use an existing pattern, which would save time and trouble.

Sophie had retreated to the small chair by the nightstand. At Maddie's approach, her lips curved softly. "Crime is a more exhausting business than I anticipated."

Maddie sat on the floor and draped one arm over Sophie's knees. "Like anything, it gets easier with practice. Though this is by far the most ambitious thievery I've ever been party to. Normally it's more a question of nicking and running. You really only need one or two brave souls for that."

Sophie reached out and tucked an errant lock of hair behind Maddie's ear. "So this is like a concerto, when you're used to playing duets or solo pieces."

Maddie leaned into Sophie's caress. "I'm sure you're right." She tipped her head backward until their eyes met. "And if I ever attempt a symphony, I'll know just who to ask."

Sophie's blush was just as delightful upside-down as right side up. "I like your friends," she said.

"They're more than friends," Maddie said. Sophie's eyes cut sharply, making Maddie laugh. "Jealous, love?"

"Should I be?" The words were tart, but her touch stayed soft, fingers smoothing along Maddie's temple.

Maddie snuggled closer. "Alice and I had a bit of a fling years ago—but that's long past. She's much happier with Judith, let me tell you." Sophie's hands stroked down on the back of her neck, making Maddie shiver pleasurably. It felt like approval. "Really it's more like . . . You know how they say soldiers bond in wartime?"

Sophie murmured acknowledgment.

"It felt like a war for a while. After Peterloo. When my mother died. When we still called ourselves the Weavers' Library and Reform Society, and it felt like nearly everyone was being arrested or imprisoned or harassed by the law. Printers, weavers, tailors, shoemakers—anyone who so much as whispered the word *reform* came in for harsh punishments. They wanted to beat us down. So we bent, rather than break." She smiled softly, seeing Cat and Emma giggling over something wry Judith Wegg had said. "These people are my family. They've been aunts and sisters and cousins to me—they're why I stayed after my mother's death, when my father ran away out of desperate grief." She craned her neck and looked up to meet Sophie's gaze. "I would do anything for them, anything at all."

"Sounds like family to me." Sophie's dark eyes gleamed with understanding. "What about Mary Slight? How'd she end up helping you with all this?"

Maddie grinned. "Mr. Giles has a habit of fiddling with the clocks in his shop. He moves the hands forward in the morning so his employees have to start early or have their wages docked, and puts them back in the evening so they work past time. The clock's in his office, you see, so it's easy for him to do on the quiet." She rested her cheek against Sophie's knee, feeling the muscles shift beneath the layers of skirt and petticoat. "Miss Slight is a clock maker. She rather objects to people who muck about with the steadiness of time. Especially using clocks that she made."

Sophie's laugh rumbled through her whole body, even the thigh beneath Maddie's cheek. She rubbed her face against it like a pleased cat.

Even the best parties had to come to a close, however. At length the lamps were extinguished and the bright decorations folded away. The guests trooped down the stairs, trying and failing to be quiet. On the landing they passed Mrs. Crewe, who watched them with the avid gaze of someone looking to find fault. The soft voices of her daughters sounded from behind her bedroom door, half-open.

Mr. Frampton paused to bow as he passed with Miss Slight on his arm, who curtsied. Judith nodded and Alice, tipsy, waved hard until Judith guided her down the stairs with a sigh half amused, half exasperated.

Mrs. Crewe turned back to Maddie and said in tones of strong approval: "That was easily the *politest* orgy I could have imagined."

Maddie's jaw dropped.

Mrs. Crewe turned sharply with her cane and shut the

door of her room behind her, cutting off any reply Maddie could have made. Sophie peered up at her expression and giggled softly.

The teasing sound warmed Maddie's heart, and a few other places. "Can you stay the night? There's still a glass of the good beer left."

Sophie ducked her head as though the invitation surprised and overwhelmed her. "I'd like that very much."

She removed her shoes and stockings as Maddie poured the last of the liquor into a single mug for sharing, then they helped one another out of gowns and stays. The beer was some of Cat's finest home brew, strong and tart-sweet. They kissed languorously, cozying up in the darkness, waiting for the bedclothes to warm enough so they could take off chemises and be properly—or improperly—skin to skin again.

Sophie stretched out on her back with her arms flung happily over her head. "You are a marvelous hostess, Miss Crewe."

"Oh, this was nothing." Maddie leaned beside her, stroking the line of her collarbone. Tracing over the rising swell of her bosom. Skating down the side of a breast and into the soft dip of her waist, the warm roll of her belly. "You should have seen the dinners we used to throw when we were the Reform Society. There were so many reform societies around, back then." Her mouth tilted upward, remembering. "Once, I saw Mrs. Buckhurst speak at the Crown and Anchor in London. You've never seen so much food devoured while people discussed who was starving on account of the price of bread." She shook her head. "Sometimes it feels as though all we can do is talk—and sometimes not even that. Hopefully we'll be able to actually *do* something soon. It's like being slowly poisoned, to know something's unjust and not be able to do anything to correct it." She looked down into Sophie's eyes, so earnest and understanding. "What about you?"

Sophie blinked. "What about me?"

"You're a musician—and a composer," Maddie said. She tapped her fingers one by one over Sophie's collarbone, repeating the melody from the duet Sophie'd taught her.

Sophie breathed out a laugh of surprise, recognizing the rhythm.

Maddie grinned. "When do the good people of Carrisford get to see you perform?"

Sophie squirmed uncomfortably. "You sound like my parents."

Maddie groaned and buried her face in the pillow. "*Just* what a girl wants her lover to say in bed."

Sophie snorted and shoved at Maddie's shoulder.

Maddie leaned into it, undeterred. "You've told me how hard it was to have a concert go wrong," Maddie said. "Don't you want another chance to get it right?"

"Of course I do." Sophie abruptly sat up and wrapped her arms around her knees. "I have a confession to make."

Maddie rolled onto her side. "Sounds ominous." What on earth could Sophie Roseingrave have to confess in such a tone?

Sophie's hands fussed with the coverlet, tugging at the velvet pile as though she were plucking each thread out one by one. "I *love* being the center of attention."

Maddie had to slap a hand over her mouth to keep her chortle from being heard by the rest of the house. And possibly by Mrs. Devereaux next door to boot.

"It's terrible," Sophie went on, with a quelling frown. "Every time I hear someone playing or singing, or go to the theater, or read concert descriptions from the musical magazines and papers, I am overwhelmed by the purest and most powerful jealousy. I want to be the one up there! I *crave* the chance to stand on stage, alone except for the piano, while everyone listens raptly. I want the audience to grow larger and larger—I want to play harder and harder pieces—I want to show off my own best work to an adoring throng and have everyone go wild with applause at the end."

Maddie could hardly breathe for laughing with delight. Finally she wheezed out: "And *why* is that terrible?"

Sophie chewed her lip. "Because: What if I don't deserve applause? I have a horror of trying to be something I'm not— and looking ridiculous for it." Her hands plucked faster. "Like the jackdaw who tried to pass himself off as a peacock, strutting about in feathers everyone could see did not belong to him."

"So you're a jackdaw now?"

"Don't be a ninny," Sophie said. "I thought it was well established that I am a sparrow. Round and brown and designed to be overlooked."

Maddie shoved herself up to her knees. "Right," she said. "That's quite enough of this sparrow talk. One, brown is a very sensible everyday color and it suits you and there's absolutely nothing wrong with that. And two—I know what kind of small brown bird you really are, and it isn't a sparrow."

"Oh?" Sophie cocked a head skeptically and her hands balled up the coverlet. "What is it, then?"

"You, my love, are a nightingale."

Sophie's eyes went wide as the world.

Maddie leaned forward. "They might look like sparrows—but only to the eye. Nobody who hears a nightingale sing would ever confuse the two."

Sophie's hands slid up Maddie's cheeks, fingers slipping into her hair and pinning her in place. Her voice was low and throbbing and undid Maddie entirely: "That is the most beautiful thing anyone has said to me in my entire life."

Maddie's cheeks ached from smiling. "We're still young. Give it time. I'll do even better, I promise you."

Sophie's mouth swallowed Maddie's smile, coaxing tenderness into something ravenous and needy. Maddie arched back as Sophie straddled her hips, the weight of her solid and exquisite, her breath tangy and earthy from the beer. Salt touched Maddie's lips and she licked it away—then realized Sophie was weeping. "What's wrong?"

Sophie broke the kiss with a sound like pain. "I want to make you feel as beautiful as you made me feel just now. Not just tell you how pretty you are." She quirked an eyebrow. "Surely people have done that before."

"I'm vain enough already," Maddie said with a low laugh.

Sophie's thumbs stroked possessively over her cheekbones; Maddie hummed at the yearning that shot through her.

"I want to make you *feel* it," Sophie repeated. "In your skin—in your heart. So you'll never forget it as long as you live. So that—so that it transforms you, just a little bit." She pulled in a shaky breath. "I suppose that's terrible too, in a way."

Maddie's arms went tight around Sophie's waist. "It's not terrible to want things."

Sophie's lips curved shyly. "I want to surprise you."

Oh, that made Maddie's heart ache. "Sweetheart," she murmured, "you already have."

Chapter Thirteen

You, my love, are a nightingale.

Sophie wore those words like a ribbon tied around her heart, bound tight to keep it from bursting with happiness as she walked home the next morning. All day every bird in Carrisford seemed to be singing at her: robins hallooing the morning, sparrows chattering in the afternoon, chickadees singing for scraps of supper outside the Mulberry Tree. She whistled back whenever no one was around to hear her and think her silly.

And when the shop had closed and she sat down to the piano to work on the waltz, the melody came like it had only been waiting for her to listen properly: a whistling warble of a tune that flew liquidly from note to note. The wall, that damnable barricade she'd once felt between her hands and her heart and the music vanished—as though it were no more substantial than a cloud. Sophie's hands felt like wings; her fingers were feathers, arching out to snatch at the sky.

Her pencil couldn't jot fast enough when she rushed to

pin the song to the staves of her sheet music. She worked until night had fallen and her eyes ached with straining against the candlelight.

She'd written down as much as she could. She could only hope the rest of it would still be there waiting in the morning.

The bedroom Sophie now shared with her younger sister was always in chaos. Julia was intensely disciplined as a musician and utterly careless in everything else, so despite her stated intentions and frequent flurries of tidying, her belongings were usually strewn over floor and furniture as though a giant hand had picked up the room like a toy and shaken it.

They'd had their own rooms in London, but after the move the children had been compelled to share. Robbie and Jasper and Freddie had the larger room, and Sophie and her sister had resigned themselves to the smaller. It felt as though it shrank an extra inch with every day that passed, leaving less and less space for either sister to feel comfortable.

The younger Roseingrave daughter was cramming petticoats and stockings into the wardrobe even now. Sophie began helping her and folding things much more neatly. Julia fixed her with a stern look. "Why won't you consider doing a concert, Soph?"

Sophie groaned. "Not you, too."

"Out of all of us, you're the best on the piano," Julia was saying. "Father's started building one again and of course he'll want to build more—and Mother wants to have Father out of the shop so Robbie can take his place and learn more of the business—but we need a market for our pianos first—and the best way to create a market is to have someone brilliant—

someone, for instance, like you—play our pianos in public. In some sort of performance. So"—Julia shrugged— "a concert."

"Father is building a piano again?" Sophie had missed that somehow.

Julia bit her lip, looking chagrined. "I wasn't supposed to let on," she confessed. "It was going to be a surprise."

The damage from Mr. Verrinder's crimes was melting away from her father like frost beneath the springtime sun. "A new piano, then a concert, then I go off to court to astonish the royals."

"Just like Mother did."

"But I'm not Mother."

"What do you mean?"

"Well . . . It's a fairy tale, isn't it? Going to court. Impressing a prince. How can that be someone's life—my life?"

"It's only a fairy tale if you tell it like one," Julia said.

Sophie blinked. "Pardon?"

Julia shrugged. "You can make anything sound like a fairy tale if you want," she said. "Once upon a time there was a poor instrument builder. He went to a concert with a friend one night—and a woman came out on stage. She wasn't the prettiest woman there—"

"—but when she sang he fell in love at the first note," Sophie finished. It was how her father had met her mother: he'd been telling the same story in the same way for over twenty years of Sophie's life.

Julia nodded. "But I asked Mother once if that was how it really happened."

Sophie's eyes narrowed. "And?"

"And . . ." Julia clearly wanted to drag out the moment and her position of superiority, but didn't have the patience. "Mother said she peeked out into the audience before she started—and there was Father, in the first row, straight as a tuning fork, eyes wide and eager. Starving for the performance. She liked the look of him, so when she went out on stage she aimed her first song directly at him." Julia's grin was mischievous and knowing. "She said there was never an easier conquest."

Sophie chuckled: she could just picture it. Her father willing to be pleased, her mother seeing something she wanted and putting everything into it. "She got Father, and a family—us," she said. "And now she wants to put me on stage, right where she started."

"So?" Julia said again. "It's not like you'll be doing it alone."

"I won't?" A moment ago Sophie had dreaded the prospect of a concert; now the thought that other people would share the stage with her rankled. She pursed her lips and rolled the stockings in her hand extra tight out of injured pride, and irritation at her own inconsistency.

"Jasper and I have been working on our duet for *ages*," Julia said. "And we have that trio with Robbie, too. Freddie's still a little young, probably—"

"You're only one year older," Sophie protested.

"Precisely," twelve-year-old Julia went on, undaunted. "And Father mentioned that music society you've joined, so we can definitely find enough musicians for a whole program." She put away the last pair of stockings and nodded in satisfaction—then ruined it by immediately stripping out of her dress and leaving it in a heap on the floor. "You'll still be the finale," she said, clambering into bed in her chemise. "Because you're undoubtedly the most impressive. But you don't have to fill the whole evening yourself."

Sophie refused to pick the dress up for her. Absolutely refused. Definitely, positively—oh, why bother pretending? She shook Julia's frock out and hung it up, then removed her own clothes and put them away as Julia wriggled against the wall to leave Sophie room on her preferred side of the bed. Sophie could only hope Julia took after her and their mother, rather than following in their father's long and lanky footsteps. She missed being able to sprawl, particularly when she felt restless like this. "Carrisford is not London, but it's not small, either. The Aeolian Club might have musicians much more talented than me—I haven't heard them all play yet. I might not look so impressive, when it comes down to it."

"I can't wait until you go to court," Julia sighed, and jabbed at Sophie with her heels. "Just think of all the room I'll have when you're gone."

The news came across the sea, and spread swiftly on the tongues of the weavers and the lace makers and the merchants: Mr. Obeney's utopia had failed. Apparently when they were assigning jobs to the assembled residents, in true egalitarian fashion, they had assumed the women would continue doing all the usual domestic work of keeping house, washing clothes, caring for children, mending, cooking, cleaning, and so on. On top of the duties women were assigned as full working members of the collective, of course. After all, they couldn't ask the men to do such petty tasks, could they?

The women had worked as hard as they could, but the strain had grown and grown until protests were voiced and arguments erupted and at last the entire experiment unraveled.

And now Mr. Obeney was coming back to Carrisford.

Maddie Crewe knew that meant one thing above all else: the Weavers' Library was running out of time.

The fire in the hearth of the Mulberry Tree's private parlor had been stoked into blazing. The heat made sweat bead beneath her gown and droplets roll down the length of her spine. Mrs. Money had shed her fur cuffs and wool coat in favor of night-blue silk, the hem heavy with ribbon medallions like children's pinwheels, and the sleeves artfully puffed.

Maddie tugged at the neck of her gray wool and wished she'd worn something lighter. Between making the punch cards for the magic lanterns and rewarping her loom for the upcoming summer's new ribbon designs, she felt as though she'd been sweating for days on end. "We'll have to show Mr. Giles something soon," she said.

"We will," Mrs. Money replied. "I've acquired a key to Mr. Obeney's factory—don't ask me how—and we can begin putting everything together as soon as the pieces are ready."

It would mean more late nights and extra work on top of their existing jobs. At times Maddie wanted to scream. She sighed instead. "Why is crime so often harder than honest labor?"

"Because it has a chance of paying much better." Mrs. Money reached out and patted her wrist. Her Limerick gloves were made of kid so fine you could store them inside a walnut shell, and they easily let the warmth of her touch come through. Maddie, sitting so close to the fire, didn't need more heat—but she appreciated the comfort all the same.

"My dear," said Mrs. Money, "you've been so gallant through all this—steady and true as the North Star. But I wonder: Have you thought about what you'll do afterward?"

"You mean when we have all that money to rely on and the Combination Acts are repealed so we can agitate properly?" Maddie laughed. "Oh, Mrs. Money, believe me, I have grand plans."

"And what do you plan to do if Mr. Giles has you arrested?"

Maddie shrugged. "He can try. But I'll look like I was just as taken in by you as he was. He'll have no proof."

"When has the truth ever stopped him before?"

Maddie had to concede the point. Mr. Giles had one of the pettiest souls in England. He would not hesitate to lash out in anger and disappointment. And Maddie had always been a target for him—she'd draw his ire even more now.

It would get in the way of the work, and just at the moment when they could least afford entanglements.

Another bead of sweat bloomed and fell, beneath her clothes.

Mrs. Money saw her grim face and pressed her argument. "I know you have goals for the Weavers' Library—but you might consider letting the other girls take over for a time. You might consider leaving Carrisford altogether."

Maddie's laugh sounded rusty even to her own ears. "And

go where? Everyone I know is here. Except my father. And who knows where he's run off to."

"You could come with me."

Maddie stared.

Mrs. Money's expression was uncharacteristically nervous. "I have more than enough to support us both for as long as you care to stay."

So she'd explained, when she'd first come back to Carrisford. She had, she said, arrived in Australia a convict and married a ship's officer—James Money, instead of the poor fictional Horace. Her husband turned merchant and built up a neat little empire before dying a neat little death. Finally free and wealthy enough to do what she pleased, Mrs. Money had outfitted herself as befit a wealthy widow, stepped onto an England-bound ship, imitated the other wealthy wives in secret until she had the high-born accent pitch-perfect, and come back to Carrisford to see if her beloved Marguerite still remembered her.

Maddie had reassured her: Marguerite hadn't forgotten her at all. But Maddie had also lied to Mrs. Money, by omission. Marguerite hadn't forgotten her beloved, it's true—but neither had she waited to be rescued.

Marguerite Crewe had been busy trying to rescue everybody else. Maddie liked to think she took after her mother in this more than anything else.

Mrs. Money sighed, and her years seemed all at once to press more heavily on her. They creased her face and grayed the thick strands of her hair. "I was too late for your mother. Let me at least protect her daughter."

Maddie's temper flared up like a match struck against

flint. "My mother would not thank me to abandon the work she devoted years to. She *died* for this. She fought because she believed she could make life better for girls like me, in towns like Carrisford. And everywhere else besides." She folded her arms. "I've been jailed before. I can accept the consequences if it means the others will be safe."

Mrs. Money's mouth was a harsh line. "You may have spent a few days in an English jail, my dear: so have I. Believe me when I tell you you have no conception of what transportation is like. Of what it will cost you."

Maddie wouldn't let herself imagine what lay behind Mrs. Money's bleak tone. It would only frighten her into cowardice. "I won't leave until I have no other choice. The Weavers' Library is all I have. They need me. How can I abandon them to save my own skin?"

Mrs. Money's voice turned sharp. "If the work cannot go forward without you," she countered, "then it is doomed to fail. You cannot base a collective on the effort of a single person. No matter how dedicated that one person may be."

Maddie's rebellious soul flared again—and then her wiser self took over. With an effort, she choked back her temper. "You're right," she said more softly. "I know you're right. Mr. Giles will want all of us arrested or worse, for taking his thousand pounds." She stared grimly into the fire. "We have to find a way to make *him* leave."

Mrs. Money's gloved fingers tapped on the arm of the sofa. Her voice was slow, wary. "That's a different project than simply fleecing a man. You have to give him something to run away from."

Maddie gazed into the dancing flames on the hearth. "If I have to, I'll burn his whole world to the ground."

"It will have to be public. Very public. Mr. Giles has done so many terrible things in Carrisford—but he's always been careful how he is perceived among a certain class of men." She leaned back, gloved hands tapping on the back of the sofa. "You need to embarrass him, at the very least. Better still, destroy his reputation so thoroughly that even the most determinedly self-deluding optimist would know there is nothing left for him here."

Maddie growled. "Sometimes I think it would be easier to kill him."

Mrs. Money nodded. "It would."

Maddie kept her eyes on the fire for a long, long moment. Coals smoldered in the depths, and red tongues licked hungrily. "It would be easier—but it wouldn't be better."

"Well," Mrs. Money said agreeably, "you don't get the money if you kill him."

Maddie snorted.

Something public, she thought. But a certain flavor of public. Not merely an ordinary afternoon. Something celebratory. But St. Hunger's Day had passed and the Oyster Feast was not until September.

They couldn't wait that long.

"If only I could invent a holiday," Maddie said to Sophie later that evening, as they walked along the riverbank that evening. "And get enough people excited about it. A certain kind of people, I mean—the merchants and their wives, the gentry with their shiny titles and matched horses and well-fed families. The kind of people who go to balls and soirées and all that rot—but only when the invitations come on thick, perfect paper, written in golden ink."

"Golden ink?" Sophie laughed.

"Oh, who even knows? I've made finery for the rich folk all my life—but I can't say as I've ever really talked to them."

Sophie watched anxiously as Maddie kicked at a clod of dirt in the path. They were out by the north bridge. In springtime, Maddie had said, this stretch of the river would be crowded with people enjoying the wary return of the sun. For now, it was only the two of them, with nobody else around to overhear. The wind off the water had a bite like a wolf; it howled along the channel below and stirred up icy waves like tufts of fur.

Maddie tucked Sophie's arm in hers, and led her downstream toward the ruins of Carrisford Castle.

"I'm worried things are getting out of hand," she said, her voice barely audible over the rush of water and the calls of gulls and diving birds. "First the plan was a simple set of lies with some small mechanical tricks—then some *large* mechanical tricks—and now it's verging on a performance, in three acts, with an interval of dancing bears and flying pigs." She kicked again at a second stone; it bounced, veering off the bank and into the current rushing by. Barely a ripple rose to mark where it vanished.

They'd reached the castle ramparts and the outer bailey: decades ago some enterprising council member had filled the ditch with earth and turned the ramparts into gardens. But right now, beneath the frosty sky, their original purpose rang true: the sloping earth looked defensive and forbidding, built to make any attacker despair.

Maddie switched sides with Sophie, so her taller body shielded Sophie from the brunt of the wind.

Sophie instantly felt warmer. She lifted her eyes gratefully—but Maddie's gaze was fixed on the tumult of the River Ethel, the swell and the current threatening to carry away anything light or delicate that happened to fall within its grasp. There was a bleak set to her mouth and a hopeless crease between her brows, as if her worries were rushing over her as coldly and inexorably as the chilly water below.

Maddie was trying to protect everyone else—Sophie would have to be the one to protect Maddie.

But how? She was no soldier, no knight. She had precisely one talent, suitable only for parlors or—

A performance, Maddie had said, *in three acts*. And: *if only I could invent a holiday*.

Sophie halted so abruptly that Maddie was jolted out of her trance. She turned and blinked down at Sophie.

Well, Sophie thought, as she pulled in a long breath, *you said you wanted to surprise her*.

"What you need," she said, very deliberately, "is a concert."

"But something like that would . . ." Maddie stopped, and stared, and started again, echoing Sophie's careful tone. "That would be very complicated to arrange."

Sophie smiled a little. "Not if you're a Roseingrave. My parents and now my younger sister have been making very determined arguments," she went on. "My siblings want a chance to show off, and my father has mentioned wanting to do something to show our family is a part of this town, and wish the best for the people here. And now it seems that giving a concert would help you out a great deal, as well."

Still Maddie hesitated, her reaction a far cry from the joy and relief Sophie had hoped to evoke.

A small note of alarm rang through her. "If it's not what you want, we can find something else."

Maddie shook her head solemnly. "It's perfect. A concert would draw in the kind of wealthy and important audience that you need for this next step." She bent closer, her mouth almost kissing Sophie's ear. Her voice was an oar, cutting through the murmur of the water. "I would rather let the whole scheme come to nothing than give you an ounce more of the hurt you've been healing from."

Sophie's mouth dropped open. She hadn't expected this. "Your friends are your family," she said simply. "And they're depending on you."

"You are my family, too," Maddie insisted. "You more than anyone."

"Then let me help." Sophie took Maddie's hands, tucking those blue mittens against her heart. "If I were able to offer you a ring and a lifetime's vow, I'd be asking you right now. But I can't—so let me do something else instead, to show you how much I—how much I care."

Maddie shook her head—not refusing, Sophie knew, but simply disbelieving.

But Sophie's stubborn Roseingrave mind—and her

heart—had already decided. "For most of this year, I've been trying to hide myself away from the world," she said. "I thought if I were quiet enough, I would feel stronger. Instead I only felt small, and ignored, and lonelier than ever. Until you. I think it's time I stopped making a habit of silence. I think it's time I stood up—on a stage—and made people listen."

"Aren't you afraid?" Maddie asked.

Sophie gave a helpless little laugh. "Terrified. But what if I do it anyway?"

And there it was—that spark of hope, bright and clear, lighting up Maddie's face like a sunrise coming over the horizon. Maddie's eyes dipped down to Sophie's mouth and then up; Sophie felt the ghost of that kiss, a promise to be fulfilled as soon as they were alone and safe.

"So now you're an accomplice," Maddie murmured, and on her tongue it became the sweetest of endearments. "Tell me: How much time do you need?"

Sophie pulled in a breath of cold, bracing air. "One month."

Chapter Fourteen

The next morning, Sophie had screwed up her courage and told her family she agreed to a concert in one month—provided all the Roseingrave children would perform, not only herself. Mrs. Roseingrave looked satisfied and Julia smug; the boys were either thrilled (Freddie), terrified (Robbie), or overflowing with questions (Jasper, to whom Julia had apparently revealed nothing).

Her father's face had the sort of intense euphoria she'd only ever seen when he'd worked out something clever to try with a piano action.

She squirmed, knowing that they would all be much less happy—and Jasper would probably have *even more* questions—if they knew the concert was also a ruse to cover an elaborate criminal scheme. Mr. Roseingrave clearly took Sophie's fidgeting as a sign that her nerves were still getting the better of her. "Practice, my dear," he said. "You'll feel much more up to it once you get a little more practice in."

Unfortunately, the next morning, Mrs. Muchelney came into the store and bought the Dewhurst and Ffolkes.

"Harriet's gone about as far as she can on our small instrument," she said, beaming at Sophie. "Your instruction has given her so much encouragement, Miss Roseingrave. I want to see how much further she can go with a proper piano to practice on."

"A very proper piano," Sophie said, stroking one hand over the beloved cherry case. Some part of her had known she would have to part with it eventually—her father had repaired it specifically to sell it, after all—but her first impulse was still a wild urge to fling herself over the instrument like a soldier defending his queen from an assassin's blow.

At least she would get to visit it when she gave Harriet her lessons. It might sting a little at first, but the thought of Harriet's face lighting up when she realized she had this wonderful instrument for her very own . . . Well, that was going to be worth seeing.

As Mrs. Muchelney arranged for the delivery of the instrument, Sophie asked, "Mrs. Muchelney, do you think your daughter might perform in a concert we are planning?"

"A concert?" The woman blinked rapidly, clearly taken aback. "But she has only just started learning!"

"It's a family concert," Mr. Roseingrave put in. "There will be players of all abilities—Sophie, of course, my younger children, and possibly a few ladies and gentlemen from the Aeolian Club."

The mention of *ladies and gentlemen* had the intended effect of softening Mrs. Muchelney's expression. "I shall have to ask Harriet—but I would be very proud if it were something she wished to do." The widow made her farewells and departed for home. Within the hour, the cart and footmen had come and loaded away the Dewhurst and Ffolkes.

Sophie ached at the absence of the piano in the shop as though a tooth had been pulled from her jaw.

Her father patted her arm. "Come, my dear—there's something I've been meaning to show you."

He left Robbie in charge and towed her into the back repair room. Familiar smells of wood and sawdust, varnish and turpentine and metal wound around her. A large canvas hulked in the back corner; Mr. Roseingrave put one hand on this and smiled at his daughter. "I've only just finished this."

He swirled off the canvas as though raising the curtain on a much-anticipated new opera.

Sophie gasped and clutched her hands to her chest.

She'd forgotten Julia had spoiled this surprise already: a new piano. No, not just a new piano—a new *Roseingrave*, a grand, with the name and the telltale rose logo painted in gold on the fallboard. The case was fine spruce with a gorgeous varnish the shade of fresh honey, and when she set one hand to the keys and played half a scale her heart soared at the sweetness of the instrument's voice.

The only other time she'd fallen in love this fast was with Maddie Crewe. "Is this the new action?" she asked, raising the lid to peer beneath.

"It is," her father confirmed. "With improvements, of course."

"Of course." Sophie ran her hands over the case, the

wood sleek and slippery beneath her fingers. "Whoever she'll belong to is very lucky indeed."

Mr. Roseingrave chuckled. "Sophie, my child," he said fondly, "she's for you."

Sophie could only gape at him.

He laughed again at the surprise on her face. "We may not be able to send you to court just yet, but at least we can provide you with an instrument to practice on until you can get there. Besides . . ." He leaned in. "If the concert goes as well as I hope, we may be sending you away sooner than you think. But!" He pulled up a piano bench. "Until then, you'll have a piano that's as worthy of you as anything these two hands can create."

"It's far too much," Sophie protested. But not very hard. She was caught in the full-fledged grip of piano adoration.

"Nonsense," her father said firmly. "You can't prepare for a concert if you have no instrument to practice on, and there's an end. Oh, and I was wondering," he went on. "What would your Miss Crewe say if I commissioned her to weave a set of programs in silk? We could sell them on the night for a souvenir. People so like souvenirs—even when a concert is not particularly memorable." He grinned proudly at her. "I have a feeling this one will be the furthest thing from forgettable, though."

He didn't know the half of it. Sophie grimaced, as the truth squirmed painfully in her gut.

What would her father say if he knew Sophie was using the concert to cover distinctly criminal purposes? That she hadn't agreed to the event because she felt she was ready, or because she wanted to perform—she did want to, but that hadn't been her main motive. Her father thought she was finally ready to face the world as a musician and a composer, after a long and painful year.

He was wrong.

She was doing this because she loved Madeleine Crewe, and that was the plain truth of it. Maddie was persuasive and beautiful and strong, and Maddie had asked for Sophie's help. So Sophie would give it—even if it meant betraying someone else she loved.

Even if that betrayal felt like she'd swallowed acid and it was slowly burning its way through her from the heart out.

"Sophie?" her father said, peering close. "Is something the matter?"

She couldn't do it. She had to tell him.

She closed her eyes, and opened her mouth.

The side door of Mr. Obeney's factory creaked heavily, and thudded shut behind Maddie like a sepulcher stone falling into place. Moonlight crept through the long windows slashed into the roof and turned the support beams skeleton silver. Miss Slight and Mr. Frampton had been working since the afternoon, but Maddie was the first of the weavers to arrive. The others followed shortly, and by the time Mrs. Money came striding in, the factory's partial resurrection was complete.

Two weeks had passed since Sophie had agreed to a concert and the rest had begun other preparations. They'd set up on the riverward side of the building, where nobody would be likely to see or hear what they did. Half a dozen of the silent old looms had had modified Jacquard heads attached by Miss Slight and Mr. Frampton. The magic lanterns hidden there spilled rainbow light onto the bone-pale threads of the warp, their heat and smoke masked by more visible lanterns placed between looms.

Miss Slight had also thought to add small panes of glass at carefully calculated angles underneath the shed. As the threads moved and the shuttles flew, the glass surfaces sent back flashes of light into the eyes of anyone looking closely: Maddie could stare directly for only a few seconds before her eyes began to water and she had to blink. Like the others she wore a factory-girl's uniform: at Alice's suggestion the pinafores had been artfully streaked with watercolor in various hues to imply they'd been working these looms for longer than a single night.

Mrs. Money looked around and nodded in approval, the feathers in her turban bobbing decisively in the light of the single lantern. The hat had been Maddie's idea. Feathers were wonderfully eloquent: they made a woman look fussy and flighty and vulnerable. By making them tremble just so, you could undermine any statement you made, giving the listener the opposite impression from your actual words. And Mr. Giles would think it was all his own cleverness in noticing, and would trust it better than any lie her lips could utter.

Each weaver now bound a strip of black muslin over her eyes—Mrs. Money would tell Mr. Giles it was to protect their sight from the effects of the unstabilized dye, but really it was to help make the other weavers less immediately recognizable—and less plausibly culpable.

Maddie wanted nobody at risk except herself.

At Maddie's call, the weavers set to work. Beaters thumped against the weave and the shuttles snapped accompaniment. Just enough light came through the blindfold to make clear the familiar parts of the loom, though any of them could probably have managed the work with their eyes closed. It had been years since Maddie had worked in a factory, but once you had, the pattern of it became part of you. Her body fell into it without her brain having to direct her limbs.

Alice and Judith began softly singing one of the old songs, the one about a maid well loved; their voices soared above the percussion and sent goose bumps shivering up Maddie's forearms.

She joined in at half volume, one ear cocked for the arrival of their quarry. But when the knock came, and the door creaked open, behind Mr. Giles's unctuous greeting were several other voices.

He'd brought friends.

Maddie would have frozen in surprise, the shuttle thunking to a telltale stop, but fortunately the rhythm of the song had her in its grip and her hands automatically kept time with the other girls while her brain scrambled to catch up to events. She wanted to snatch the black band from her eyes to see what was happening, but didn't want to attract the attention of breaking ranks with the others.

So she had to be content with listening as hard as she ever had in her life.

There was Mrs. Money's voice, exclaiming in surprise, and Mr. Giles's smooth tones attempting to plane her distress away like a carpenter smoothing out a knot from a piece of wood. Introductions were made, a series of names Maddie only half caught—but she heard enough of the voices and vowels to know that these were not any of his employees or shop assistants. These were wealthy men, educated, their plummy tones speaking of public schools and private tutors, of lineages as long as the noses down which they'd peer at someone of her lowly status.

In a word, Maddie realized, Mr. Giles had brought *investors* along with him tonight. Men who sowed money about like seeds, and reaped someone else's labor as if it were their proper harvest.

Judith brought the song to a close, and did not start another. Maybe she too was trying to listen to what was being said. Maddie could only be grateful.

Mrs. Money was explaining the fake weaving process, while the learned and wealthy men harrumphed in habitual skepticism. ". . . Daytime weaving forestalls the need for blindfolds. The unfixed dye is not so harmful to the eye in sunlight."

At the lower edge of her blindfold, Maddie saw a pair of gentleman's shoes take several steps back from where he'd been approaching the looms. She bit down on a smile: let self-preservation keep any of them from looking at warp and weft too closely.

"How soon could they have a supply ready to sell?" Mr. Giles was asking. "Mr. Sterling knows of a modiste in London who would be very interested in an exclusive license."

"The looms produce at the usual broadcloth rate," Mrs.

Money said easily. "With six looms working nights, I should expect you could have half the ladies in London wearing this cloth by Christmas."

"And what if you could expand the number of looms?" Mr. Giles pressed.

Maddie recognized that tone. That was his *I have an audience and now I shall impress them* voice. She'd heard it often enough—and she'd learned to dread it. It meant he'd found an opportunity. And whenever Mr. Giles found an opportunity, someone else was bound to suffer for it.

Mrs. Money's response was quelling, but not too harsh. "It's somewhat impractical to expand the production line at present," she said, adding wryly, "especially considering that you own neither the process itself nor the property we're standing in."

"Ah," Mr. Giles breathed, as Maddie strained to hear. "But what if we did?"

A long pause, as the Jacquard punch cards rattled like boxes full of bones. "I am afraid I don't follow," Mrs. Money said.

"I intend to make Mr. Obeney an offer on his factory," Mr. Giles said.

Maddie sucked in a breath, the sound masked by the hiss of the shuttle from one side of the loom to the other.

"Oh?" Mrs. Money put just the right amount of interest in her voice: affected, as a business partner must be, but not outraged or opposed or strident. Maddie wasn't sure she could have held onto her control, in the face of such shock and provocation.

Mr. Giles, a factory-owner? In charge of the work and wages of hundreds of people, mostly young women and girls? Mr. Giles had been bad enough as a draper and an employer—as the master of a place the size of this one, his control would be inescapable.

And the first thing he'd do would be eliminate his enemies. Band together with Mr. Prickett, who was quite terrible enough on his own. Force independent hand weavers like herself—and Alice, and Judith, and so on—out of business any way he could. They'd all end up back in the factory, she could feel it coming, like a storm just cresting the horizon.

It was a thought to chill the soul.

"Do you think," Mrs. Money was saying, "that Mr. Obeney is likely to sell?"

Mr. Giles scoffed contemptuously; Maddie jerked twice as hard on the shuttle handle. "Certainly, if we offer him a high enough price."

"I wasn't aware that you had such a fortune at your disposal."

"That is where these gentlemen come in," he purred back. "They are men with a wealth of financial experience, who know a good opportunity when they see one." The investors murmured approval of this flattery. Mr. Giles finished up: "Fortunes favor the bold, madam." More approving murmurs from the investors, then: "Gentlemen, now that your curiosity has been answered, shall we retire somewhere and finalize the terms?"

"A moment, Mr. Giles," Mrs. Money put in.

"Of course." The investors rumbled out the door to their

carriages, promising to wait. "I hope you're not having second thoughts, Mrs. Money."

Mrs. Money gave a light laugh that had the perfect amount of false anxiety in it. Maddie could almost see the feathers trembling on her headdress. "In fact . . . I was thinking I ought to raise my price, since it is now clear you will be making rather an adventure of this."

"Come now," Mr. Giles said, smooth as syrup. "Your late husband was a brilliant chemist—but you are still a grieving widow, unsuited for the rough world of business and the cruel nature of competition. You have only to accept your reward, and then take a well-earned rest from all this tedious labor." The sound of rustling paper. "I have written a letter of credit for the Carrisford Bank where you may draw upon—"

"No," Mrs. Money interrupted.

Maddie was all but holding her breath. This was the tricky part, the money: they'd spent a long, long time arguing about it. Banknotes were numbered, and could link the crime to the person who tried to spend them; cash was untraceable, held its value, and could be disbursed as needed to workers on strike in need of funds. It would be easy enough for Mrs. Money to redeem any paper for hard currency and give the cash to the Weavers' Library—but if they did that, they'd have no opportunity to create the kind of public scene that would send Mr. Giles running far, far away.

Until Judith Wegg had laughed and said: "If we need both, why don't we just ask for both?"

"My price has now doubled," Mrs. Money said.

Mr. Giles's syrupy tone crystallized a little with irritation.

"Madam, I cannot believe you would change the terms of a bargain made in good faith—"

"I also emphasized the importance of secrecy, did I not?" She harrumphed, a sound of such petty, irritating fussiness that Maddie had to choke back a hysterical giggle. "I do not appreciate my private business being made known to so many strange gentlemen. *Especially*," she went on, "when I know my Horace worked so hard to keep it from his rivals. So now the price is: one thousand pounds for the factory key, which will get you the looms, the color-changing equipment, and the remaining stock of silk you've seen demonstrated. Play it right, and Mr. Obeney will never have to know you started the work before you bought the place." A jingling sound, as she extracted the key from her purse. "And another thousand pounds for my husband's notes—which include the chemical formula for the dye, and complete instructions for the fabric process. And you'll have to make your choice quickly, Mr. Giles. I intend to miss as little of the London Season as possible this year. Particularly since I want to be there to witness your miracle fabric take the *ton* by storm."

"The *ton*," he echoed, with a little gasp at the end.

Oh, well played, Maddie thought. It was an image impeccably designed to fire the mind of a man with commercial ambition and envy of the aristocracy. Blindfold be damned: she could *see* him yearning for it, visions of duchesses and debutantes swirling across the parquet, all wearing the silks he sold them, their gowns flashing from pink to blue to gold to green in a rhythm to match the steps of the waltz . . .

"As a pledge of good faith," Mrs. Money said more softly,

"I will give you the key right now, in exchange for the letter of credit that you mentioned."

"Well," Mr. Giles said at last. "Perhaps you are not so unsuited for high finance as I'd implied."

"Heaven forfend," Mrs. Money said, and only Maddie heard the wry note beneath the mask of feminine reticence. "Do we have a deal, Mr. Giles?"

Maddie waited for his answer, her shuttle thumping *left-right, right-left* in front of her like an anxious heartbeat, the rhythm echoed by the other girls' looms unseen in the darkness around her.

And then: "Done," Mr. Giles's voice said. A single note, so low it was almost lost in the thrum of machinery.

The rush of success sent the blood soaring through Maddie's veins; she only dimly heard Mr. Giles take his leave. Mrs. Money waited at the door until the rattle of horses and carriages showed the investors and Mr. Giles had all departed. "All right, girls—you've done it," she called out, and as one the weavers let go the handles of their flying shuttles, and pulled the black cloth from over their eyes.

Maddie blinked against the rainbow lights from the colored lanterns, which was searing after so much darkness. Alice was chattering happily to an amused Judith about how well the illusion had worked, as she began taking down the magic lanterns from the Jacquard heads. The other girls were drifting toward the spot where Mrs. Money stood in the pool of ordinary lantern light by the door. The looms would have to be stripped of their silk, but that could wait for the moment.

"Who were those other men?" Mary Fisin asked, twisting the blindfold nervously between her hands.

"Nobody good," Mrs. Money said grimly. "Not if they're interested in a deal as underhanded as this one."

"I don't know if I can afford any more enemies," Alice said.

"They won't be enemies," Maddie said. "They'll be quite helpful to us, even if they don't realize it."

Everyone spun to stare at her: Judith with arms folded, Mrs. Money blinking in surprise, Alice squinting from the coruscation of the magic lantern in her hands, the other members of the Weavers' Library.

Maddie smirked, her mind pulling scraps of thought into a pattern, as the threads of the looms around her shimmered like harp strings. "We are going to invite these men to the concert. You said yourself, Mrs. Money, that we need to embarrass him publicly. We'd planned on doing that already. Now if we make sure his investors are in the audience, we'll have some very interested eyes when Mr. Giles's true character is revealed. If they think he's lost all their money . . . Won't they demand he pay it all back?"

Alice began to grin, and Judith with her. Mrs. Money nodded, and even anxious Mary Fisin's eyes brightened.

Maddie rubbed her hands, anticipating. "Time for one last performance, everyone."

Chapter Fifteen

Maddie had been glad of the commission for the concert program, since it let her put to use the cream silk they'd bought for the false factory demonstration. Her loom had been warped properly for the work and the design punched onto the Jacquard cards—but today, instead of weaving more of the delicate design, Maddie was taking a day to help finish preparations for the other, secret performance that they were planning.

Mr. Samson had been to London and back, and now he had brought his finds to Maddie's—along with Miss Narayan. The Narayan shop had always been a bit too costly for Maddie, but she knew they had the best reputation for tailoring in all of Carrisford. "So nice to meet you," she said, shaking the slim brown hand Miss Narayan held out to her as Mr. Samson introduced them. "And we very much appreciate your help with this." She led them into the front room, and turned. "Did Sophie—did Miss Roseingrave tell you what we needed your help for?"

Miss Narayan's dark eyes were bright with curiosity.

"She and Mr. Samson have been very mysterious about it, Miss Crewe."

"Allow me to dispel the mystery, then—we are plotting a crime."

Miss Narayan's eyes went wide.

Maddie went on: "We are planning to rob Mr. Giles of everything we can. In the open, where everyone can see."

"How subtle," Miss Narayan laughed.

Maddie's lips quirked in acknowledgement. "And now that I have told you that, I ask for your help."

"And if I refuse?"

Maddie spread her hands. "Then I simply ask you not to tell anyone what we're planning to do."

"As if anyone would listen if I told them something so outlandish," Miss Narayan muttered. She narrowed her eyes, and turned to Mr. Samson. "And you have been a part of this?"

"Since Miss Crewe first asked for my help a few months ago," he confirmed. His expression was somber, his gaze earnest. "You may have heard my family is thinking of moving into manufacture?"

"That's what they say," Miss Narayan replied.

"Well, they happen to be right. My father has been trying to purchase Mr. Obeney's factory from the manager for fully a year now—but Mr. Giles has put words in the man's ear and gold in his pocket, and the factory sits empty when it could be putting people to work. And now we learn Mr. Giles is talking of buying the place himself."

The seamstress folded her arms. "And your father, does he want you to help him run this factory?"

"He and my brothers will—but I've convinced him my talents are better served by taking over the secondhand trade."

Miss Narayan nodded thoughtfully, and turned back to Maddie. "What is it precisely you are asking of me?"

Maddie smiled softly. "Alterations. At whatever price you care to name."

Mr. Samson broke in. "I've told Miss Crewe there's no better seamstress in Carrisford. Particularly if you're working with delicate fabrics and eveningwear. But more than that: we needed someone we could trust." He swallowed, lifting his chin. "And I'd put my life in your good hands, Miss Narayan, if you asked it."

The seamstress's eyes widened. "And if I need time?"

"Then I'll wait." He smiled, as she stared. "As long as you need. I'll wait."

Miss Narayan's soft lips parted on a sigh that was too soft for Maddie to hear.

"What *we* need," Maddie said eventually into the silence, "is six identical gowns. What we have—are these." She waved at the wealth of fabric heaped on Emma's worktable, a heap of Pomona green frocks and flounces in a dizzying variety of fabrics. Silks and satins mostly, with a few cotton and muslin dresses. The more one looked, the more the difference in the dyes became pronounced: one having slightly more yellow, another slightly more blue.

Miss Narayan cast one last searing glance at Mr. Samson then moved forward, sorting thoughtfully through the chaos of fabric.

"This hue was extremely popular last season," Mr. Samson

explained, after clearing his throat, "so there were plenty of castoff gowns to choose from. And Mrs. Money seems like the kind of woman to be fashionable, but not to the point of buying a completely new wardrobe every season." His smile hitched up on one side as his voice turned wry. "Especially in a backwater like Carrisford, where nobody of significance is around to see her."

"Nobody but all of us," Miss Narayan said drily, and tilted her head. "How much scrutiny are they expected to withstand? If they must look identical side by side it will be a very different amount of work than if they are passing on opposite sides of the street."

"Let us say: as identical as you'd make them if they were on a theater stage," Maddie said.

Miss Narayan's smile widened. "That gives us a little flexibility," she said, and rubbed her hands together.

"And you won't be working alone," Maddie said. "My friend Emma will be helping—she's as quick with a needle as anyone you're likely to find, though most of her experience is in garment construction rather than alterations. And she'll be making slippers to match."

"Only one final question," Miss Narayan said. "How much time do I have?"

"One week," Maddie said softly.

The seamstress snorted. "You just added fifty percent to my rates, if that's how fast I've got to work."

"Done," Maddie said.

Emma was out with John and Cat for her evening off, so Maddie helped Miss Narayan—"Call me Gita, since we're now in league together"—consider the whole of the project. They began sorting through the gowns, comparing sizes, embellishment, length, and color. "We need one to be presentable very close up, a garment some fine lady would wear in the evening if she wanted to look impressive—but the others can be less precise."

"One true bride, and five imposters," Gita said, with a chuckle. "Well, that makes things simpler . . . Do you have any trimming around I could use? Any ribbon or lace or silk scrap? Gold or silver, for preference."

Maddie ran up and came down with a quarter bolt of gold silk.

Gita stopped and stared at the richness of the silk, liquid and smooth and enchanting. "Where on earth did you come by this?"

Maddie swallowed. "It's all that's left of the last broadcloth my mother wove, before she died. I've been saving it for something special."

Gita peered at her. "Wouldn't you prefer to make this into something you could wear?"

Maddie bit her lip, and shook her head. "My mother lived and died believing that what we did together was more important than what each of us did alone. She might not approve of the crime aspect, but I know she'd be proud we could use some of her work to make life better for everyone in Carrisford." She stroked one hand down the silk, then pushed it into Gita's hands. "That's more important than whether or not one person looks pretty."

Gita looked askance at this, but accepted the fabric with

no further objection. Within an hour, the seamstress had sketched out a plan for the taking apart and reassembling of the various gowns into things that would more or less look similar. This skirt with this bodice, that neckline in the other fabric—it was all a bit dizzying but it gave Maddie hope the scheme would work. "The trim is the key," Gita said, tapping the gold silk. "If you put the same embellishment on the same places in all the gowns, most people won't look too closely at the fabrics unless they're given a reason." She narrowed her eyes at Maddie. "So whatever you do, don't give them a reason."

"I'll do my best," Maddie promised, and heard Cat's voice and John's and Emma's laughter as the trio returned home. "Now let me introduce you to everyone else, and we can get to work."

Chapter Sixteen

Show up after sunset, Sophie's note had said. So Maddie had worked on her attic loom until the last fingers of daylight slipped below the horizon, then grabbed a quick supper and walked the dusky streets to the Roseingraves' shop. It was one of those nights where the fog poured in from the sea, and the streets were filled with curling wisps like fingers reaching out to grasp the unwary. Maddie walked fast enough that she sweat a little beneath her cloak, and had to pause to catch her breath outside the instrument shop window.

Even from the outside, she could tell something was different. She knocked, and heard Sophie's call of "Just a minute!" from inside. She had time for several long breaths to help her racing heart to settle before the door was pulled open, and Sophie's small, eager self was there to greet her. "Come in," she said, and stepped back.

Maddie followed her into the shop—and gasped.

A few scattered candles like stars gave a faint, fey light to the space. The tables and shelves of sheet music and smaller instruments had been moved out against the walls and windows, making room in the center of the shop for a lone chair with a cushion. One small table stood beside it, bearing a tankard that was sweating nearly as much as Maddie was. The chair faced a piano, one Maddie hadn't seen before, pale wood shining gold in the candlelight. The piano was placed at right angles so that the person in the chair could see the musician's hands and profile as they played.

She turned to Sophie, amazed. "What is this?"

"What else?" Sophie ducked her head, but couldn't hide the glee in her expression. "It's a concert."

Maddie's jaw dropped.

Sophie's eyes flicked up, then away again. "I thought since you were going to be so busy on the night, that you might . . . that I . . . ." She sighed, and straightened, and visibly gathered her courage. Chin lifted, hands clenched tight, eyes daring. "I wanted to play this piece for you all the way through," she said. "Just once. I wanted to do it when you were able to pay attention. Not when half your mind was running through how to wrap things up with Mr. Giles and Mrs. Money and—and . . . ." She buzzed like a tuning fork, vibrating with anxious energy.

Maddie took a seat in the chair, spreading her skirts out with a regal flourish, and picking up the tankard. She held the cool metal in both hot hands like a chalice, took a sip of her favorite cider, and asked: "What's the piece?"

"I call it: 'The Hellion's Waltz,'" Sophie said solemnly, before her smile burst out again in helpless pride. "And it's the best thing I've ever composed."

Such a frank, plain statement, where Maddie knew Sophie must have been painfully tempted to deflect and demur. Those *It's just tunes* or *I'm sure it still needs work* must have been so difficult not to say. But instead Sophie was offering Maddie her honest thoughts on her own work—even if they sounded overproud or boastful.

That was a boldness she knew must have cost Sophie.

Maddie's heart threatened to overflow, fizzing like the cider on her tongue. She set the drink aside, pressed her hands to her knees, and nodded.

Sophie shook out her hands, stepped up to the piano, and took a seat. Her fingers fluttered briefly over the keys, and she closed her eyes for a moment. She opened her eyes, breathed in, and struck the first notes.

Maddie trembled as the waltz filled the room. Light at first, a flirt of a melody with sinister undertones beneath. A second tune came in, low and persistent, chasing after the first. They circled one another, closer and closer—until finally they fell into a harmony that was all the more glorious for being unexpected.

Maddie gasped silently as she realized: this was about *her*. Sophie was telling their story through music, in a way that people could understand, but without any words to expose or condemn.

And all of Carrisford would hear it.

The waltz's rhythm picked up, more notes pouring from Sophie's flying fingers. The two melodies danced faster and faster, grace notes and trills popping up like sparks. Maddie was agog, leaning forward in her chair, fearful it was all going to come tumbling down. How could human hands do anything like this? Up and up, higher and higher—the tune grew breathy with altitude—they were going to run out of piano soon—Maddie herself felt like she teetered on a precipice, faint with vertigo—but Sophie paused on the peak and then brought everyone gently, carefully back to earth with a long glissando that ended on a chord like a sigh of spent pleasure.

She pulled her hands from the keys and looked over at Maddie, eyes shining.

Maddie burst into wild applause, clapping so hard her hands ached with it.

Sophie blushed a deep rose and wrapped her arms around herself.

Applause was insufficient. Maddie was up and out of her chair before she knew it, striding over to Sophie, her hands cupping the composer's face and thumbs tracing away the teardrops that had yet to spill down Sophie's cheeks. "That was the most incredible thing I've ever heard," she said. She bent and kissed her, her body blocking anyone outside who might see, heedless of anything but the one truth pulsing through her like a heartbeat:

Anyone who could compose a waltz like that deserved to be kissed, as often and as thoroughly as possible. If Maddie had to spend the rest of her life making sure this particular precept was fulfilled, then so be it.

"Thank you for playing for me—thank you for writing such a gorgeous, wild piece of music." She felt Sophie's lips curve beneath hers, and echoed the smile. "You could kill someone, writing waltzes like that. How on earth did you fit all those notes in?"

Sophie broke away with a sputter of a laugh. "It's not nearly as out of control as it sounds, I assure you." Maddie's skeptical expression must have said enough, because Sophie turned back to the instrument and began picking out one of the threads of the final melody on the keyboard—slowly, all the tones precisely in place. "A performance is really just a trick," Sophie said. "It's supposed to feel natural and expressive, even magical. None of the effort or the hours and hours of practice are supposed to show."

"How long have you been working on this?" Maddie asked.

Sophie's eyes were bright with reflected candlelight. "Since shortly after I met you."

Maddie threaded wondering fingers through the errant locks of Sophie's brown hair. "So you chose to write a waltz for a woman you'd only just met?"

Sophie leaned into the caress. "No—the waltz suggested itself." Sophie's smile widened in pure, honest pride. "I *chose* to make it as good as I possibly could. A slight shift of melody here, a slight tweak there. Small choices add up." She ran through a couple variations, showing how the tune had shifted over time. Then her fingers slowed. "I went to Mrs. Narayan's shop for a gown for the concert." A few more notes, a minor key. "She told me you'd given her your mother's silk for the copy gowns."

Maddie traced one finger down the side of Sophie's neck.

"I saved it for something important," she replied. "What's more important than family?"

"What indeed," Sophie murmured.

"I can't wait to hear your waltz again at the concert." Maddie wrapped her arms around Sophie's shoulders, nuzzling into the crook of her neck. "In a proper hall, with the audience wrapped around your clever fingers. Just like I am."

Sophie's smile wobbled at little at the corners. "Of course."

They had dinner with Sophie's family and made their way back to Maddie's attic. The room was crowded now with piles of silk programs, plain silk backgrounds with deep blue text. Roseingrave was prominent, as was For the Benefit of the Weavers' Library and Cooperative Society.

And, to Maddie's gratification, her beloved lit up at the border of tiny songbirds that framed the text. "Not sparrows," Sophie said.

"Nightingales," Maddie confirmed. "And oh, how they'll sing . . ."

Later, in the darkness with dawn so far off, Maddie lay on her back and stared up at the shafts of moonlight on the ceiling. They crept slowly along the plaster, bending around the beams, slicing across the heavy frame of the loom.

Sophie rolled over and snuggled close, chilled. Maddie felt as much as heard her, Sophie's lips moving against the side of her shoulder. "Still awake?" she murmured.

"Just thinking."

Sophie stretched. "About what?"

Maddie slid an arm around her waist and pulled her close. Sophie's small, round form fit perfectly against the curve of Maddie's waist and hip. "What if it's not enough?" she asked.

Sophie made a sound indicating confusion.

Maddie tried again. "We're taking out the worst villain of the lot—but the system will stay in place. They used to smash machines, you know? Before, when the power looms were new, the handloom weavers sabotaged a lot of the factory machinery to protest the way the power looms had replaced them. It landed a lot of those weavers in jail or worse—and the power looms stayed all the same. Because the machines aren't the system."

"I must have dozed off a little," Sophie replied with a yawn. "Because my poor brain couldn't make any sense of what you just said."

Maddie let out a breath. "The problem was never the power loom—it was the people who wanted power looms because they were cheaper and produced faster. It was the way all the factory owners were chasing profits at the expense of workers' wages and livelihood—their health and happiness. The *problem*," she said, "is when people think the factory is more important than the people who work there."

"Something like that is happening in music," Sophie said after a moment. "Mr. Broadwood's piano factory in London can make five new pianos in a single day. And that's just with people—nobody's invented a machine for building pianos yet."

"So what will your father do when they *do* start building machines to build pianos?"

"Build a better piano-building machine, I expect," Sophie

said, with a faint laugh. "And the faster they make pianos, the more people they will need to tune them." She paused. "But you already did something like this. When the factories began making cheaper broadcloth than you could weave, you switched to ribbon making."

"Because they haven't yet made a machine for designing patterns," Maddie said. "A Jacquard head can't punch its own cards. Yet," she added grimly.

The moonlight gleamed on the metal Jacquard head, as though it were listening.

Sophie stroked a line over her collarbone, fingers soft and soothing. "Yes, there are probably more inventions coming that will upset the way things are done. But you've changed course before. And you don't have to do it alone." Back and forth her fingers went, the slide of them slightly hypnotizing Maddie. "What if you came to court with me?"

Maddie blinked into the moonlight. "Have you decided to go, then?"

"Well . . ." Sophie's fingers paused briefly, then resumed their pace. Back and forth, back and forth. "Not as yet. But maybe sooner than I originally thought. A lot of it depends on how things go tomorrow night. But . . . I've been thinking a great deal about what my mother said. About running out of time, and not letting my best playing years slip me by. And if I were to go, I'd like to have a companion with me—someone who knows me, and who I could trust among so many strangers. We can tell people you're my maid—or better, my assistant, someone steady and respectable who manages my schedule and keeps my wild artistic impulses in check. You could even keep designing patterns, so you would have an income of your own. Though I don't know if you could bring the loom."

"No," Maddie whispered, anguished. "I couldn't bring the loom." Not unless she took it apart, piece by piece, and reassembled it somewhere else. But she couldn't picture it anywhere else—it had always stood here, a testament to her mother's drive and ingenuity and skill. Maddie couldn't imagine a way to move it that wouldn't feel like destruction.

But what good was a weaver without her loom? What was Maddie, if not a weaver?

Sophie's fingers stopped stroking and slid around Maddie's shoulder, gripping tight. "I don't want to lose you."

"You're not going to lose me," Maddie said at once, looking down into Sophie's eyes, which were liquid silver with moonlight and worry. "And you know I'll never lie to you."

"I know." Sophie's answering smile was haunted. Maddie kissed her lips free of it, and found a better way to spend the last hours of the night.

Chapter Seventeen

The concert evening was clear apart from a few trailing wisps of cloud, as though the sky itself had put on handmade lace for the occasion. Everyone appeared in their very best: the gentry, the merchants, and the factory families. The only difference was the latter would bundle their finery back to the pawnshop on Monday morning, until Friday's pay could redeem the good clothing for church.

Sophie had Julia help her into her concert gown of pale blue silk with a net overlay. The net was extremely fine and had been embellished with white embroidery in the shape of long, graceful plumes; they feathered over the bodice and short sleeves, and trailed down the center of the gown to the hem.

It made Sophie feel quite angelic, which was both gratifying and pricked at her conscience.

Julia was in white, with a spattering of small gold wings like bees, and very proud of them she was. Jasper had a waistcoat made of the same material, and had been strutting about in it all afternoon until Mrs. Roseingrave made him change to a less imperiled one to eat supper in. "Are you ready?" Julia asked.

Sophie took one last breath and braced herself. "As ready as I'll ever be."

Mr. Roseingrave had hired a carriage for the night, and a wagon had taken Sophie's piano over earlier that afternoon. Once the Roseingraves arrived—a noisy group, as the twins and Freddy were near bursting with excitement, with only Robbie silent and ashen-faced—she hurried to test her instrument was in tune and make her final anxious adjustments.

The Carrisford Moot Hall was an old building lately refurbished: the room a long rectangle with the organ at one end, rows of pillars down either wall, and a sky-blue arch of ceiling above. It was so precise a match for the hue of Sophie's gown that she almost wished she could fly up and disappear into it.

But that was her nerves talking. They jangled like overstretched wires down her arms and in her belly, and there was no way of putting them in better tune.

The hall blazed with light, most of it by the old Gothic window where the piano had been situated along one of the long walls, rows of chairs facing it. At the back of the rows were tables with bowls of punch and trays of sweets. The members of the Weavers' Library were serving, bright and lively in various hues. At one of these tables, Alice sold silk souvenir programs and accepted donations for the Weavers' Library. Sophie and the other performers clustered at the back, many holding instruments with damp hands and murmuring softly to one another.

And there, sitting in the second row, tapping one foot on the floorboards, was Mr. Giles.

Sophie estimated the tempo of his agitation by the speed at which he tapped. She knew, because she'd helped write the note, that Mrs. Money had sent word to him this afternoon that one of his investors, on the side, had made her an offer for the formula of the color-changing dye.

I knew we couldn't trust them, the note had said.

They have betrayed you. Horace's rivals must have found out: they have long been looking to steal his secrets and claim the credit. They must not get hold of his formula! Horace's legacy must not be so tarnished!

I cannot linger here past tomorrow—but nor do I dare meet you anywhere quiet, where they might ambush me before I have a chance to deliver Horace's notes to you. If you have the thousand pounds—even if it must be in banknotes—bring it to the concert at the Moot Hall tonight.

I will be wearing green, my mourning year being past. Find two seats in the front row, and I will join you once the music has begun. One last act for my Horace's honor, and I will shake the dust of this town from my feet.

Mr. Giles's coat, Sophie noticed, was bulging a little on one side. As though he had a second heart hidden there. He would occasionally reach one hand up to touch it, defensively, as he waited with ill grace.

Slowly, the hands on the clock crept forward, and the chairs in the hall filled with people both new and familiar.

Every carrying laugh and cough wound Sophie tighter, until she worried her joints might actually burst with the strain.

Miss Narayan wore an amber velvet that made her brown skin glow as if lit from within. She and her aunt were in the precise center of the chairs, with Mr. Samson a tall figure in between. Mrs. Roseingrave was wearing deep blue satin; she walked slowly to the front row with the elder Mr. Frampton and spoke to Mr. Giles. While Sophie watched closely, Mr. Giles moved over at her request, so that Mr. Frampton with his cane could settle into the aisle seat, with Mrs. Roseingrave beside him. Two empty seats separated Mrs. Roseingrave from Mr. Giles: the spaces reserved for Mr. Roseingrave, and Mrs. Money.

Sophie saw Mr. Giles touch his coat again, and felt her heartbeat skip double-time.

Sophie's mother rose from her chair and murmured something to her friend. Moments later she was giving Sophie an encouraging maternal kiss on the cheek. "Feeling brave, my dear?"

"Only if bravery feels precisely like nausea," Sophie murmured back in a burst of frankness.

Her mother smiled. "Old performer's secret: if you're going to be sick," Mrs. Roseingrave whispered, "be sick and get it out of the way." She embraced Sophie hard, kissed her husband, then returned to her seat.

Sophie shook out her hands at the wrist and flexed her fingers. She wouldn't be playing for a while yet, but she worried if she ran away to retch somewhere she'd just keep running and never come back.

She couldn't even think it. Too much depended on her.

Restless, she made her way over to where Harriet Muchelney stood. The girl's sheet music was fluttering in her shaking hand, and her eyes were so big they glowed white even back here where the light was dim. "My cousins Lucy and Stephen came up from London," she said faintly. "It's a very long way to travel. And they brought a *countess* with them."

A lot of expectation there. Sophie could sympathize. She put a steadying hand on her student's shoulder. "How are you feeling?"

"Terrified," Harriet whispered.

Sophie leaned down and whispered: "Me too."

Harriet's surprise was clear; her eyes widened further. "But you've done this before?"

"Not quite like this," Sophie said. "But I do know: it's a little terrifying every time. And now you know something about performing—this is just how it feels before you begin." She squeezed the girl's shoulder. "It doesn't mean anything about how you're going to do. That's entirely up to you."

The girl swallowed audibly. "What if I hit a wrong note?"

"You might," Sophie allowed. "But you just keep going."

"What if"—Harriet bit her lip— "what if I forget how to play?"

"If you get lost, you can just stop, and then start over."

"From the beginning, or—?"

"From anywhere you like. And it might feel awful. But just try again, and keep going. Because here's another secret . . ." She leaned close. "The audience wants to see something interesting. And if you play very well, that's interesting. And they'll clap for you. But if you hit a wrong note, or lose your place—if you have to stop and start over and try again—if you make a mistake but keep going and then make it to the end anyway . . ." Sophie smiled. "They'll clap *even harder*. Because if you play perfectly, you've conquered a piece of music. But if you play imperfectly, and still finish, you've conquered fear itself. And every audience in the entire world wants to see that."

"They'll clap harder?" Harriet asked.

"I've heard them," Sophie said.

Harriet gave a small smile, and her music didn't rattle quite so hard in her hands.

Mr. Roseingrave grinned at his daughter. "Are you ready to create a sensation, my dear?"

Sophie straightened her shoulders. "As ready as I can be."

"Then let us begin."

Mr. Roseingrave cleared his throat, moved to the front, and raised his arms. The audience chatter faded away into silence as he strode into the bright lights of the small stage. "Ladies and gentlemen . . ." he began.

His introduction was mercifully brief, and at the end he resumed his seat in the audience, his wife patting his knee. Jasper and Julia were up first, the crowd cooing over their matching garb and improbable confidence. They raised their violins—Jasper gave a silent count—and the duet began. Sophie had heard it a hundred times as they practiced at home, but here in this space it sounded unfamiliar, as though it had been created just for this moment.

As soon as the first notes sounded, Mrs. Money walked into the room. Her Pomona green gown bore rosettes of bright gold on the bodice, and no fewer than three tiers of flounces along the hem. She made her way along the side, unseen.

Sophie marked time by watching Jasper and Julia, who were outdoing themselves. Soaring strings and small, quick fingers, and two instruments that were fortunately in good tune: the audience applauded so much at the finish that Jasper's grin nearly split his face, and even bold Julia looked surprised and slightly shy at such a wealth of approval.

While everyone applauded, Mrs. Money slipped into the empty seat in the front row, clutching at her purse as though she feared to lose it.

Now it was Harriet Muchelney's turn on the program. She turned half-wild eyes to Sophie.

Sophie nodded briskly and smiled. "It's up to you now."

Harriet's spine straightened, and she nodded back. If her walk to the piano bench was a bit of a martial march, well, that was only to be expected.

Sophie held her breath. Despite her bold words to the girl, Miss Muchelney's success was a test for her teacher as well. This was Sophie's first student in Carrisford, and her ability to attract others would hang on what happened in the next few minutes.

The piece Harriet had selected (with Sophie's help) was a simplified version of a waltz in A minor: she only had to worry about the white keys, and it sounded dramatic and eerie and sinister in a way that had called to the girl's fierce soul. Miss Muchelney sat on the bench, wiped her hands on her skirts, and reached for the keys.

Sophie had to remind herself the human body needed to

breathe. She sucked air in, conscious more than she had ever been before of the way her lungs expanded in her chest, and the muscles that moved all of it in and out.

Harriet launched into the waltz as though declaring war.

It wasn't graceful, it wasn't lyrical, and half the audience reared back in polite surprise at the volume—but her rhythm was good, the sound filled the hall to the corners, and she wrung every feeling she could from the melody. It was blood-thirsty, somehow, and brave, and it threw caution absolutely to the wind.

She played every note perfectly, if emphatically, and reveled in the small bits of showiness at the end.

Before the notes of the last chord faded from the air, the applause was already deafening.

Harriet rose and bowed, her cheeks flushed, her lips parted, the wonder of it clear on her face: this applause was all for her. From the back came the sound of her brothers yelling her name; she flushed and gave them a little wave, and laughter rolled over the applause.

Sophie had fallen in love with performing herself in just this way—albeit with a much smaller audience—and from the wings she clapped until her hands stung, fit to expire from mingled relief and pride.

In the front, Mr. Giles turned to murmur a few words to Mrs. Money, and she held up a quelling hand, peering suspiciously around at the audience.

Mr. Frampton and Miss Slight followed, playing one of Spohr's sonatas for harp and violin. The bell-like tone of the harp and the voice of the violin were an exquisite combination, and Sophie managed to soothe her nerves a little in the shiver of the strings.

She peered out at the audience again when the sonata finished, and spotted Maddie Crewe for the first time. Maddie was across the aisle from Mrs. Money; her gown was a silvery gray color that brought out the rosy tones in her skin and the auburn in her hair. Starlike spangles were scattered along the neckline and down the skirt. They sparkled as she clapped, her eyes diamond bright. She flicked a quick glance across the aisle, where Mr. Giles sat, not even applauding, clearly so caught up in his dreams of unearned success that he was unwilling to even *pretend* to enjoy the performance. Waiting for the important part—which is to say, the part of the evening that involved and affected him.

How profoundly selfish, Sophie thought.

More performances: Robbie and Freddie, the Aeolian Club. Sophie managed to resist the urge to chew her nails down to the quick. And when she stretched her hands for the hundredth time, trying to keep them busy, she realized: she hadn't actually thought about Mr. Verrinder in weeks.

She'd been too occupied practicing her waltz, kissing Maddie Crewe, and plotting to defraud Mr. Giles. Only one of those was truly virtuous, but they'd all been enjoyable. More than enjoyable—they'd made her feel like the strongest and truest version of herself.

Maybe this was what healing felt like.

One final quartet finished playing, and carried their instruments away. The piano was once again alone out there, shining like a torch in the candlelight.

Maddie Crewe leaned forward in her seat, roses blooming in her cheeks.

She had woven the silk programs; she had known the order of performances. She knew Sophie would be up next. The finale, the last great spectacle of the night.

Maddie was eager for it, the curve of her lips evident even at this distance.

Sophie gazed at the woman she loved more than she'd ever thought possible, and like her mother so many years before, she knew she was doing all this tonight for one reason and one reason only: to enthrall and enchant one particular audience member. In the hope she could steal Maddie's heart so thoroughly they would spend the rest of their lives tangled up together.

And she realized: this was what Mrs. Roseingrave had talked about. This was one of those perfect moments that happened only so often in the course of a musician's career.

There was nothing to do but give it everything she had.

Sophie strode into the light and curtsied to all of Carrisford. She sat on the bench and smoothed out her skirts so her feet could reach the pedals unimpeded.

The waltz unfurled in her mind like a map to the next ten minutes.

She felt Maddie's gaze on her, warm with approval.

She breathed in deep, raised her hands, and began to play.

Maddie had suspected it, but now she was sure: Sophie Roseingrave was a musical genius.

She'd heard "The Hellion's Waltz" once before, so she ought to have been prepared. But it was one thing to hear it played in a close and intimate setting, for an audience of one—it was quite another to be sitting in a throng as Sophie's incredible hands pulled note after note out of the piano shining under the lights. The audience was rapt, utterly entranced by the skill of the composer and the performer, the air thick with the peculiar tension that happens only when hundreds upon hundreds of people are all holding their breath with wonder.

It was such a shame they wouldn't get to hear the ending.

As the third and final section started up—the two melodies singing together, harmony ringing out honey-sweet in the Moot Hall—Mrs. Money made her move.

Maddie had watched her closely the whole night, sitting beside their victim. Mr. Giles had tapped his foot impatiently through every performance in such a way as to make Maddie reconsider the wisdom of murdering him and throwing his body in the river. And now, as the final movement of the final piece rang out, and everyone's attention was fixed upon the small figure on stage, the evening's real performance began.

Mrs. Money took a few folded sheets of paper out of her purse, wrapped them quickly in her silk souvenir program, and handed it to Mr. Giles. He, in turn, passed her a small purse, with a cord she quickly looped over her wrist.

Then Mrs. Money rose and crept to the side, ready to make her way out of the hall.

Mr. Giles tried to tuck the silk-wrapped bundle in his

coat, but it was just large enough to be awkward. He fought with it. Mr. Roseingrave noticed the gesture, and from across the aisle Maddie could just hear him say: "Oh! Oh, dear. Your program is badly creased, Mr. Giles—do let me offer you a fresh one."

And he plucked the silk from Mr. Giles's hand.

Maddie's every muscle tensed.

"Give that back, sir!" Mr. Giles hissed—too loudly. People from the second and third row shushed him, frowning at the unmelodious interruption.

Mr. Roseingrave had already cast his eye upon the paper, enough to read what little was written there. Maddie's hands clenched, as the piano maker's eyes flicked up again, narrowed in offense. His tone was a shade louder than before, as if he had briefly forgotten he was at a concert. "I beg your pardon, sir, but this is not a gambling hall."

"*What?*"

Mr. Giles's exclamation rippled through a quarter of the audience. More heads turned, and an irritated whisper rose from the crowd.

On stage, Sophie's hand slipped, and the first wrong note marred the waltz.

Mr. Roseingrave held out the papers, as Sophie struggled on. But the weight of attention had shifted now, to the drama playing out in the front row.

Mr. Giles snatched the pages from the piano maker's hand and peered at them, shuffling through them slowly and then faster and faster. Maddie knew what he saw there:

every page bearing the same three letters, tall and bold and mocking:

IOU

Maddie watched realization dawn on his face and turn it a pale and sickly green.

Concert utterly forgotten, Mr. Giles leaped up from his seat and raced down the aisle. Mr. Roseingrave hurried after him. Listeners cried out as the figures blocked their view, and a few voices called out objections.

The spell that had held the audience rapt was finally shattered. Sophie's waltz broke off entirely.

She twisted on the piano bench, her face horrified as the murmur of the audience grew more urgent. People were standing up, turning to face the back of the hall, craning their necks to see what all the fuss was about.

The sudden break in the music left a gap—something had to fill it.

Maddie stood from her chair and began making her way toward the exit.

Mr. Giles reached the back and looked wildly around. Finally, his gaze lighted on Alice. where Alice stood guarding donations like a dragon guarding its hoard. "Where is she?" he demanded, anger making his voice heedlessly loud.

The audience all swiveled to see.

Alice—fair, slight Alice, who looked so fragile and meek, and who was anything but—could only shake her head.

Mr. Giles cursed.

The murmurs of the crowd acquired a disapproving color. Maddie saw one gentleman she knew to be a trustee of the Carrisford Bank of Savings come up to take Mr. Giles gently by the elbow, whispering something softly in his ear.

"No!" Mr. Giles shook him off, his eyes wide and white, the red coming and going from his cheeks as he grappled with this disaster. He demanded again, turning wildly toward all corners of the room. "Where is Mrs. Money?"

Heads shook, shoulders shrugged.

By the door, Maddie pulled in a breath. "She went this way!" she cried.

And turned to run.

They found her easy enough to follow, thanks to all those silver spangles on her dress. By the time Maddie reached the street, there were a handful of people running alongside her: Mr. Giles sprinting with all his panic and power, Mr. Roseingrave with his long legs eating up the ground, quick and lithe Alice. They slowed a little as they poured out the doorway, searching for signs of the older woman's flight.

"There!" Alice cried, pointing. A green-clad figure at the end of the street, running left to right. Gold rosettes stood out against the green bodice, and the hem bristled with flounces.

Judith Wegg—not Mrs. Money—but not even Maddie could tell from so far away.

With Maddie in the lead, the crowd took off in pursuit.

Another corner, another dress—impossibly far ahead. "How could such an old bitch move so fast?" Mr. Giles hissed, panting. Maddie didn't spare the breath to reply; she was busy trying to keep at the head of the hunt.

They passed by the Mulberry Tree, blazing like a beacon in the night. A few gentlemen several sheets to the wind stopped to holler in outrage as the crowd roared around and past them.

"To the left!" Maddie panted, pointing to where a green-clad woman sprinted toward St. Severus.

Mary Fisin, Maddie thought as she wheezed for breath, had a surprising turn of speed.

They followed for another two turns before the figure vanished once more. They were close to the castle now, and the crowd was flagging. Mr. Roseingrave dropped out and was replaced by a young man who looked like a consumptive clerk but who ran like the wind. Alice was now at the head of a tangle of older boys baying with delight like a group of hounds let loose on the tail of a fox. "She's heading for the river!" one of the boys cried, as the figure in the green gown dashed across the top of the old ramparts.

It was Mrs. Money in truth this time—the twists and turns Maddie had taken had given the older woman plenty of time to get here ahead of her pursuers.

The crowd burst out of the streets and onto the rampart just in time to see their prey hasten down the river stairs toward the rushing water. A small boat was tied to a dock there—the woman scrabbled into it, the skiff bobbing and bucking in the current. She reached for the metal cleat where the boat was tied and began yanking at the ropes.

The ramparts were high enough above that everyone could see what happened next.

The mooring rope came free and the woman pulled her

wrist away—but the purse had caught on the cleat, and tore in two with a sound that made half the listeners flinch.

One thousand pounds in Carrisford bank notes burst out into the air and were immediately snatched up by the wind.

They spun tight and thick at first, then less so, some of them landing on the surface right away and some of them dancing down more leisurely. But all of them, all of them lost in the cold rush of the river, a fortune borne away beneath the roiling waves.

Mrs. Money's boat was caught by that same current, too swift for any runner to catch. She sat there, head bowed and hands empty, as the River Ethel carried her away.

Chapter Eighteen

Sophie basked in the chaos in the concert hall.

Everyone was talking. As the story of Mrs. Money's perfidy spread through the audience, it quickly came out as well that in order to meet her price Mr. Giles had mortgaged his shop to the Carrisford Bank—the trustees of whom were almost all present in the audience. The gentlemen held a hurried and anxious conference to one side of the hall. It was clear they were most upset to see their faith had been so misused. They had entrusted him with a great deal of money in a very short span of time—but evidently Mr. Giles's judgment was not to be relied upon.

Sophie watched the hungry sharks turn to rend one of their own.

Mr. Roseingrave returned and explained what had become of Mrs. Money. "I know just how you gentlemen feel: I have been the victim of a very similar swindle not so long ago . . ." His open face and kindly manner had the usual effect as he told the story. The relieved trustees shook his hand and clapped him on the back and thanked him for his sympathy.

Sophie went to compliment Miss Muchelney on her performance, and saw Mr. Frampton and Miss Slight slip out the side door, with Miss Narayan and Mr. Samson following soon after. She held her smile and did her duty until the Moot Hall was mostly empty, with only Roseingraves and members of the Weavers' Library left. The latter began vanishing as well. Sophie fought against impatience and exhaustion both. It had grown late by now, but they had not played the finale quite yet.

Sophie and her father bid good-night to her mother and siblings, and walked down the road to St. Severus's Church.

The graveyard that had seemed so stark and sinister before now glowed sweet and silver in the moonlight. Tombstones with faded letters listed as if they, too, had been worn out by the evening's events. Night birds called out from the nearby trees, and old snow crunched underfoot. Sophie and her father went along the path and around the corner, past the great marble stones of the wealthy and to the smaller, humbler set of plots where the weavers and tailors and shoemakers were buried.

Everyone was waiting for them, gathered beneath the concealing branches of an ancient willow. Mr. Samson and Miss Narayan, Miss Slight and Mr. Frampton, Alice Bilton and Judith Wegg and the rest of the Weavers' Library.

And, of course, Maddie Crewe, her silver spangles now

hidden beneath her cloak. Beside her, wrapped in a dark shawl and a plain hat and wearing anything but Pomona green: Mrs. Money.

Sophie and her father joined the loose circle around one small gravestone. "Well?" Sophie asked, hardly louder than the breeze. "Did it work?"

Maddie's lips opened in a silent laugh. "Almost too well. Mrs. Money's 'escape' looked so real I almost believed it myself."

Mrs. Money's head tilt was as proud and pleased as an actress curtseying for an ovation.

"And you, sir," Mrs. Money said to Mr. Roseingrave. "You missed your calling, not taking to the stage."

Mr. Roseingrave flushed and ducked his head. "Oh, I think I've suffered enough nerves tonight for a whole life's worth as an actor," he said.

"How did it go with the bankers?" Maddie asked.

Sophie chuckled. "The last we saw of them, they were trading tales of Mr. Giles's unreliability, and wondering that he should have gone on so long without being called to account before this."

"They're sure to consider him poison after this," Mr. Roseingrave put in. "I imagine it will be quite difficult, if not impossible, for him to repay them such a sum."

"They'll take his shop," Judith said, satisfaction rich as velvet in her voice.

"Good," Mrs. Money said. Her vowels had lost their aristocratic patina, and were now as true and honest in accent as Maddie Crewe's.

"I only wish we could have ruined all the trustees, too," Alice put in. "They were perfectly willing to go along with his scheme, underhanded as it was, so long as they profited from it."

"Next time," Maddie Crewe promised, with a wicked smile.

Mr. Roseingrave, to his credit, only blanched a little at this promise of future crime. "Are you coming home, Sophie?" he asked.

"Not just yet," Sophie said. She was still quaking too much for sleep.

Her father nodded, bowed to the gathering, and began his cheerful walk back through the stones. One by one, the others followed, until only Mrs. Money, Maddie, and Sophie were left.

The organist of St. Severus's began her evening's practice: haunting music and lantern light spilled through the tall stained-glass windows, designed to mimic the effects of woven cloth. Bright bands of every color slanted over and under one another in a dizzying spectrum. Sophie watched the colors fall protectively over the small grave, and let her eyes trace the letters carved there: MARGUERITE CREWE, BELOVED WEAVER, MOTHER, AND FRIEND.

The organ notes floated in the air, soft as moonlight at this distance.

Mrs. Money's eyes were clear as she looked at her lover's grave; her tears had been shed long since. "I suppose I should be making my escape in truth," she said. Earlier this week she had presented Mr. Giles's letter of credit at the bank; that thousand pounds, in cash, now belonged to the

Weavers' Library, with Mr. Giles none the wiser and thus unable to ask for it back.

Jenny Hull's vengeance was complete.

Mrs. Money's hand rested briefly on the gravestone in a final farewell, then she straightened and looked at Maddie. "Last chance—if you feel the need to flee Carrisford for a while, come by the Mulberry Tree an hour after dawn."

Sophie's heart stuttered in her chest.

Mrs. Money didn't wait for a reply, but strode off into the night.

Maddie was still staring down at her mother's headstone. "I swear every time I come here, the letters are worn down a little more," she said. "I don't want her memory to fade with them."

Sophie swallowed the lump in her throat, as the willow tree shivered in the breeze overhead. "My mother is urging me to go out into the world—and you feel yours would want you to stay. Where does that leave us?" But she was afraid she knew. It always came down to this: Sophie wanted someone more than they wanted her.

The moonlight, the graveyard, even the music—it was a farewell scene, and it made Sophie's heart ache.

Maddie spoke low. "Do you want to know a secret? My mother died angry. She didn't regret attending the meeting at St. Peter's Fields, but she was *furious* that her life was ending in such a fashion. It was like theft, she told me. The soldiers who killed her stole the rest of her life. From her, from me, from all of us—she had so much more work she wanted to do. The Weavers' Library has always honored her sacrifice, and I have tried to carry on as she would have, but . . ."

Sophie reached out and took Maddie's hand, then gently took both hands when she felt how chilled Maddie had become.

Maddie turned and drew their joined hands up. "I think if I tried to live the rest of her life in her place, that would be a kind of theft, too. I'd be stealing from myself—and I know I would have regrets, very strong regrets, about what I'd have to sacrifice." She pressed her lips to the back of Sophie's hands, one after the other. "But I promised I'd never lie to you, so let me say it clearly. I love you, Sophie. I can't give you up. I don't want to stay here if you're leaving." She pulled in a shaky breath. "If you ask me to come with you, I'll say yes."

Sophie feared she was dreaming. Here was fierce, beautiful, audacious Maddie Crewe offering her heart and her future. The Sophie of one year ago would have felt too small and sparrow-like to accept, would have worried this was something she had to earn instead of a gift freely given.

The Sophie of this moment, however, was an opportunist. Her flirtation with worthwhile crime had taught her to see the true value of things.

There was nothing in all the world she valued more than Madeleine Crewe.

So she bounced up on her toes, pulled Maddie down for a thorough kiss, and grinned in the moonlight. "I love you, too," she said. "Come with me."

"Now?" Maddie laughed.

"Now—and every day after."

Maddie swooped Sophie up in her arms and whirled her about, there among the gravestones and the stained-glass rainbows. She was still laughing when Sophie kissed her again; Sophie swallowed up the sound of that laugh until it lit her up like the flame inside a lamp.

Maddie set her down at last, and for a moment they simply breathed together, as the sound of sacred music filled the air around them.

Chapter Nineteen

Mr. Giles, it transpired, had been extremely busy extremely quickly with the full amount of the loan from the Carrisford Bank, which exceeded even what Mrs. Money had demanded: with this vast sum he had consulted expensive experts on factory production and bought his usual gifts and bribes to smooth his way into this new branch of the industry. Many of these expenses were unrecoverable, and as the trustees began making stern sounds about the courts and the magistrates his desperation mounted by the hour.

In the end, Mr. Giles had to sell everything—his wares, his shop, his house, his furniture. He did make a case before the magistrates, and tried to call the Weavers' Library members as witnesses to prove they'd helped defraud him. But every girl stood before the bench and testified she'd been hired to work the loom, had been blindfolded, had no idea the dye didn't work as promised, or how that fraud had been sold to him by the deceitful Mrs. Money.

The magistrates, who'd had several quiet meetings with

the trustees, turned a baleful eye upon Mr. Giles. Furious and disgraced, he left town to go live with a cousin somewhere in Cornwall, and everyone spared a moment to pity the cousin.

The elder Mr. Samson once more made an offer on the empty factory. Mr. Obeney, still grieving the loss of his utopia, sold hastily and moved away, while Mr. Samson began updating the old looms and hiring weavers and overseers, negotiating hours and wages with the Weavers' Library—now once again the Weavers' Library and Reform Society, the old name revived as soon as the ink had dried on the repeal of the Combination Acts. Full of funds and bolstered by legality, they were already strategizing about Mr. Prickett's silk mill, the employees of which were threatening a strike.

The chief strategist would be not Maddie Crewe, but her stepmother: Mrs. Crewe had learned of the silk mill's many faults of management from her observant daughters, and was earnestly and rather terrifyingly set on correcting them. The Weavers' Library had used some of Mr. Giles's own cash to purchase his empty storefront and made it the center of a cooperative retail society. Soon lace makers, shoemakers, tailors, piece workers, and others became members to show goods in the fledgling store, while Mrs. Crewe and her two daughters kept eagle eyes on stock and customers alike.

The running of the Weavers' Library and Reform Society was now left to Judith Wegg and Alice Bilton, and Maddie was still staggered by the relief she felt at stepping down from a job she'd seen as a duty for so many years.

And then, six months after the concert, Mr. Frampton

the elder had a letter from a friend and former fellow musician in Westminster. A gentleman he knew had a daughter mad for the piano but terrified of performing in public, and he wondered if Mr. Frampton might know someone who would know how to teach her.

Mr. Frampton was happy to say that he did, and passed along Sophie's name. Several letters later, Sophie had a job, a new pupil, and a journey to pack for. Harriet Muchelney's teaching would continue under the auspices of Mrs. Halban, an older woman with kind eyes who brooked absolutely no nonsense.

The week before the journey, the Aeolian Club and the Weavers' Library threw a farewell soiree for Miss Sophie Roseingrave and Miss Maddie Crewe.

It was a lively mix of weavers, trade folk, and musicians, and inevitably someone called for a dance. The pattern books were tucked out of harm's way, the chairs and tables were pushed aside, and someone pulled out a guitar and launched into a sprightly piece. Three couples formed the first set: Miss Narayan and Mr. Samson, Mr. Frampton and Miss Slight, and Maddie and Sophie.

Sophie glowed in a rose silk dress, her cheeks pink with small beer and delight. You'd never know by looking just how nervous she was to leave her family, but Maddie had no doubt Sophie would rise to the challenge.

She and Maddie stepped and spun in perfect unison through the familiar figures of the dance—every arch of Sophie's arm, every lift of her foot seemed to tug invisibly at Maddie's heartstrings. She barely felt the floorboards beneath her shoes: at the end of the row she half expected to turn and find they'd danced away from the earth and into a field of stars.

But perhaps that was just that her heart felt so light and buoyant. In a week's time she was going out into the wide, wide world with a woman she loved more than she'd ever loved anyone. There might well be more villains lying in wait—but Maddie had faced down villains before. She was the furthest thing from afraid, because she knew she wasn't alone.

Sophie's eyes sparkled, and she hummed a harmony that only Maddie was close enough to hear.

Maddie curtsied at the dance's end, skirts billowing around her. The dress was one she'd altered specifically for Westminster, so she might carry her past with her into the future. White silk with gold rosettes—the embellishments made of her mother's weaving, which Gita Narayan had saved from the copycat Pomona green gowns. One rested like a talisman just over her heart; the ones on the hem of the gown floated between ribbons of deep blue nightingales, cut from souvenir programs of the Roseingrave concert. Every time she looked at them, her heart took flight.

What couldn't she and Sophie do, so long as they did it together?

She took her beloved by the hand, and waited for the next song to begin.

ABOUT THE AUTHOR

OLIVIA WAITE writes historical romance, fantasy, and science fiction. She is currently the romance fiction columnist for *The New York Times Book Review*, where she writes reviews and thoughtful essays on the genre's history and future. To learn more and sign up for her newsletter, please visit oliviawaite.com.

Discover great authors, exclusive offers, and more at hc.com.